MURDER AT WEDGEFIELD MANOR

Books by Erica Ruth Neubauer

MURDER AT THE MENA HOUSE

MURDER AT WEDGEFIELD MANOR

Published by Kensington Publishing Corp.

MURDER AT WEDGEFIELD MANOR

ERICA RUTH NEUBAUER

www.kensingtonbooks.com

For Beth McIntyre.
For everything, for always.

This book is a work of fiction. Names, characters, businesses, organizations, places, events, and incidents either are the product of the author's imagination or are used fictitiously. Any resemblance to actual persons, living or dead, events, or locales is entirely coincidental.

To the extent that the image or images on the cover of this book depict a person or persons, such person or persons are merely models, and are not intended to portray any character or characters featured in the book.

KENSINGTON BOOKS are published by

Kensington Publishing Corp.
119 West 40th Street
New York, NY 10018

All Kensington Titles, Imprints, and Distributed Lines are available at special quantity discounts for bulk purchases for sales promotions, premiums, fund-raising, and educational or institutional use. Special book excerpts or customized printings can also be created to fit specific needs. For details, write or phone the office of the Kensington special sales manager: Kensington Publishing Corp., 119 West 40th Street, New York, NY 10018, attn: Special Sales Department, Phone: 1-800-221-2647.

Library of Congress Card Catalogue Number: 2020945316

The K logo is a trademark of Kensington Publishing Corp.

ISBN-13: 978-1-4967-2588-2
ISBN-10: 1-4967-2588-3
First Kensington Hardcover Edition: April 2021

ISBN-13: 978-1-4967-2590-5 (ebook)
ISBN-10: 1-4967-2590-5 (ebook)

10 9 8 7 6 5 4 3 2 1

Printed in the United States of America

Acknowledgments

Huge thanks to John Scognamiglio, my editor extraordinaire, as well as to Larissa Ackerman, my outstanding publicist. I'm so lucky to work with the two of you. Thank you to Robin Cook for her patience. Further thanks to the rest of the Kensington team who work so hard to get books into your hot little hands.

Ann Collette, my amazing agent, who regularly makes me feel grateful that she chose me.

Zoe Quinton King, my dearest of friends and editor. Together we make an amazing team. I'm grateful for you every day. So much love to you.

To my dear friends Katrina Niidas-Holm and Chris Holm. Without the two of you, I wouldn't have had a first book, let alone a second one. I am so grateful for your friendship, support, and encouragement, and the occasional pie. (Or poor beverage choice.) I miss your faces. Love you both to the moon and back.

I'm so grateful for my Midwest ride-or-die ladies: Jessie Lourey, Lori Rader-Day, and Susie Calkins. They keep me inspired, encouraged, and laughing. I love you.

It was super weird to launch a debut novel during a pandemic, but so many people rallied and did a great deal to help. I thank you all from the bottom of my heart, with special shout-outs to Jess Lourey, Johnny Shaw, Elizabeth Little, Susie Calkins, Lori Rader-Day, Keir Graff, Jon McGoran, Laura Benedict, Juliet Grames, Tasha Alexander, Andrew Grant, Bryan Quertermous, Sarah Weinman, Eric Beetner,

Jon Jordan, Catriona McPherson, Steph Gayle, Jim L'Etoile, Halley Sutton, Claire Booth, Sherry Harris, and Jim Higgins.

Thank you to the booksellers who pivoted and went virtual with me. I hope to meet you one day in person (if I haven't already). Special thanks to: Daniel Goldin and Chris Lee at Boswell Books, McKenna Jordan and John McDougall at Murder by the Book, Anastasia Soroko at the Savoy Bookstore, Barbara Peters and the Poisoned Pen staff, and Karyn and Kelly at Fountain Books.

Immeasurable thanks for friendship, love, and support to Tasha Alexander, Gretchen Beetner, Keith Brubacher, Kate Conrad, Hilary Davidson, Dan Distler, Matthew FitzSimmons, Daniel Goldin, Andrew Grant, Glen Erik Hamilton, Carrie Hennessy, Tim Hennessy, Megan Kantara, Steph Killen, Elizabeth Little, Jenny Lohr, Erin MacMillan, Joel MacMillan, Pat McCarville, Mike McCrary, Katie Meyer, Trevor Meyer, Pam Nelson, Lauren O'Brien, Margret Petrie, Nick Petrie, Bryan Pryor, Andy Rash, Kyle Jo Schmidt, Jay Shepherd, Becky Tesch, and Bryan Van Meter.

Thank you to Patrick McCarville for taking a chance. I'm a lucky girl.

Thank you and big love to my amazing family, Rachel and AJ Neubauer, Dorothy Neubauer, Sandra Olsen, Susan Catral, Sara Kierzek, Jeff and Annie Kierzek, Justin and Christine Kierzek, Josh Kierzek, Ignacio Catral, Sam and Ariana Catral, Mandi Neumann, Andie, Alex, and Angel Neumann. Special thanks and love to my dear friend Gunther Neumann, who is truly a rock.

And finally, Beth McIntyre, a.k.a. Betty, Bob, B-Mac, Bethlehem, Bea, etc., etc. Thanks for being the jelly to my peanut butter, the Ernie to my Bert. *Peach emoji*

Chapter 1

England, 1926

One wheel of the biplane slammed into the ground, the wings tipping precariously, before the second wheel made contact and the little plane righted itself, hustling along the soft dirt track before coming to an untidy stop. The engine roared, the propeller a blur before my eyes.

My heartbeat evened back out as well. I had thought for sure we would crash.

"Not bad for your first landing!" I heard the shout as I turned in the seat to look at the man seated behind me. "Do you want to go again?"

I felt a grin split my face. Yes. I wanted nothing more than to go again.

"Push the throttle in just like I showed you. Steer with the pedals. Let's go!"

I pushed the de Havilland forward, steering awkwardly with the pedals beneath my feet, the plane twisting too far to the right before I got the hang of them. I turned the aircraft around and started in the opposite direction down the track, this time with a light wind at our backs. My body was tense until the plane lifted into the air and sailed over the tree line. Even then it was difficult to fully relax, despite knowing the instructor had a matching set of controls at his seat and would take over if we found ourselves in serious trouble.

It felt as though an angel's breath could blow us either up or down—and the few scudding clouds below us wouldn't do anything to soften our fall. But soaring above the English countryside, rolling green hills dotted with grazing sheep, leaves turning gold and orange, I felt every care slip away. My heart filled to bursting with a sense of freedom, of open air and endless possibilities. After too short a time, I brought the plane back around to Lord Hughes's estate and lined up with the dirt track running along the edge of his property.

This time the landing went much more smoothly, both wheels gently kissing the ground together before rolling us to a stop. A small group had gathered in the adjoining green space, awaiting our return.

"Much better! That was nearly perfect." Group Captain Christopher Hammond pushed his goggles back as the engine stopped, revealing his twinkling brown eyes. He hoisted himself out of the back seat as I pushed my own goggles back onto the leather helmet strapped firmly to my head. I couldn't help the smile that refused to leave my face.

Until I saw the look on my aunt Millie's.

"I don't know why you insist on taking these lessons, Jane." Millie's voice carried across the distance. She flatly refused to come anywhere near the shiny yellow biplane, as though mere proximity might catch her up and carry her into the sky. "It's incredibly dangerous. And if you crash and die, how will I explain it to your father?" I nearly asked if having to give an explanation would truly be the worst part of my dying in a plane crash, but held my tongue instead.

"It's perfectly safe." Group Captain Hammond offered me a hand and helped me dismount from the front seat as I gingerly stepped onto the lower wing and then alighted onto the ground. "The Moth has an excellent safety record." Hammond winked at me before turning toward where Millie stood, arms crossed and scowl affixed.

"Hrmmph."

Lord Edward Hughes, the owner of the estate we stood on, patted Millie's arm before coming forward to shake the group captain's hand. "Good show, Hammond. Do you need help stowing it?" Lord Hughes was still a handsome man, despite being a few years senior to my aunt Millie. His gray hair was thick, and he was tall and lean like his daughter Lillian, his love of the outdoors and sports giving him an air of ruddy good health. Lord Hughes's small white dog leaped around in circles before chasing over and flinging itself at Hammond's legs. He bent down and gave the creature a scratch behind the ears before finding a small stick to toss. Rascal took off after it, tongue flapping in the breeze.

"No, Your Lordship. I'll just roll it into the barn for now. We'll probably need to refuel before we take her back up. Did you still want to go this afternoon?" Hughes nodded enthusiastically as the gentlemen walked around the aircraft, discussing logistics and the little plane. Lord Hughes and the group captain were long-standing acquaintances, and Hughes had invited the experienced flight instructor out to his estate for an exchange of sorts—Hammond would get an extended vacation in the country and Hughes would pay for flight lessons.

I removed my leather helmet and shook my auburn bob back out. It was almost a disappointment to be back on solid ground. I turned from the men and met Millie's continuing glare with a smile. There was no way to explain to my aunt how soaring in the sky was the precise opposite of the claustrophobia that had plagued me since my marriage. Much like there was no way for me to explain to her how terrible my marriage had been.

"Shall we head back to the house?" Millie turned on her heel without answering and I trotted to catch up with her.

I could see my breath in the crisp morning air. For once, England favored us with pure blue skies, and the bright sunshine cut through the chill. Millie and I traveled the well-worn path between the house and the barn that housed several cars as well as the airplane I'd just landed—Lord Hughes had the Moth on an extended loan from one of the Royal Aero Clubs. Beside the makeshift garage sat the stables, which now housed only two horses, the rest of the herd having been sold off years ago.

We approached the manor house, a large gray stone building with a portico and white marble columns gracing the front entrance. It was a large and utterly imposing home, especially compared to the compact brick houses I was used to back in Boston. Coming from the rear of the building, Millie and I let ourselves into a small entrance off the kitchen where there was an area to leave our long wool coats and scarves. I sat on a bench and pulled off the heavy boots that I borrowed from Lillian, as well as the thick wool socks, and changed back into my own flats. By the time I had finished, Millie had already disappeared down the hall. I decided to leave her to her mood instead of following her.

I poked my head into the warm kitchen where the smell of freshly baked bread scented the air. The large room had obviously once supported a much larger household and staff, but now was the sole domain of Martha Fedec. Lord Hughes had updated a few items to make Martha's work easier, including the plumbing system. A state-of-the-art stove stood to one side, the large stone fireplace gracing one wall now largely unused, and the racks of pots and pans hanging above the scarred wooden table shone with their newness.

Martha looked up from her large pot bubbling on the stove and glanced at me. "In or out, Miss Jane. Doorposts are the devil, you know." I didn't know, but did as she said and stepped fully into the room.

"Smells delicious in here, Martha."

Now Martha beamed at me, red curls peeking out from beneath her sensible white cap. She was tall and thin, the opposite of what you would expect of such an excellent cook. Flour dusted the apron that covered her gray dress and was smeared across one pale cheek. She had been running Lord Hughes's household for years, and her clear skin and brisk manner made it impossible to tell if the woman was thirty-five or fifty. Or anywhere in between. And her vague accent—as well as her affinity for hearty stews—made me wonder where she originally hailed from.

"You will have some for dinner. Along with red stew. But for now, there is still some food laid out in the breakfast room if you're hungry." I smiled and thanked her, leaving her to work in peace.

Since our escapades in Egypt, including Millie's near-miss with death, my aunt decided that she wanted to spend time in England with her daughter, Lillian, instead of returning home to America as we originally planned. I was happy enough to go along with the change of plan, wanting to better acquaint myself with my newfound cousin, and so we found ourselves at Lord Hughes's estate in the countryside of Essex. It was a quiet life, unless of course you were interested in golf. Lord Hughes had set up a detailed course on the sprawling grounds for Lillian to practice on, and the girl spent the majority of her waking hours doing just that. Lillian's enthusiasm for the sport knew no bounds, and when the weather was poor she needed another way to use her clubs—thus the putting setup in what used to be the great hall.

I had no interest in the sport. Or any sport, really.

Days at the Hughes estate, fondly called Wedgefield by the family, had come to look much the same for me, a far cry from the danger and excitement of our trip to Egypt. The quiet had initially been something of a relief, but that had quickly passed only to be replaced by a restless energy I couldn't seem to shake. Luckily, Group Captain Hammond was on hand to teach me to fly—we went up every morning, weather permitting. In the two weeks since our arrival I had already logged twenty hours and felt fairly confident in my takeoffs. I hoped before long the landings would feel just as natural.

Afternoons found me either walking the grounds or curled up in Hughes's comfortable library with a good book. Lord Hughes had an excellent selection of current novels, and I was able to find a few murder mysteries to while away the time I spent on the ground. Even solving a real-life murder hadn't dampened my enthusiasm for the genre.

My mind wandered to that recent mystery and my partner in solving it, and I quickly pushed the thought away. It wasn't any concern of mine what Redvers was up to, or even where he was in the world. I hadn't heard anything from him since my arrival in England, nor did I expect to. With a firm shake of my head, I took myself to the breakfast room for a post-flight snack.

CHAPTER 2

The afternoon passed lazily, and following a pleasant dinner that night, our party moved into the drawing room. A fire had been lit and it chased away the slight chill that had descended when the sun dropped behind the hills. Lillian and her friend Marie immediately moved over to the new radio and began fiddling with the dials.

"Aunt Millie, would you care to start a game of mah-jongg?" I moved over to the table near the fire where the game was already set up.

"Only if Lord Hughes agrees to join us." Millie flashed a rare smile at him, and he smiled in return. It was moments like these when I wondered if what had transpired years earlier between Millie and Lord Hughes was being rekindled. It still stunned me that my short, plump aunt with her sharp tongue had engaged in an affair—resulting in Lillian—with the pleasant aristocrat before us.

I grimaced. Best not to contemplate the issue too much.

"Of course." Lord Hughes turned. "Group Captain Hammond, will you make our fourth?"

"Delighted."

We sat down to play, and my aunt Millie began shuffling the tiles, "the twittering of the sparrows" as they called it. As she dealt the tiles to each of us, Flight Lieutenant Simon Marshall strolled into the room and joined Lillian and Marie.

The girls were picking through a large stack of records near the gramophone, the radio having been abandoned when nothing caught their fancy. Lillian greeted Simon cheerfully and immediately began passing him records to help sort through. The young man's clothes were neat, a button-down shirt with the shirtsleeves rolled up, and a pair of stylish brown suspenders attached to his often-mended tweed trousers. He was just one of several veterans that Lord Hughes employed on the estate. From what I understood, Simon took care of the cars and anything mechanical, having served as an aircraft mechanic during the war before being field promoted to flight lieutenant. I hadn't spent much time with the young man, but he seemed indispensable to the family.

Lord Hughes took his turn at the tiles as the girls put on a jazz record from the Kit-Cat Club. Simon pushed several upholstered armchairs to the side of the room, and took turns swinging each of the girls into a frenzied Charleston, although it was obvious to anyone that Simon preferred Lillian. I watched the trio from the corner of my eye, and I could see that Marie had noticed Simon's special attention to Lillian as well; as Marie watched them dance, her eyes narrowed and her arms crossed before her chest. But Simon's good humor and easy grace on the dance floor were hard to resist, and when it was Marie's turn to take a spin around the floor, Simon quickly had her smiling again.

"Pung!" Millie crowed. With her first hand, she already had a run of three tiles—the five of circles. I returned my attention to the game.

Play went around the table, and as Lord Hughes studied his hand of tiles before him, Millie turned her attention to Hammond.

"So, Group Captain Hammond. You served as a pilot during the war?" I wondered where Millie was going with this line of questioning.

"I did." Hammond shifted in his chair. I knew he was uncomfortable discussing his time in the war, as many veterans were.

"And you never married?"

I rolled my eyes. Her machinations to see me remarried were never subtle.

"I was, but we divorced after the war." Hammond's voice was even and he regarded Millie with a polite smile.

I almost laughed at the pained expression on Millie's face. The group captain's declaration brought her interrogation to an abrupt end, as I'm sure he knew it would—Millie could never sanction my marrying a divorcé.

Millie focused on her tiles, and Hammond stood. "Drinks, anyone?"

"I'd love one." I gave Hammond an apologetic smile. "A gin rickey if you would." The group captain gave me a wink and excused himself to the well-stocked bar cart where he was quickly joined by Lord Hughes. Hammond was easygoing and hard to ruffle—as I well knew from spending time in the air with him. I didn't think Millie's question had truly bothered him, but I was still chagrined at her clumsy attempt to set me up. Again. Millie refused to accept that I wasn't interested in a second marriage and was quite happy with my hard-won freedom. And while the group captain was attractive—with brown hair and even, pleasant features, he was also the same height as I was. In fact, back to back I might have stood an inch taller.

And there was the matter of a tall, devastatingly handsome man whose memory lurked in the back of my mind. Even though I batted any thoughts of him away as quickly as they came.

Hammond returned with my gin rickey and a tall boozy concoction for himself. Lord Hughes regained his seat carrying a whiskey highball for Millie and a snifter of Scotch.

Knowing Lord Hughes, it was an expensive single malt aged for decades in some fancy barrel. He was a simple, down-to-earth man, but he appreciated fine liquor.

In that respect, he and Millie had much in common.

With the pause in the game, Millie had turned her attention to the young people dancing madly on the other side of the room. She watched as Simon spun Lillian and then dipped her low, his attention on the neckline of her modest dress. I could feel Millie bristle beside me. The music paused for a moment and Simon and Lillian collapsed into chairs beside Marie, cheeks flushed and laughing.

"Edward," Millie's voice was loud and carried across the room. "Do you think it's proper for one of your *servants* to be socializing with the girls?" I could feel my breath catch as everyone in the room froze.

Everyone but Simon. The young man paused only a moment before bolting out of his chair, rage deforming his usually pleasant features. His face had colored to nearly the same color as a ripe tomato, and he stalked across the room, fists clenched.

"What the hell do you know?" Simon shouted.

Chapter 3

Millie's eyes widened and she carefully set down the tile she had been holding in her hand, never taking her eyes off the suddenly volatile figure before us. The clack of the tile was like a gunshot in the silent room.

"And who gives a bloody fig what you *Americans* have to say about a damned thing?" Simon stopped just feet from the table, fists clenched at his sides. "What have you *Americans* ever done for us? Huh? Tell me that, Mrs. High-and-Mighty." Simon's voice had continued to rise, and now that he had finished, his harsh breathing was the only sound in the room.

Group Captain Hammond calmly pushed back from the table and went to Simon, placing a hand on his arm. Simon shook him off, still breathing heavily, but Hammond continued to stand before the young man, saying nothing, gazing calmly at him. After a moment, some of the rage drained from Simon's face and he abruptly turned on his heel and left the room.

After a few beats, I let out a breath I hadn't realized I'd been holding.

"Millie! How could you?" Lillian's wail broke the silence. Her tone of accusation made me wonder whether she had welcomed Simon's attention. I could see from Millie's face that she wondered the same thing and did not like the prospect at all.

With another small cry, Lillian bolted from the room. Millie was starting to push back from the table when Lord Hughes put a hand on her shoulder, letting it rest there.

"Don't," Lord Hughes said quietly. "They'll be all right."

"Are you certain?" Millie settled uncertainly back into her chair as her hands fluttered in her lap. "I'm not sure she should be alone with that young man. What a temper he has!" It was rare to see Millie so unnerved, but I knew her love for Lillian had changed her, softened her in some ways. However, I also knew that she was unlikely to take any responsibility for his outburst in the first place.

Hammond moved back toward our table. "He'll be fine in a moment. He's just . . . easily set off." The group captain paused, and I could tell he was trying to decide how much to say. "It's been difficult for many of the men since the war."

We were all quiet for a moment before Millie plunged ahead. "But what did he mean about Americans? I mean, we certainly did our part. Why does he seem so . . . venomous toward us?"

Hammond and Lord Hughes exchanged a brief look, and I could tell there was more to the story than they were willing to say. I made a note to myself to ask Hammond about the exchange later. Perhaps he would give me the full story—I knew Lord Hughes would decline to "trouble the ladies" with such details.

"Of course, you did," Lord Hughes said comfortingly. "Let's just forget the whole thing, shall we? We can't let this ruin our evening." Millie sighed and gave a vague wave of her hand before reaching for her highball. I was a little surprised that she didn't demand further explanation, but she was obviously distracted with thoughts of Lillian.

As we awkwardly turned our attention back to the game—with difficulty—the sound of an engine racing pierced the night. Headlights from one of Lord Hughes's vehicles washed over the drawing room windows as the car raced down the drive, gravel spitting in its wake. A moment later Lillian returned, her face pale and drawn.

"Well, he's legged it. Again."

Lord Hughes seemed unconcerned that one of his expensive cars had just been taken from the estate at high speed. "He'll burn it off and come back in a few hours. He always does." Hughes glanced at Lillian with a reassuring smile before he returned his attention to his tiles. "Chow," he said, laying a run of tiles before him.

Marie had been pacing near the gramophone, but now she came forward and claimed Lillian from the doorway, leading her back to the record player. Lillian sat, staring distractedly out the windows while Marie tried to tempt her back onto the dance floor. Marie finally gave up and flopped into the chair beside her, letting the record play itself out. She lit a thin cigarette and smoked it in silence.

For a moment, I, too, gazed out at the inky darkness beyond the bank of windows and gave a small shiver. I hoped Simon would drive safely.

The following morning, I woke a little later than usual. With all the excitement, Hammond and I had decided to delay our usual early flight until late morning, and I had to admit that I was glad for the extra time in bed. It had taken me longer than usual to fall asleep, and I'd found myself listening for the sounds of a car returning. I didn't know the young man, but I was still concerned for his safety. I wondered if Millie had had any trouble sleeping since it was her outrageous statement that had set him off in the first place; if I were her, I would have felt at least somewhat responsible for Simon's well-being. But knowing my aunt, I doubted it had given her even a moment's worry.

Donning a simple knit dress, I freshened up and headed down to the breakfast room. The space was filled with warm light which reflected off the golden hue of the walls. Portraits of solemn-faced men and women, whom I assumed were Lord Hughes's ancestors, hung from the walls, observing us as we ate. After filling my plate at the side table with eggs, toast, and a slice of English bacon, I took a seat across from Lillian who was poking at her baked beans.

"Good morning, Jane." Group Captain Hammond gave me a warm smile as he took the seat to my left.

"And a good morning to you, Chris." Hammond had insisted I call him by his Christian name on day two of our flying lessons. Farther down the table, Millie's eyebrows raised at the familiarity and I caught one corner of her mouth tipping up in a smug smile, before she remembered his admission the night before and grimaced instead. I returned my attention to my morning coffee and ignored her altogether.

Lord Hughes perused the pages of *The Morning Post*, one of three papers that he received daily. His hand occasionally dipped below the table as he slipped a bit of food to Rascal, who was taking his role as a foot warmer very seriously. The tension from the night before hadn't completely dispelled, and we ate in silence, the clinking of silverware and the rustling of the newspaper the only sounds. I was just about to excuse myself when an unexpected voice from the doorway broke the spell.

"Good morning, everyone. I hope I'm not disturbing you."

My heart leapt into my throat at the sound of that deep, rumbling voice, and I turned slowly to face him.

Redvers.

Chapter 4

My pulse stuttered then began racing and I wondered if I looked as foolishly lighthearted as I suddenly felt. But as I studied his face, I could tell that something was amiss. He gave me a brief, warm smile, but his face quickly regained its somber appearance as he turned to the rest of the table.

Millie greeted him. "Glad to see you, Mr. Redvers. Do you know everyone here?"

"I believe I'm acquainted with everyone."

I was barely listening. "What's wrong? Has something happened?" I asked.

He looked back at me, then to Lord Hughes. "There's been an accident."

Millie gasped and I heard a fork clatter to the table. I turned and noticed that Lillian's face had lost all color.

"Simon," she whispered. Marie covered Lillian's hand with her own for a moment before Lillian shook it off and clenched both her hands together in her lap.

"I'm not sure who it is, but there was a car accident near here. I'm afraid the driver didn't survive."

There was no doubt in my mind who the driver was, and looking around the table told me there was little doubt in anyone else's either. Next to me, Hammond's face had turned stony and impassive—a far cry from his usual friendly appearance. He pushed his chair out and stood before I could say anything to him. In addition to being a flight instructor, he also worked tirelessly to find jobs for veterans—I recalled that the group captain had recommended Simon for his position here on the estate. Hammond had to feel responsible for Flight Lieutenant Marshall in many different ways.

"I'll go with you," Hammond said quietly.

I pushed back my chair as well, placing my napkin alongside my half-eaten plate of food. "I will, too."

"Jane," Hammond said at the same time my aunt did. I silenced both of them with a fierce look and turned to catch Redvers' eyes narrowing at the group captain. Before I could wonder at his reaction, I shrugged it off and moved toward the door.

"Let's go."

The three of us climbed into Redvers' hard-top black sedan in silence, Hammond insisting that I sit in front with Redvers. I fidgeted with the skirt of my dress, suddenly feeling awkward at seeing the man after what felt like an eternity, although it had been less than two months. My distress over Simon's fate warred with my elation that Redvers had suddenly appeared—although in retrospect my aunt had not seemed terribly surprised to see him. I briefly wondered if she had something to do with his arrival at the estate.

Redvers shot me a sideways glance.

"I'm sorry this isn't under better circumstances."

"As am I," I said, suitably somber, though I found myself wanting to fling my arms around the man and thank the heavens for his solid and reassuring presence.

It took us only a few minutes of driving narrow roads cut through rolling farmland to reach the scene of the accident. As we rounded a large bend, I could see the Lambda crushed against a large oak in a small grove just off the road. Redvers pulled onto the grassy verge, leaving enough room for cars to get past us. Glancing around as we climbed from the car, I wasn't surprised that Simon hadn't been found until now. We were somewhere between the estate and the small village, and the road wasn't much traveled. Lord Hughes's estate was fairly isolated and there wasn't another house for miles.

"It looks like he came around the curve and lost control." Redvers walked around the car and the three of us moved forward, surveying the scene. Hammond tried to shield me from the grisly display with his body, but I moved swiftly around him, even though I could have seen perfectly well over his shoulder. He didn't have the height or build to block much.

"Are you sure you should be seeing this, Jane?"

I ignored the man as Redvers assured him I had seen worse. I shot him a grateful smile before turning back to the scene before us.

Two police officers and what I assumed was the local doctor were already attending the crash, but without any sense of urgency. The entire front of the vehicle was smashed like an accordion, the driver's body crumpled against the steering wheel. Even from the distance we stood at, I recognized the thatch of curly dark hair and the clothes Simon had been wearing the night before. I didn't need to move any closer to the car to be certain—I was happy to maintain a respectful distance and let the officials on the scene do their jobs.

"Do you recognize him?" Redvers looked between Hammond and I. We both nodded our heads.

"It's Simon Marshall," I said.

"You're sure?"

I shot Redvers a dark look and he merely nodded.

"Flight Lieutenant Marshall was a very good driver," Hammond said slowly. "And he knew these roads well. I'm surprised he would have crashed at all."

"When did he leave last night?" Redvers was surveying the road in the direction we had come from.

"It was dark," I said. "But I'm not exactly sure what time he left. I didn't see a clock."

Hammond shook his head. "I didn't either. But really, the dark shouldn't have mattered."

"Unless something jumped in front of the car."

I sighed. If that were the case, I doubted we would be able to discover what that person or animal might have been. But I considered the scene. "If something jumped in front of him, he would have hit the brakes, correct?" The men nodded in agreement. "And if he'd braked hard what would that do to the road?" I thought I knew the answer, but I wanted to double-check my suspicions.

Redvers cocked an eyebrow. "Well, Mrs. Wunderly, that would have left some impressions in the dirt, I would think. On the road as well since the tires would have locked."

I ignored his formal use of my name and looked at the unmarked road and the path the car had taken to its fatal meeting with the tree. There was disturbance to the ground, but nothing like I expected to see from a car with its brakes slammed to the floor. No dark ruts or torn earth. "I don't see any evidence of that. Wouldn't locked tires have done much more damage?" I looked up and found that Redvers' dark chocolate gaze was already locked on me. A flush crept up my neck.

Just like old times.

"We need a mechanic to take a look at the car." Hammond began moving closer to the accident but stopped abruptly. Glancing over, I could see that Simon's battered body was about to be moved and I turned away, my breakfast a leaden lump in my stomach.

Redvers nodded. "I'll be sure to recommend that to the police. Did he have any family we need to notify?"

Hammond shook his head sadly. "No. I'll . . . talk with Lord Hughes and see what we can do for him."

Hammond and I returned to the car while Redvers quickly touched base with the man in charge of the scene. Our ride back to the house was silent, each of us lost in our own thoughts. The car had barely stopped before Hammond got out and headed into the house. Redvers and I both got out as well, but paused for a moment on the drive.

"What are you doing here?" I asked.

"Aren't you happy to see me?" Redvers' eyes twinkled.

I rolled my own eyes and his face split into a grin. I didn't want to boost his ego by admitting to him—or myself—just how happy I was to see him, despite the little skip my pulse did every time our eyes met. Our time apart hadn't changed my reaction to him.

Although I shouldn't be so pleased to see him. Our parting kiss at the Mena House in Egypt had been a brief break in good sense on my part—the good sense to stay away from handsome and charming men. It seemed I needed a solid reminder of that.

"You can hardly be here to investigate a car accident."

"Well, we don't know whether it's an accident or not, do we? Not yet, at any rate."

I wrinkled my nose at him. I suspected he didn't believe it was anything more than a tragic accident. But as for why Redvers had mysteriously appeared on Lord Hughes's doorstep, I had more than a sneaking suspicion about who might have called him.

"Do you know Lord Hughes, Redvers?"

"We've met before."

"Mmm-hmm." That much was obviously true. "It's nice that you're acquainted."

"It is, isn't it?"

"But I would wager that Aunt Millie is the one that called you."

Redvers widened his dark eyes innocently. "I'm certain I don't know what you mean."

I fought a smile as we moved toward the house. I normally hated my aunt's interference and her endless attempts to marry me off, but if she had alerted Redvers to our presence in the countryside, I found I wasn't upset about it. Suddenly, Rascal came flying down the drive, flinging himself at Redvers' legs.

"Down, boy." Rascal ignored me, and I looked at Redvers, only to find him staring at the dog with his mouth open. "He must have gotten out when Chris opened the door."

"Yes, but what *is* it? Is it a *sheep*?"

I laughed. I'd had much the same reaction when I first laid eyes on Lord Hughes's unlikely canine. His fluffy white fur was indeed shorn in a way that made him look like an undersized sheep. "It's a Bedlington terrier."

"But why does it *look* like that?"

"I don't know why they shave Rascal that way. Something to do with the breed." With a shrug, I moved toward the door and Redvers trailed along beside me. Next to him, Rascal bounded merrily, his tongue flapping in pure joy. I could hardly blame the poor dog for taking to Redvers so quickly. I couldn't help but feel a bit merry at his side as well.

The house was quiet when we entered, and we found the family gathered in the drawing room—the same room where we had last seen Simon Marshall before he raced off to his sad end. It seemed rather morbid but somehow fitting that we would gather here again since it was Simon's fate we needed to discuss. The furniture had been moved back to where it belonged, and Martha had set out a tray of tea and sandwiches that were going largely untouched. The only sounds were my aunt and Lord Hughes speaking in hushed tones near the window. As I watched, Hughes reached out and took Millie's hand for a moment, holding it gently in his own.

Looking away, I noticed there was a newcomer to the party. A young man wearing a fine wool suit was seated on an upholstered love seat next to Lillian, patting her arm. He had dark blond hair and fine features with a long patrician nose; he might have been considered classically good-looking, except his icy blue eyes were a shade too close together.

Lillian stood as soon as she saw us. "Was it Simon?" I nodded and she sank back down into her seat. Lord Hughes came forward, patting Lillian's shoulder as he passed, then reached out to shake Redvers' hand.

"Good to see you, Redvers. Glad you could join us."

"I'm sorry I had to be the bearer of bad news."

I gave my head a little shake. It seemed that Lord Hughes had anticipated Redvers' arrival, which meant he was likely complicit with Millie's plan to bring him to the estate.

"And this is my nephew Alistair. He's only just arrived." The blond young man stood and came forward, shaking both our hands and giving an appropriately subdued smile. I could now see Alistair was long and thin—he reminded me of a greyhound. I glanced at Redvers, but it appeared that here, finally, was someone he didn't already know.

"Rotten thing to happen," Alistair said. "I'm just glad I can be on hand for Lillian." He looked back at her, sending her a reassuring look before turning back to us. "I know how much she enjoyed Flight Lieutenant Marshall's company." Something about the statement struck me as disingenuous, but I studied Alistair for a moment and he appeared sincere.

I glanced around the room, but both Hammond and Marie appeared to be missing from our gathering. Lord Hughes noticed my interest.

"The group captain went to make some phone calls and take care of the . . . arrangements."

I nodded. "And Marie?"

Lord Hughes shrugged. "I believe she went to her room."

I wondered if Marie was irritated with the attention Lillian was receiving from yet another young man. She was devoted to Lillian, but she also didn't care to share her affections.

A distant jingle broke the silence and a moment later Shaw came into the room. Another veteran of the war, John Shaw was tall with spectacles and a rather pronounced dark unibrow. He was somber and adept at his role as butler—even Millie had been unable to find fault with the job he did, although I could tell his pronounced working-class accent troubled her. His familiarity with the letter *H* was fleeting at best.

"Sorry to disturb ye, but there's a phone call for Mr. Redvers."

Redvers followed Shaw from the room, and I watched them depart, hoping it wasn't news that would take Redvers away after he had only just arrived. Because it would be inconvenient for him, of course, coming all this way only to leave again so soon. It had nothing to do with my wanting to spend time with him. But my stomach did a small flip all the same.

Frustrated with where my thoughts had wandered, I raided the tea tray, finding that Martha had thoughtfully set out a small pot of coffee for me. I helped myself to a lukewarm cup before I joined Millie and Lord Hughes near the window.

"Millie, did you happen to summon Redvers here?" I studied my aunt's face. "It seems strange that he would appear out of the blue otherwise."

Millie gave a casual shrug and Lord Hughes was suddenly very interested in studying the curtains. "What matters is that the man is on hand for this tragedy. Isn't that right, Edward?"

Lord Hughes murmured something agreeable and I shook my head. I didn't need any further proof; I had found my culprit.

Moments later, Redvers returned to the room, face grim. He came and sat in the chair next to mine, and Lillian and

Alistair rose quickly and stood behind the couch where Lord Hughes and Millie were seated.

"That was the police inspector. He'll be joining us shortly."

The inspector's impending arrival wasn't the only reason for the phone call—I could tell by the look on Redvers' face. "The inspector has learned something, hasn't he?"

Redvers' eyes met mine. "I'm afraid the brake cables were tampered with."

Chapter 5

A collective gasp went around the room, but I merely nodded. I wasn't as surprised as the rest, especially after hearing what Hammond had to say about Simon's driving abilities. I had also seen for myself that it didn't seem as though Simon had braked at all going around that corner. I felt familiar sparks of interest flare up, and immediately felt guilty. Simon had been a nice young man troubled by his experiences in the war.

"The police inspector will be here soon," Redvers said. "He'll want to speak with everyone."

I had no doubt that the police would conduct the investigation with due thoroughness, but my mind was crowded with questions. I couldn't help voicing them.

"Lord Hughes," I turned to where the Lord sat, pale-faced. "The car that Simon was driving. Did he use it often?" The first thing I wanted to know was who the saboteur had been targeting in the first place. If it was a vehicle that Lord Hughes used regularly, Simon might not have been the target at all. A quick glance at Redvers told me that he approved of my line of thinking.

Lord Hughes thought for a moment. "It was the blue car?" I forgot that he hadn't seen the crash and owned multiple vehicles. Redvers and I both nodded. "The Lancia Lambda. That was my oldest car. It handled well on the roads but wasn't especially fast. I let Simon tinker with it . . . he thought he could make it faster and more efficient. Frankly, the boy liked to have a project and I was happy to give him one. He was a smart lad, especially with mechanics."

I processed that for a moment. "So, he was the only one who used the Lancia?"

"Yes, I only really use the black Bentley. And Lillian doesn't drive, of course." Redvers and I exchanged a look. If the saboteur was familiar with the family's habits, it looked as though Simon was in fact the target.

Behind Millie and Lord Hughes, Lillian had been quietly shifting from foot to foot as we talked, but seemed unable to stay in the room a moment longer. "If you'll excuse me, I think I'll head outside."

I cocked my head at her. It was hard to tell if she was merely upset that someone who worked for her father had been killed, or if she took Simon's death more personally. As, say, a love interest. It was difficult to tell since Lillian wasn't one to wear her emotions on her sleeve—or anywhere else you could see them. But her reaction so far had me leaning toward there having been some sort of attachment on her part.

"Of course, dear," Millie told her. "The fresh air will do you good."

I was about to say Lillian should stay put so the inspector could interview her, but at Millie's fierce look I held my tongue instead.

Lillian started to turn away when Alistair placed a hand on her arm. "Do you want some company?" His brows knitted together anxiously. Lillian gave him a wan smile and patted his hand.

"No, thank you, Alistair. You're the butterfly's boots for asking. Truly. But you should stay here with the others." I wondered briefly if Alistair would catch on to her unspoken message—Lillian wanted some time to herself. His jaw moved several times as he appeared to be working it out before he graciously nodded.

"Absolutely, Lillian. Whatever you say."

Lillian gave another weak smile and left the room. Alistair stood awkwardly for a moment, unsure of whether he should take a seat or not. He shifted from foot to foot before finally coming to a decision.

"I think I'll just unpack my things, if no one minds."

"Of course, Alistair." Lord Hughes nodded at the young man. "I'm glad you're here. This is difficult for Lillian."

"I'll do what I can, Uncle." Alistair gave a short bow and left the room. We were quiet for a moment, lost in our own thoughts.

Redvers cleared his throat. "How long has Flight Lieutenant Marshall worked for you, Lord Hughes?"

Hughes rubbed his chin. "I think three years or so. Group Captain Hammond refers men who need employment—it's tough for some of the men to find jobs, let alone keep them."

Millie looked at Lord Hughes. "It's good of you to give them work, Edward."

The lord's face colored slightly. I wondered if it was Millie's use of his given name, or if it was the compliment that embarrassed Lord Hughes. I didn't know the man well enough to say either way.

It was also an interesting statement, given Millie's remark the night before. I wondered if she had the slightest bit of self-awareness about the trouble she had caused. Blame for the young man's death couldn't be laid at her feet, but she had certainly served as a spark to the flame.

Redvers continued. "Is there anyone you can think of who would have wanted to hurt Flight Lieutenant Marshall?"

Lord Hughes slowly shook his head. "He was a good lad." Millie raised her eyebrows and Hughes tilted his head in acknowledgment of her silent statement. "He did have a temper, but I believe it was just residual shock from the war.

When he had one of his . . . episodes . . . Simon would take a car and race around the countryside for a bit then come back right as rain. As though nothing had happened."

"This happened more than once, then." It was possible whoever sliced into the brake cables knew about this habit of Simon's.

"Every few weeks or so. It was happening with less frequency, to be honest. I thought the country air was finally doing him some good. As well as having steady work. That's one of the reasons I thought it was so important for him to have a project. It helped him feel useful again."

I considered that. Unemployment among the men who served in the Great War was still high. And it must have been difficult to come back after serving your country to find that your job—and nearly all the jobs—were taken by someone else. In some cases, by someone who hadn't been fit enough to serve. The whole thing must have felt like a slap in the face.

I thought about the other staff employed on the estate. The gardener, Sergeant Barlow, whom I had seen multiple times working on the grounds, was obviously a veteran, as was the butler, Mr. Shaw. Barlow was missing his left hand, and although Shaw seemed intact, who knew what shadows followed the man in private. Millie was right. Lord Hughes was doing a service to these veterans by giving them employment.

Then I recalled Simon's comments from the night before.

"Lord Hughes, why was Simon so resentful of Americans?"

Redvers and Hughes shared a look. Hughes cleared his throat and I could tell he was going to gloss over the truth yet again.

"I think some of the boys were simply a little resentful that it took so long for the Americans to join the fight."

I looked at Redvers.

He shrugged. "And then the Americans took a lot of glory

for riding in to the rescue when our boys had already been fighting for so long. Living in the muck and watching their friends die. Only to see the Americans come in like conquering heroes and have the world fawn over them. It was a lot to stomach."

That was closer to the explanation I was looking for. I glanced at my aunt, and for once she was quiet, studying her cup of tea. Lord Hughes shifted in his seat, lips pursed in mild displeasure.

I looked over and could see that Redvers had moved on to another topic and his mind was churning. "Lord Hughes, the lad's been here three years, but the war's been over for longer than that. Do you know what Marshall did in between?"

Hughes shook his head. "I believe he worked at a mechanic's shop in London. You'll have to ask Group Captain Hammond for the details."

We heard a murmured exchange in the hall, then Hammond entered, casting a quick glance behind him before crossing the room to us.

"What will you have to ask me?"

"What Simon did between the end of the war and coming to work here for Lord Hughes." I smiled at Hammond, and gestured for him to join us. He gave me a rueful smile and remained standing.

"I have some more phone calls to make, I'm afraid." He shook his head. "I'm not entirely sure what Simon did after he was discharged. You'll have to talk to his commanding officer, Air Commodore Ward." Group Captain Hammond turned and gave a glance back at the doorway before returning his attention to us. I cocked my head at him, but he gave his a little shake in response to my unasked question.

I could hear some activity at the front door before Shaw came into the room once more.

"Inspector Greyson is 'ere."

Chapter 6

The inspector strode into the room, the ends of his long black coat flapping. He was tall and slender with a severe face, long nose, and slightly ruddy cheeks. I recognized him from the accident scene—he was the man Redvers had spoken to about inspecting the car. His gray eyes seemed to take in everything, and I shifted in my seat even though I knew I had nothing to be anxious about. Police still made me nervous after my numerous interrogations in Egypt. Lord Hughes rose to greet the newcomer, and I went back to the tea tray to pour myself some more coffee.

Lord Hughes made the introductions, and when the inspector came to me his face broke into a surprising smile. It brightened his severe features and made him look almost handsome. I found myself giving a cautious smile in return.

"Ah, Mrs. Wunderly. You were at the accident scene earlier, were you not?"

I cleared my throat. "I was."

"I noticed you right away."

I tipped my head slightly. Was the man flirting with me? I glanced over and saw that Redvers' jaw had tightened.

The inspector gave a shake of his head. "Although I must say it was no place for a woman. Mr. Redvers, I'm quite surprised you allowed it."

If the man had been flirting with me, he had just sunk his own ship.

Redvers didn't bother to respond as the inspector took in the rest of the room. "And where is the other man who was with you?"

"Group Captain Hammond. He's just making some phone calls."

The inspector nodded and motioned for us all to take our seats. He pulled over a small leather chair, seating himself strategically at the head of our little group before he proceeded to ask us the same questions that Redvers and I had covered, making notes in a little notebook with a worn brown cover. When he finished, he rose and shook hands with Lord Hughes. "I'll have to speak to your daughter and the rest of your staff later, but this should do for now."

Lord Hughes nodded. "Of course."

"Redvers, would you accompany me out?"

Redvers stood. "Certainly."

My mouth twisted a bit and the inspector came over and shook my hand once again. "It was a pleasure, Mrs. Wunderly. I'm sure I'll see you again." I smiled weakly in response.

As the men left the room, Millie caught my eye and raised a speculative eyebrow, but I could only give a little shrug in reply. It had become obvious that the man was flirting with me—and I'd noticed during our interview that his hand was naked of any kind of wedding band. Not that I had any interest in the man romantically; it was merely an observation.

Since the inspector had asked Redvers to see him out, I assumed he wanted to discuss some aspect of Simon's death with Redvers. I only hoped Redvers would tell me what they talked about later. Even though I had come to trust the man, he was known to keep details to himself. I was sorely tempted to follow them, but I managed to stay in my seat, even when Lord Hughes followed the other men out.

I gritted my teeth and turned to my aunt. Millie had been

uncharacteristically quiet during the interview, and I now found her gazing into the teacup perched in her lap, her animation from only moments before completely melted away.

"Aunt Millie?" I asked quietly so as not to startle her.

"Will you look into this, Jane?" my aunt asked, equally as quietly.

"I would have thought you would prefer me to stay out of it." Millie had not cared for it one bit when I began investigating the murder of a young woman at our hotel in Egypt. And I had been a suspect at the time. I wasn't sure I would be able to keep my nose out of things now, but I was curious as to why my aunt would have such a change of heart about my involving myself in something so salacious as a murder investigation.

Glancing around and seeing that we were truly alone, Millie turned back and regarded me.

"I don't want anything to disturb Lillian," she said. "She's in training, and . . ." Millie trailed off, looking back into her cup. We were quiet for a moment before she raised her eyes to mine. I couldn't help but be concerned at my aunt's uncharacteristic behavior.

"I don't want anything to happen to Edward, either."

It took me a split second to remember that Edward was in fact Lord Hughes. "You don't think he could have anything to do with this, do you?"

"No!" Millie's voice was loud in the empty room. "No," she repeated in a subdued tone. "But what if that car was meant for him? I . . . I'm simply asking if you could keep an eye on things. Perhaps ask some questions."

I was surprised that my aunt was asking it of me. But before I could answer her one way or another she spoke again.

"Please, Jane." Her voice was soft and pleading.

My aunt never said *please*. At least, I could not remember her ever saying it to me. I couldn't stop my eyebrows from inching up, and I looked at her in wonder. It was unlikely that I would be able to resist working on a new puzzle anyway, but the fact that my aunt had basically begged me to help was shocking. I could hardly stay out of it now.

"Of course, Aunt Millie. I'll . . . keep an eye on things."

Her shoulders slumped a bit, but the tension in her face remained. We were quiet for another moment, then a crafty look replaced the worry. I winced into my coffee cup in anticipation of what was coming.

"You know, it seems the inspector was more than a little interested in getting to know you, Jane. It seems you haven't lost all your attraction."

I was not going to thank her for the backhanded compliment.

"It wouldn't hurt to flirt with the man a little bit. Maybe it would make Mr. Redvers sit up and take some notice." She sat back and gave a satisfied nod. "If you made some effort, I'd wager we could have you married in no time."

I sighed. Even when some things changed, others remained stubbornly the same.

Redvers came back and we decided to take a walk around the grounds. The sun had disappeared behind heavy gray clouds, leaving a frosty chill in the air. I pulled my felt cloche hat snugger around my ears, huddled into my wool coat, and sent up a grateful thanks that the inevitable rain hadn't started yet.

"What did the inspector have to talk to you about?" We crunched through fallen leaves as we headed away from the open fields of Lillian's golf course and toward the woods lurking behind the stables.

Redvers' mouth quirked up. Likely because he knew I wouldn't be able to go a minute without asking him. It was annoying that he had been proved correct.

"Nothing important. He and his men are going to search

the garage where the car was kept." Redvers stopped and nodded at the building in question. The door was ajar and I could see the lights were on. "I imagine they're in there now."

"Was that all?"

"And he wants me to keep an eye on things for him here."

I gave an unladylike snort. "That's almost exactly what Millie asked me to do. Keep an eye on things for her." I was quiet for a moment. "I think she's worried. Either that someone we know is responsible or that someone she loves might be next."

"She certainly seems more worried than she did when you were being investigated."

I pursed my lips. "I noticed." It gave me a slight pang, but I moved on. "So, what would have her that concerned? Lillian?"

"Lillian doesn't seem to have a motive."

"No. She really seems to have cared about the young man. This is the most emotional I've ever seen her, I think. Except perhaps when Millie was hurt." We crossed a small stone bridge spanning a lazy stream and continued meandering among the trees. Farther along, the woods became quite thick, even menacing with its dense foliage, but here there were clear paths among the scattered maple and birch. Sparrows chittered at us as we passed, irritated at the intrusion.

"Do you think she was interested in Simon?"

"It's hard to say. Lillian is so difficult to read. But I think she was genuinely fond of him." I adjusted my hat against a sudden gust of wind. "If we're talking motive, do you think it's Lord Hughes that Millie is concerned about?"

"It would make more sense. But why would he kill his mechanic?"

"Because Simon was interested in his daughter? It seems there would be better ways to put an end to that, though. Maybe Millie is just worried that something else might happen."

We had neared the edge of the woods, and I could see a putting green to our left. I went a few more steps before I realized Redvers had stopped. I turned back. "What is it?"

"Jane," he started to say. His voice rumbled through me and my stomach clenched in anticipation.

"Hello there!" I jumped as I heard the shout. Peering around a tree I saw Lillian waving her club from the green. She must have just come over the hill and spied us among the trees. Redvers heaved a sigh as I gave a half-hearted wave back.

"What were you going to say?" I was both desperate to know and terrified at hearing whatever was on his mind. I didn't for a moment think it was about the investigation—especially since he was now grumbling under his breath.

"It can wait" was his only response. Aloud, anyway.

I was certainly conflicted about Redvers. My first marriage had been a disaster of epic proportions and I wasn't looking to make another catastrophic mistake. I still bore the scars—literally—from that debacle, and I was quite comfortable with my decision to never marry again. I enjoyed being single.

But I also enjoyed Redvers' company. And there was nothing conflicted about that kiss—it had rocked me to the very tips of my toes. But repeating it would be a terrible idea.

Wouldn't it? It would. It absolutely would.

We walked out onto the green and drew near to Lillian. She was absently swinging the club as she waited for us. The wind ruffled her hair and painted her cheeks red, but she didn't seem the slightest bit cold. "Have the police come?"

"They have. I believe Inspector Greyson is searching the garage as we speak."

Lillian thought that over for a moment. "I suppose they'll have to speak to me." She didn't appear nervous. Simply matter-of-fact.

"They will at some point." Redvers and I were both studying the girl.

"I'm very sorry about Simon," I said softly.

Lillian glanced up, then back down at her club. "Thank you." We waited a moment for her to go on and we were not disappointed. "He was such a nice young man and had such a rotten time in the war. And he had no family left . . . he was all alone."

I nodded sympathetically, but my attention snagged on what she said. "Did Simon talk to you about his time in the war?"

"Just a bit. Whatever he saw . . . well, that's why he would take the car out and tear around the countryside."

"What did he say about it?"

Lillian shook her head and gave me a direct look. "I won't betray his trust."

I thought that was a rather silly sentiment given that Simon was dead—possibly murdered—but pressing her on the issue now didn't seem the best course of action. I would talk to her again when her feelings weren't quite so raw. Hopefully Simon had mentioned something about his time in the service that could point us in a direction that didn't lead directly to someone on the estate.

"Were you . . . interested in Simon, Lillian?"

She was quiet for a moment. "I know he was a bit sweet on me. And I liked his flirting, I really did."

We waited expectantly.

"But Father would have never let me marry a servant. Even if he was a hero during the war."

"So, you had feelings for him?"

She shrugged. "It was nothing serious, really. I don't ever want to marry."

I would unpack that last statement later. But Lillian having tender feelings for Simon explained her strong reaction to his death.

"Jane," she started, then stopped, glancing at Redvers.

This was getting to be a habit with people. One that was getting old fast.

"Yes?"

Lillian shuffled her feet, then continued. "Will you look into this? I know the police are investigating, but will you as well?"

"I can ask some questions. But why, Lillian?"

"I'm just worried about Millie. My mother."

Chapter 7

You could have knocked me over with a feather. I was under the impression that Lillian still didn't know who her birth mother was, although she had dropped the "aunt" when referring to Millie some weeks ago. The fact of her parentage was no surprise to me—I'd learned that Millie was Lillian's natural mother during our time in Egypt. Millie and Hughes had had an affair resulting in Lillian, and Millie had given the baby over for adoption to Lord Hughes and his wife. The first time Lillian had met Millie was at the Mena House and the two had grown quite close, although I didn't think Millie had shared her secret with Lillian yet. It appeared the girl was more perceptive than I gave her credit for.

But I wasn't sure what to address first. Ask how Lillian knew Millie was her mother? Or why Lillian thought Millie might be involved in what had happened to Simon? Thankfully Redvers jumped in to fill the silence and made the choice for me.

"Do you think Millie had something to do with this?" Redvers' voice was gentle, as though Lillian were a horse that might bolt at any time. She had seemed reluctant to talk in front of him, and by speaking up, Redvers was reminding her that he was still with us. I held my breath for a moment, but she cocked her head, thinking the question over.

"I'm not sure." Lillian banged her club against her sturdy

boot a few times. We all watched the movement. "She didn't like Simon's interest in me, that's for sure. But I can't see her hurting someone." I didn't share her illusions about my aunt. If pushed hard enough, I had no doubt Millie would cause someone harm, and not just with her sharp tongue. But I keep that to myself. "I just . . . I don't want anything to happen to her."

There we agreed—I didn't want anything to happen to Millie, either. We were all quiet for a moment before Lillian sighed. "I don't want you to think I'm not worried about Father also. But he's more used to this sort of thing."

"What sort of thing?" She couldn't mean that he was accustomed to murder inquiries.

Lillian waved a vague hand. "You know, taking care of himself."

I was quite sure that wasn't what she meant at all, but before I could ask her about it, her face closed down and she turned toward the house. "I'm going to go in. I'll see you before dinner."

We watched Lillian move toward the house before I tipped my head in the opposite direction, back through the woods we had come out of. Redvers nodded and we moved back under the canopy of trees.

"Everyone seems to suspect everyone else." Redvers moved easily along the path. I was glad he was with me, as dark clouds had begun to descend and an ominous gloom had gathered in the forest behind us. It gave me a slight shiver to think about what might be lurking there unseen.

"I would prefer to think they are just concerned for each other." I stuffed my hands into my pockets as we walked, wishing I had remembered my gloves.

"It's interesting that everyone assumes it was someone on the estate, when it could have been anyone, really." I thought about the layout of the grounds. I was sure the house was locked up at night, but the outbuildings were all but abandoned once night fell. "It would be very simple to sneak into the barn and damage the brake cables; it's not like there are a lot of people about, especially after dark."

Redvers nodded. "I'd noticed the same thing."

"And we don't know enough about Simon's background. Any number of people from his past might know he was employed here. It would be easy to stake the place out and learn enough about the family to know which car to sabotage."

"Anything is possible."

"What do you think Lillian meant about Lord Hughes being used to this sort of thing?"

"I haven't the foggiest. Although I'm not sure she quite knows either."

I sighed. "We just don't know enough about anything right now."

"Not even enough to make your usual wild guesses?" Redvers shot me an amused glance.

I rolled my eyes. "Not even that."

We were quiet for a few moments, and I wondered if Redvers was going to bring up whatever he was going to say earlier, but we continued on toward the garage in silence. I honestly didn't know if I was disappointed or relieved.

But there was one thing I knew for certain. And it couldn't hurt to admit it.

"I'm glad you're here, Redvers." And it had nothing to do with the creepy woods, or even Simon's murder.

Redvers' smile was like the sun breaking through the clouds on a dreary English day, and nearly as dazzling. "So am I, Jane. So am I."

It was only a little farther to the gray stone barn where Lord Hughes kept his vehicles along with the yellow Moth biplane. I could see a handful of policemen moving about the area but none of them acknowledged our arrival.

Inspector Greyson met us at the door. He smiled broadly

at me before giving me a small wink, which left me feeling unsettled. "Lovely to see you again, Mrs. Wunderly, but don't you think you would be more comfortable in the house?" He glanced up at the sky. "The weather is rather unpleasant."

"Have you found anything?" Redvers ignored the man's solicitousness toward my personal comfort. I found myself mentally cheering him.

"Not much." He shifted on his feet and glanced my way. It seemed the inspector was happy to see me but was reluctant to talk about the investigation in front of me. It was quite irritating—I would much prefer if things were the other way around. I would trade flirting for a good chat about a case any day.

"I'll just relay the information to her later on," Redvers said impatiently.

Greyson frowned, but continued. "I believe we've found the knife it was done with."

I thought that was a bit more than "not much," but once again I managed to hold my tongue. I caught Redvers' sideways look out of the corner of my eye—he was obviously expecting a snide comment as well. I faced Redvers with an angelic look of innocence on my face, which elicited a quiet snort. The inspector looked between the two of us for a moment, a puzzled look washing across his face. Finally, he cleared his throat and moved on.

"We found a pocketknife with what looks like damage to the blade. The kind of damage you might see from sawing through a brake cable. It was engraved with the initials *ERH*."

I frowned and was about to open my mouth, but the inspector cut me off.

"Obviously Lord Hughes's initials, but it's impossible to say who used it. Practically everything in this place belongs to the man. And it would be easy to set him up by leaving it at the scene. We'll try to get fingerprints."

I had to admit I was impressed, despite my personal irritation with Greyson. It seemed the inspector wasn't going to be jumping to any quick conclusions. I admired that and felt more than a little relieved since Millie's fears were beginning to look justified. With the discovery of the knife it looked like Lord Hughes was in fact being set up for Simon's murder, since I couldn't imagine he was actually responsible.

At least if the man was being framed, it was unlikely he was also being targeted. The damaged brake cables were likely meant for Simon after all.

With that bit of information learned, we decided to leave the police to it, although I doubted they would turn up anything else of note in their search. Greyson promised that he would see us back at the house later—he would need to talk to Lord Hughes about the knife, regardless of whether he thought the man was guilty of using it.

Chapter 8

Martha met us at the back door, her thin face drawn and her tone clipped.

"Mr. Redvers, I had Queenie get your room ready. You will be two doors down from Mrs. Wunderly."

"Is Alistair staying as well?" I wondered if the young man would stick around with so much turmoil in the house.

"He'll be across the hall from you."

"Who's Queenie?" Redvers asked.

"Queenie Powell. She's one of the girls from town who comes in to clean. We haven't had live-in maids since before the war."

"Ah. Well, thank you, Martha."

With a sharp nod, Martha bustled back to the kitchen. I wondered if it was the arrival of extra guests that had the normally unflappable woman out of sorts. I wanted to ask her if she knew anything about Simon, but it seemed like a good idea to wait until she was more herself and willing to talk.

I left Redvers to get settled in, and wandered through the downstairs rooms, unsure of whether I was looking for someone or trying to avoid company altogether. I came to a stop in the drawing room and gazed out the window. From where I stood, I could see the gardener moving easily about his work despite his handicap. I wondered if anyone had bothered to talk with him yet—he was the sort of person that faded into the background and was easily overlooked. I would have to go back outside, but there was no time like the present to chat with the man.

When I first arrived, Sergeant William Barlow had been introduced to me, but I had only caught glimpses of him since. He had a quiet demeanor, kept to himself, and unlike Flight Lieutenant Marshall, didn't join the family for any socializing. I wasn't even sure he stayed in the house like the rest of the staff, although I didn't know where else he would bunk down. I wondered if he didn't feel as welcome given the color of his skin, or if he simply preferred his own company.

My feet crunched on the gravel pathway, announcing my approach. Sergeant Barlow stood from his work slowly, where he had been mulching the rose bushes. There was a profusion of roses on this side of the house in a rainbow of colors. They had begun to die back already, but you could see how glorious the garden must be at the height of summer.

"Sergeant Barlow," I said softly. "How are you?" I could see where the man's left hand had been removed and sewn up, a scarred stump the only remnant of his loss. Light scarring marred the same side of his face and neck, the light marks pronounced against his smooth dark skin.

Barlow faced me and gave a lopsided smile. "I'm well, Mrs. Wunderly. What brings you to my rose garden?" The gentle roll of his West Indies accent washed over me as he gestured with his clippers. "It's not at its best right now, as you can see."

"But I can see how well tended it is. It must be lovely in the summer." I paused in front of a garden bench facing Barlow, tucked my coat securely beneath me, and took a seat on the cold stone. "I suppose you heard about Flight Lieutenant Marshall."

The sergeant's face fell. "Yes, Miss Martha told me about it. It's a terrible thing. Although I'm glad no one in the family was hurt as well."

I thought that over for a moment. "Do you think it was meant for one of them instead?"

The sergeant shook his head. "No, Simon was the only one who used the Lambda. But Miss Lillian sometimes rode with Simon. When he wasn't in a temper."

I nodded and paused, considering how to proceed.

"Did you know Simon well?" I finally asked.

"As well as anyone, I suppose. He liked to seek me out and talk when he was in his cups." As quiet as the sergeant was, I imagined those were very one-sided conversations.

"Did you serve together?" I didn't know anything about either of their time in the war, and was nervous to broach such a sensitive subject. Especially with a man who had obviously suffered as much as the sergeant had.

"No, ma'am. People with my color skin served with our own kind. Not at first, but later."

"Oh." My face flushed a bit at my ignorance.

"It's nice that you didn't assume, ma'am." He smiled at me kindly; then his face turned thoughtful. "But I'm not sure his being a veteran had anything to do with his being killed."

"What makes you say that?"

Barlow studied me for a moment before giving a small shrug. "Well . . . Simon had bragged to me a few weeks ago that he had . . . found out some information."

I shifted, the cold from the bench beginning to seep through my coat, and waited for the sergeant to gather his thoughts.

"About Lord Hughes."

My mouth gaped open. I stared at Barlow for a moment, but he seemed to be finished. "Do you know what it was?"

Sergeant Barlow shook his head. "I don't—he wouldn't

tell me, even though I asked him several times. But I know it wasn't anything good."

I'm afraid I was still imitating an open-mouthed fish, so he went on. "I don't believe Lord Hughes had anything to do with his death, ma'am. He's a good man. I told Simon to take care with whatever it is he'd learned. We're all lucky to have these positions, but especially me." He gestured to the end of his left arm, then to his face. "Many of the black soldiers who wanted to stay couldn't—there are very few jobs for us here. I was lucky to get this position, especially without the hand."

I could do nothing but smile and nod in sympathy. Frankly, I had thought it absurd when I learned Lord Hughes had a one-handed gardener, but the man seemed quite capable, and made good use of the rest of his arm. I hadn't even thought about how much more difficult the man's race would make it on top of that. I'd assumed relations between the races were more egalitarian in Britain than they were in the States, but I had assumed wrong.

"Did Simon ever say anything about his job before he came to work here?"

Sergeant Barlow tipped his head and was quiet for a moment. "I know he worked at a shop that was closed down. He told me that he wasn't involved, but there was some trouble with the owner. I think the man might be in prison." Barlow shrugged. "Either way, Simon was out of a job."

That was definitely an avenue to explore. Perhaps Simon hadn't been as innocent as he claimed in whatever sent his boss to prison.

"What did you do during the war, Sergeant?" The words were out before I could think over the wisdom of speaking them.

He was quiet for so long, I thought he might not answer me. "I was part of the Artillery Corps, ma'am. We fought in

Turkey." He was silent for a moment, surveying the grounds around us. "I like the quiet of tending to the gardens. And the horses." I nodded, although he wasn't looking at me.

There was something else I was curious about. "You're not from England, Sergeant Barlow. Why didn't you go home after the war?"

Something sharp and painful flashed in his eyes. I only saw it for a fleeting moment before the man's face shut down and smoothed back into his normal amiable expression. "My people are gone, ma'am. There's not much left for me there."

He looked to the sky. "You should get inside, Mrs. Wunderly. It's going to rain soon." I looked up at the clouds and saw that they had gathered in earnest.

"Thanks for your time, Sergeant."

"Call me William, ma'am." He placed his clipper into a waiting handcart and moved to gather his other tools as well.

"And call me Jane."

"Yes, ma'am."

I smiled. There was no way he would call me by my first name, no matter how many times I insisted.

I headed back into the house and muttered a curse under my breath when I realized I'd forgotten to ask whether Barlow had seen anything unusual on the grounds—like a stranger creeping into the barn late at night to do damage to some brake cables. But a glance outside told me that the rain had in fact started. My question would have to wait until later.

Perhaps the sergeant hadn't been merely trying to get rid of me and my questions.

Chapter 9

I attempted to hunt down Redvers. I wanted to discuss what Barlow had told me about Simon—maybe Redvers would have an idea about what kind of information Simon could have had about Lord Hughes. But I couldn't find the man in any of the numerous downstairs rooms, or anywhere else for that matter. The door to Lord Hughes's study was closed, but I could hardly knock and disturb the man when he was the topic I wanted to discuss. I headed upstairs and rapped on Redvers' door, hoping to find he was still getting settled in. I thought it seemed unlikely, and I was correct. There was no answer and a twist of the doorknob got me nowhere.

With a huff of frustration, I went to my own room and found the door unlocked. I puzzled over that—I was certain I had locked it before I'd left. Had Martha or Queenie come in to do some cleaning and forgotten to lock up behind them? Entering, I cast a glance around and saw nothing out of the ordinary—everything was just as I had left it. Hands on hips, I turned and spied the large four-poster bed situated across from the large windows. A small white note graced my pillow.

Meet me before dinner for drinks. Library. –R

I almost smiled before I realized that meant he planned to disappear for the rest of the afternoon, and muttered something unflattering under my breath. I walked over to the door and looked closely at the lock—no signs of a scratch. I made a mental note to ask him later how he managed that.

A sudden chill raced through me. If the lock was that easy to pick, would someone else have an equally easy time getting inside? I obviously wasn't a target for what happened to Simon, but the thought still left me feeling unsettled.

I haunted the library for the rest of the afternoon, pretending to read a book, but really staring out the window at the increasing rain, thinking things over. Everyone had secrets, so it stood to reason Lord Hughes did as well. But whatever Simon learned, was it enough to kill over? Was I being foolish in assuming Lord Hughes was innocent?

There were plenty of other people on the estate, including a handful of servants who may have known each other during the war. Did one of them have a reason to kill Simon? And why slice the brake cables, and risk someone else being killed? Why not take a more traditional route to murder? It would have been hard to peg exactly when Simon would use that car again. And if he had found the problem before taking the car out, which he might have done since he worked on the car frequently, chances were good the plan wouldn't have worked at all. It was a risky move altogether. And what was the reason Simon's previous place of employment had been shut down?

I had nothing but questions. And a growing list of people to talk to, including the elusive butler and a suddenly snappish Martha.

I didn't hear any footsteps, but I caught a whiff of a woodsy cologne, and I turned, one eyebrow arched like Garbo. "We have to stop meeting like this."

Redvers' mouth twitched. "Preparing for your silver screen debut?"

I laughed. "You don't think I'm ready?"

"I think you'll need more paint for your face."

I feigned outrage. "Are you saying I need to wear more makeup to be attractive?"

Redvers' mouth gaped open a bit and a flush of red stained his cheeks. He pulled at his collar with one finger. "No, not at all . . . what I meant was . . ."

He trailed off and I laughed. "Redvers. You seem to be flustered."

He narrowed his eyes at me, and I laughed again before deciding to put him out of his misery. It was just so rare that I was able to turn the tables and make *him* blush for once. A warm glow spread through me that we seemed to be able to pick up where we had left off with each other in Egypt.

I grinned, then noticed his hair was damp.

"You've been outside."

"I could have bathed."

I sniffed at him from my seat. "No. You smell like rain."

He shook his head, his composure regained. "Rain doesn't smell like anything. Did you find anything out from the gardener?"

I almost asked how he knew about my conversation with Barlow, but decided it was pointless. I stood and moved to the bar cart instead. It was time for a drink. "I did."

"And are you going to share, or will you be keeping that information to yourself?" Redvers joined me at the cart, and the scent of fresh rain and clean pine came with him.

I wrinkled my nose at him but continued anyway. "It seems as though Simon learned something about Lord Hughes, but Sergeant Barlow didn't know what."

"Well, that could cover a lot of ground."

I agreed. "I hope this isn't another case of blackmail."

Redvers grunted his assent as he poured himself a healthy dose of scotch. "Gin rickey?"

I smiled, pleased that he remembered, and passed over the glass that I had been holding absentmindedly. "Yes, thank you."

"You know, gin is considered very déclassé by the aristocracy—I'm surprised Lord Hughes stocks it."

"Well, I'm glad he does. Perhaps he did it for me." I watched as he handily prepared my drink. "Barlow also thought there was something fishy with Simon's last place of employment—that the owner might have landed himself in prison."

Redvers paused at what he was doing and looked at me. "Did he say how?"

I shook my head. "He didn't know." My mind jumped ahead. "By the by, how did you break into my room earlier? I know I locked my door."

"These locks are quite easy to get through. Too easy."

"I'm going to have to put a chair under my doorknob at night."

Redvers considered that. "Not a bad idea. Of course, it will make it difficult for you to get out. Or let someone in."

Both our faces flushed crimson as we considered the implication of what he had just said—that I might want to *let* someone into my bedroom. At night.

Before my face could redden even further, I quickly changed the subject. "So, where were you this afternoon?"

"I was taking a look around the outbuildings."

"Without me? You know I hate it when you snoop without me."

Redvers continued as though I hadn't spoken. "There appears to be a large room above the stables, but it was locked tight."

"You couldn't get in? I didn't think there was a lock that could outsmart you."

"I'll need better equipment. The locks were more complicated than those in this house, and used a lot less often."

"Is that unusual? The locks being more complicated?"

"Somewhat."

"I wonder what they're keeping out there."

Our discussion was interrupted by Millie charging through the doorway. "What are you two doing in this room? We usually gather in the drawing room." She caught sight of our drinks as she came toward us. "Are you drinking already? Excellent."

Redvers and I exchanged an amused look as my aunt helped herself to a whiskey highball. I briefly wondered if my aunt was the reason Lord Hughes seemed to keep a bar cart in nearly every room.

"Have you learned anything yet, Jane?" Millie asked.

"Not yet. It's only been a few hours, Aunt Millie." Millie gave a sniff and turned to Redvers.

"Well, I'm glad you are here, Mr. Redvers."

Redvers grinned at her. "I am, too, Mrs. Stanley."

"Well, why are we standing around in here?" She gave a dramatic shiver despite her thick woolen dress and shawl. "There's a lovely fire in the drawing room. Come along now." Millie marched us down the hall, into the drawing room, and over to a grouping of seats near the fireplace. "Although maybe you shouldn't sit so close to the fire, Jane. You look a bit warm already." I patted my face—I thought my blush had long since faded. Redvers' certainly had.

We were joined by Group Captain Hammond, who went straight to the bar cart, fixed himself a drink, and then joined us where we now sat. He stood beside my chair, refusing a seat but resting one elbow on the seat back behind me. Millie frowned at him, but he ignored her.

I turned in my seat to look up at him. "Are you sure you wouldn't like to sit?"

"I'd rather stand just now. But thank you. It's been a trying day."

"I'll bet," I said sympathetically. "Were you able to make all the arrangements you needed to?"

The group captain nodded but didn't elaborate further.

We were soon joined by the rest of the party, and then moved in to dinner.

Redvers sat beside me and Hammond seated himself across the table. I noticed Alistair negotiated around Millie in order to be seated on one side of Lillian. Marie quickly sat down on the other side, as if daring anyone to challenge her.

"Nothing fancy tonight," Martha bustled in and served each of us the first course, a delicious mushroom soup. "I did not realize we would have so much company." The poor woman still looked flustered.

"It looks wonderful, Martha," Lord Hughes told her.

There was a pause in the conversation, and Hammond addressed me.

"Do you want to go up in the morning? If the weather improves?"

"Certainly. You know I would never miss an opportunity." I smiled.

Redvers looked back and forth between us, brows furrowed. "Go up?"

"Jane has been taking flying lessons," Millie informed him, her voice seething with aggravation. "And surely you can't mean to fly anymore. Now that the car has been tampered with." She gestured to Lord Hughes, who was wisely concentrating on his soup. "Edward has already agreed to take a break from lessons until this can be cleared up."

"The car being tampered with doesn't necessarily have anything to do with the Moth, Aunt Millie."

"They were kept in the same place!" Millie turned to Lord Hughes for help, but he was concentrating on the bowl before him, pretending that he couldn't hear us. I wondered if he had actually agreed to stop flying, or if he was merely placating my aunt.

"You've been taking flying lessons?" Redvers sounded somewhat incredulous.

"Yes. I have." I stared him down, daring him to say anything further.

He returned my gaze for a moment before nodding. He looked across to Hammond. "You'll be sure to go over the aircraft especially well before takeoff, won't you?"

"Of course. I normally do a thorough inspection, but I'll be even more attentive going forward."

With that, Redvers nodded again and turned back to his soup. I was shocked that he wasn't going to argue any further. From the apoplectic look on Millie's face, I could tell she was equally as stunned. She spluttered a few times, but the rest of us ignored her.

A small smile crept over my face.

Throughout the rest of the meal, I watched as the rest chatted. Alistair paid particular attention to Lillian, and even managed to coax a laugh from her once or twice. Marie startled at the sound each time and shot daggers at Alistair.

"If looks could kill," Redvers muttered to me.

"Alistair would be next." I was thoughtful. "I wonder if the boy should be careful after all."

Redvers didn't answer, but I could see him assessing the young people at the end of the table.

The second time Alistair managed to elicit a laugh from Lillian, Alistair caught me observing them, and shot me a slow wink. I offered a weak smile in return and watched as Marie took the opportunity to turn Lillian's attention to herself. I turned back to the gentlemen at my end of the table.

"Did you serve during the war?" Hammond was asking Redvers.

"I did," Redvers said.

I was very interested in where this line of questioning might go. I'd always wondered, but had never found a way to ask.

The group captain's eyebrows went up when Redvers failed to elaborate.

Redvers gave Hammond a direct look. "I served in a . . . different capacity."

"Ah." Hammond nodded, and turned the conversation in another direction.

The party broke up early after dinner, everyone feeling uncomfortable about playing games so soon after Simon's death, and I found myself prowling around my room, not quite ready to call it a night. The book on my nightstand wasn't holding my attention, so I got up and went to the window, cracking it open and letting some of the cold night air rush into the room. I peered past the curtain to the stable and barn beyond and wondered if the police had left anyone out there to guard the buildings. It was the scene of a crime, after all.

Or were the remaining vehicles—and the little airplane—all alone in the dark, where anyone could tamper with them?

Chapter 10

The next morning, I rose early and rushed to the windows, hoping the skies would be clear enough for the morning's flight. I was in luck. The low-hanging clouds had cleared overnight, leaving a gray sky but a high enough ceiling for us to fly. I freshened up, dressed, and hurried downstairs, my worries of the night before brushed aside in the light of day. If anyone had been tampering with the plane, we would be able to tell before I even got into the cockpit. I was sure of it.

It was too early for Martha to set out breakfast, so I went straight to the kitchen. Shaw was just leaving, and I nearly stumbled into the man coming through the open doorway.

"Mr. Shaw, I'm glad I ran into you." It seemed the man was never around except when someone was at the door. "I would like to speak with you later . . . perhaps after breakfast?"

"If ye like, Mrs. W." He barely paused before disappearing down the hall. I followed him with my eyes, then crossed into the kitchen with a shake of my head. I suspected it would take a small miracle to find the man later.

"Mrs. Wunderly! I do not have breakfast ready yet!" Martha wiped her hands on her apron, then tucked an errant red curl back behind her ear.

"That's quite all right, Martha. I just need some toast and coffee and I'll be just fine. And I can get them myself."

"That will not do. Not in my kitchen." Martha shooed me with both hands toward a stool at the large wooden table dominating the center of the room. I sat and she poured me a cup of coffee from the pot already bubbling on the stove. She took a step back toward the stove, then reconsidered and left the entire pot before me on the table.

"Martha, you're a dream." I wrapped my hands around the cup and took a whiff of the delicious caffeinated air. She laughed as she buttered some bread and placed it on the stove-top griddle pan. A few minutes later I was happily munching on perfectly browned toast. Rascal had abandoned his usual post at his master's side and was warming himself by the stove, but came to sit next to me while I ate, big brown eyes sadly watching every crumb disappear into my mouth.

"Rascal! Here." Martha handed the dog a hunk of bone, and the dog trotted back to his post near the stove, tail wagging, and set to work on it. She went back to bustling around the kitchen, and as I watched her my eyes brushed across a wicker basket on the counter.

"Is someone having a picnic today?"

Martha went still for a moment, before turning her thin frame toward the sink. "Why would you ask that, Mrs. Wunderly?"

"Erm . . . because of the picnic basket."

Martha's hands were busy washing a baking pan and there was a long pause before the woman answered. "I thought I heard someone say they want to take some food out later. Perhaps Miss Lillian. She likes to have a treat when she is out on the lawn swinging those metal sticks."

"Sure, of course." Had Martha behaved strangely when I mentioned the picnic basket, or was I imagining reactions where there were none? Simon's murder had me suspicious of everyone.

Martha's soapy hand suddenly flew toward the window

above the sink. "Shoo!" she cried as she vigorously flung bubbles at the pane of glass. A black bird took flight from where it had come to rest on the windowsill.

Martha's face darkened. "Bad luck, that is." She looked at me, hands gripping her apron. "Be careful today, Mrs. Wunderly."

Before I could respond, Group Captain Hammond entered the kitchen, goggles and flight helmet in hand. "Ready?"

"Nearly!" I slugged back the rest of my coffee. "Martha, I'll finish the pot when we get back."

Martha nodded. "Of course. I will set it aside for you and reheat when you return."

I scooped my own gear off the table and bundled into my coat and scarf before we headed out toward the stable. I thought about Martha's warning but quickly dismissed it—the woman was notoriously superstitious. A bird landing on the windowsill had nothing to do with a sabotaged car. It occurred to me that her superstitions seemed far more suited to an older woman, and I wondered again just how old Martha was and where she came from.

As we crested the small hill behind the house, I could see Redvers coming toward us. As he drew near, I called out to him.

"What are you doing out so early?"

"Just taking in the fresh morning air." He gave us an easy smile, and I narrowed my eyes at him. "I'll see you both after your flight." He smiled and touched his tweed cap before continuing on.

"You two seem rather close," Hammond observed mildly. I shot him a sideways look to see if I was missing some hidden innuendo. I hadn't picked up anything but friendly interest from the group captain—was it possible I had missed something? I hoped not.

"We met in Egypt. He helped me out . . . with a problem." I changed the subject. "Chris, what did Redvers mean last night when he said he worked in a different capacity during the war?"

The group captain laughed. "You don't know? I suppose he wouldn't say anything about it."

"Of course not. And I'm not privy to the code, although naturally I have my suspicions. I would just like some confirmation that I'm right."

Hammond looked at me and sighed good-naturedly. "It usually means they worked in military intelligence in some way but aren't allowed to talk about it."

It's what I had suspected, but it was nice to have it confirmed. It also explained a lot—Redvers' refusal to discuss his current job status also made sense if he had continued on in a similar capacity with the government. He was incredibly tight-lipped about it, although I realized he needed to be. I almost laughed when I remembered his insistence that he was a banker when we first met. I'd been right to disbelieve him.

We rolled the little yellow Moth out of the stone barn and pulled her wings forward. This model of airplane had wings that folded back like a nesting dove, to make storage easier. When you wanted to fly, you pulled the wings forward and reattached them. It made me nervous that they weren't permanently attached in position, but Hammond assured me that they were secure when locked into place. Of course, that didn't stop me from checking and double-checking them—wings were a rather necessary part of staying up in the air.

Wings secured, Hammond and I went over the rest of the airplane thoroughly, both inside and out. Despite my paranoia and the ominous warnings, we found nothing out of place or damaged. With a deep breath, I climbed into the cockpit and started her up. The engine turned over like it was waiting for me.

Takeoffs were now completely under my direction and control with no help from Group Captain Hammond. As we rumbled along the dirt strip and then soared up over the tree line, I realized I had been holding my breath, hoping that we wouldn't plummet back to the earth even though we had checked the Moth over thoroughly. Once in the air I started breathing freely again, that same sense of freedom opening up inside my chest.

Today's lesson was banked turns. We had done shallow turns before, but these tipped the airplane nearly on its side to make quicker, deeper turns. I loved it. We spent more than an hour in the air practicing, the control stick sensitive to my every whim, before the clouds started to descend again and we were forced to cut our morning short. I brought the plane around and lined up with the long dirt strip. This landing went even more smoothly than it did the last time.

"You're really getting the hang of things," Hammond said when we shut off the engine and climbed out. "Those last couple turns were a thing of beauty."

"Thanks." I beamed. I had some ways to go before I could apply for a license, but I was feeling more confident in the cockpit every time.

And I remembered to send up thanks that we managed to get through the flight without crashing from some undetected problem. Whoever our saboteur was, they hadn't touched the Moth.

Yet.

Chapter 11

I helped Hammond collapse the wings and we pushed the aircraft through the open doors and into its usual spot in the barn. It had been some time since the structure had actually been used to house animals—Simon had made the space into his mechanic's workshop years earlier, opening up the ground floor until it resembled a warehouse. There were a few bales of stale hay still lying about, but workbenches had been set up along the back wall and were covered with tools. The police had had plenty to sift through the day before, although it was hard to see where they had been among the usual disorder. If anything, the place looked a little tidier.

Lord Hughes's Bentley was parked on the opposite end of the space, near the second large door. The place where Simon's Lancia Lambda had once been stowed alongside it was a glaring reminder of the young man's fate. With a sigh, I turned and saw that Alistair had pulled his sleek black and red motorcycle with its sidecar into the barn as well, tucking it just behind the sliding door.

I waited for Hammond to finish closing up the stable before we headed back to the house for breakfast. Walking back, I thought I would use the time to ask him some questions about Simon Marshall. He hadn't seemed ready to discuss the young man earlier, but I hoped he would be more willing now that the initial shock of his death had worn off.

"Chris, you said you didn't know much about Simon's life after the war. But I was under the impression you found the position here for him."

The group captain smiled. "I did. But his commanding officer was the one who recommended him to me."

"Air Commodore Ward?"

Hammond's eyebrows shot up. "You have quite the memory. Yes, it was Air Commodore Ward." I waited to see if he would continue without my prompting him. I wasn't disappointed. "Flight Lieutenant Marshall . . . Simon . . . wasn't in my company during the war, but I had seen him around. The lad was a genius with mechanics. He could fix anything."

The group captain blew out a breath that we could both see in the cool morning air. We crunched on for a few yards before he continued.

"And even though he was an aircraft mechanic, he was sent forward to do vehicle repairs—I know he saw his share of action. That's how he was promoted to flight lieutenant. When the war ended, he was able to hold down a job for a few years, but the shell shock eventually snuck up on him."

I had heard that sometimes men seemed fine when they returned but that the problems associated with shell shock didn't surface until years later.

"From what everyone has said, he was overall a good soldier. He just needed a less . . . regimented job."

"I would think a regimented position would be helpful."

"It's different for everyone."

I was curious about something less to do with Simon Marshall and more to do with the man I had spent so much time with over the past few weeks. "How did you get into this—helping men find jobs?"

Hammond stuffed his hands in his pockets and ducked his head. I knew that he didn't like to talk about himself and preferred asking after others. I suspected his easygoing demeanor hid a bit of shyness. I waited patiently.

"My father was a rather prominent solicitor. He ran in all types of circles. And through my commission in the Royal Air Force, and running one of the London Aero Clubs now . . . well, I know a few people. I just try to keep my ears open and match up people and positions."

I could see Hammond moving easily in any number of circles. "Well, it's an amazing thing you're doing for people."

Hammond's cheeks flushed slightly as we drew near the house.

"Did you help Sergeant Barlow find his position here as well?"

"I did. That was a more difficult placement. Not many people would hire a black man—the race riots were years ago, mostly right after the war ended, but even still. But when I suggested Sergeant Barlow, Lord Hughes didn't even blink at the man's race, or his missing hand. He doesn't care as long as the man is competent." Hammond's red cheeks faded as he returned to our earlier subject. "Anyway, Air Commodore Ward always spoke well of Flight Lieutenant Marshall."

"And he has no family?"

"I spoke to Ward last evening after I left you. Apparently, there was once a fiancée, but by the time Marshall made it home after the war, she had married someone else."

"That's terrible."

"It happened a lot." The group captain's voice was a bit short at this, and I decided not to pursue the subject. From the tone of his voice, I suspected it was hitting a bit close to the mark regarding Hammond's postwar divorce.

"So, you've been with the Aero Club since the war?"

Hammond's face lit up. "I have. It's how I'm able to 'borrow' a plane to do private lessons here and there. I was one of the founding members of the London branch."

"When will you have to go back?" Selfishly, I hoped it

wouldn't be for a few weeks yet. I still needed quite a lot of flight hours before I would be comfortable doing a solo flight.

"Oh, not anytime soon. I might need to go back for a weekend to check in, but Lord Hughes is paying the club plenty for me to be here." Lord Hughes typically took flight lessons from the group captain in the afternoons and let me have my time in the mornings. Hughes had been reluctant to let me take them at all initially, but when he heard Millie's objections, he had winked at me and took my side. I think he had a bit of the devil in him and occasionally liked to needle her, although it would have been a different story entirely if I wasn't a widow. Somehow that status gave me slightly more freedom of choice than being a single woman as far as His Lordship was concerned.

Back inside the house I stripped off my coat and scarf, tucking my leather gloves into the pocket. Hammond and I both left our gear on the bench for the time being and made our way to the breakfast room. Just before we reached the door, Hammond touched my arm.

"Jane, I almost forgot to tell you. I saw something odd yesterday . . ."

Footsteps sounded on the nearby staircase and we turned to see Alistair turning the corner and coming down the hall toward us.

"Never mind," Hammond muttered under his breath.

"Good morning!" Alistair greeted us cheerfully, blissfully unaware that he was interrupting anything.

I smiled and greeted him in return, and the three of us went in together. I caught Hammond's eye and gave him a rueful smile. I was very curious about whatever odd thing he had seen, but completely understood why he didn't want to discuss it in front of anyone else. I would try to catch him alone later so he could finish whatever he had started to say.

* * *

The rest of the party was already seated, and it looked like everyone was nearly finished with their meals. Martha bustled in a few moments later carrying my newly warmed pot of coffee.

"Where are you sitting, Mrs. Wunderly?" I pointed to the open seat next to Redvers and thanked her heartily for remembering to bring it.

"Well," Aunt Millie put down her fork. "I can see where you've been." Her lips were pressed into a straight little line.

"And where is that, Aunt Millie?" I asked while I filled my plate with eggs and slices of ham. I skipped the baked beans but helped myself to a fried tomato.

"You have helmet hair. You've obviously been up in that infernal aircraft. Even when I told you it was a terrible idea."

I unconsciously reached up to touch my bob, but dropped my hand immediately. It was probably all out of shape from the tight leather helmet, but I was still on such a high from our flight that I couldn't bring myself to care. I would fix it later.

"So it is, Aunt Millie." I took my seat and calmly poured my coffee.

Redvers turned to me, one side of his mouth tipping up. "And how was your flight?"

I proceeded to fill him in while my aunt grumbled under her breath to Lord Hughes. I ignored her, and it appeared that Lord Hughes was doing the same, giving a noncommittal grunt now and again. I reminded myself not to let Millie get under my skin—she had a peculiar way of showing it, but all her fuss came from a place of concern.

"Is it raining, Jane?" Lillian's voice pierced my thoughts.

"Not yet, no. Although it looks like it may later."

Lillian nodded and pushed back from the table. "I'll get some time in now then."

"I'll join you." Alistair pushed his chair back, leaving a nearly full plate of food on the table. Lillian shrugged and the two left the room.

Marie was left alone at that end of the table, indecision plain on her face—follow, or stay and enjoy her half-eaten breakfast? With a shrug, she made up her mind and settled back in her seat again. With everyone's attention elsewhere, she snatched the slices of bacon from Alistair's abandoned plate and added them to her own.

"And what are you up to today, Jane?" Millie asked pointedly. It was a not-so-subtle reminder of what she had asked me to do.

"Well, I think I need to speak with Mr. Shaw. Lord Hughes, where can I find him this time of day?"

"Hmm?" Lord Hughes looked up from his paper at his name but had obviously missed the question.

I repeated myself and Lord Hughes looked thoughtful. "Belowstairs somewhere, I would think. I've never given it much thought." He shrugged. "He's always on hand when he's needed."

Millie shot Lord Hughes a frown and Redvers cut in before she could say anything. "A good plan, Jane. Then I think we should take a walk. Stretch our legs and enjoy the fresh country air."

"It's supposed to rain," Millie said.

"We'll take an umbrella," Redvers assured her.

Chapter 12

Redvers and I excused ourselves and set off in search of Shaw.

"Do you know anything about Mr. Shaw?"

"Not much, I'm afraid."

"Is that the truth, or are you keeping things from me again?" I had a teasing tone in my voice, but there was more than a little truth behind it as well. I could think of more than one instance where he had left me out of the loop during our previous investigation.

"Me?" Redvers put one hand to his chest. "Hold something back from you? Perish the thought."

I stuck my tongue out at him.

We headed down the back stairs into the belly of the house. I had never been "belowstairs" before and wasn't sure what we would find. At the bottom of the stone staircase a long hallway stretched before us. A little light filtered down from the tall windows at either end of the hall.

"Huh."

Redvers glanced over at me, one eyebrow raised.

"It's not quite what I expected."

"You were expecting a dungeon? I don't think they keep the servants chained up down here anymore. It's not the done thing."

I gave a little huff. "No, but it's just a series of rooms, isn't it?"

Redvers didn't answer, leading me down to the opposite end of the hall.

"How do you know which room is his?" It was so quiet down here that I felt the need to whisper.

"I asked." Redvers' voice practically boomed in response.

We came to a stop before the last wooden door and Redvers raised his hand and knocked. I could hear animated talking coming from within and frowned, wondering if Shaw had company. But when the voices snapped off, I realized the man had been listening to a radio. Moments later the door cautiously opened a crack.

"What are you all doin' down 'ere?"

The voice wasn't necessarily hostile, but I decided to let Redvers take the lead on this all the same.

"We've come to ask a few questions. About Simon Marshall."

Brown eyes regarded us from beneath his eyebrow for a moment before the door opened wider. "Fair 'nough." Shaw gestured for us to enter.

In my mind I suppose I had pictured a small, cheerless room lit by a dripping candle and furnished with a narrow bed and perhaps a dresser. The stuff of a Dickens tale. Instead, the door opened onto a comfortable sitting room filled with overstuffed furniture, a warm fireplace, and a state-of-the-art wireless radio. An inner door led to an adjoining room that I assumed was Shaw's bedroom.

Mr. Shaw caught my look of surprise and grinned. "It does pay to be the butler in a joint like this."

I took a seat in an upholstered chair near the fireplace, Redvers taking a seat next to mine. Smoothing my hand over the chair's arm, I realized the fabric was somewhat outdated, but equal to the quality you would find upstairs. I wondered if the pieces of furniture here were castoffs following an upstairs renovation. Shaw sat himself on a love seat opposite, a folded newspaper tossed onto the table in front of him. I guessed it was where he was sitting before we interrupted him.

Redvers nodded at the paper. "And how are the ponies doing today?"

Shaw reddened slightly. "I'm always on 'and for whatever 'is Lordship needs." The excited radio noise I'd heard must have been a horse race. I wondered how often Shaw slipped away to listen to the races instead of minding his duties as a butler. Of course, Lord Hughes was a fairly easygoing man and I doubted he made many demands that Shaw couldn't easily field.

Aunt Millie had remarked more than once about how changed Lord Hughes's domestic situation was since she had known him decades earlier. I could tell that the unusual makeup of the household staff bothered her endlessly, and she was troubled by how casually the staff interacted with the family. I wasn't sure why Hughes had loosened the rules in the household so much, but I did know my aunt would be apoplectic if she knew what the butler was up to down here.

Redvers changed the subject. "How well did you know Simon Marshall?"

Shaw looked relieved at the abrupt shift in topic. "Not well at all, truth be told. The lad 'ad a room across the hall, but 'e surely kept to 'isself."

The police had searched the barn, but I wondered idly if they had been through his room yet. Surely, they wouldn't have overlooked it.

"Can't tell you much more than that. I did my job and 'e did 'is."

"You don't know anything about his life before he came here?"

Shaw shook his head. "No."

John Shaw was turning out to be spectacularly unhelpful. I glanced at Redvers and saw that he was equally frustrated with the lack of information. I decided to toss in my two cents.

"What about Lord Hughes? Is there something Simon could have learned about Lord Hughes that would have been damaging if it got out?"

A slightly crafty expression flashed across Shaw's face and I thought we might have finally struck gold. But the expression was quickly replaced by one of innocence. A look entirely at odds with the man seated before us.

"'is Lordship is a good man. There ain't nothing for Simon to have found out."

Shaw ushered us out pretty quickly after that, closing the door firmly behind us.

"What on earth do you think that was about?"

Redvers was already moving across the hall to the door opposite Shaw's. Pushing it open, he stuck his head inside and I joined him at the doorway.

"Well, I suspect Shaw is up to something besides betting on the horses."

"Do you think it has anything to do with Simon's murder?"

He shook his head. "Hard to say."

We both moved into Simon's room and took a look around. It was a single room, unlike the butler's suite, but still more cheerful than I would have imagined. Light from a window near the ceiling filtered down onto a bed with a patchwork quilt dominating the far wall. A large chest of drawers stood next to a sink, and a comfortable-looking chair sat in the corner.

"The police have already been through here."

"And you know that, how?"

"Greyson told me."

"Of course, he did."

Redvers grinned at me before moving to the dresser and

opening the top drawer, poking through the contents. I wandered over to the bed and peeked beneath, finding nothing but a few balls of dust.

I sighed, glancing around again. "Not much here." I walked over to the chair and picked up the tome that had been placed pages-open over the arm. It was a book on etiquette for the upper classes. I put it back down, wondering what use a mechanic had for such a thing.

Unless he had grander aspirations.

Redvers closed the drawer he had been looking in. "No, not much to see."

It was time to move our search outside. "Maybe we'll have better luck in the stables."

Chapter 13

"But first," I told Redvers when we were back in the hallway, "I think we need to figure out where Sergeant Barlow sleeps. I don't want to break into his private rooms if that's who's staying out there."

"I already asked Lord Hughes this morning. Barlow has another one of the rooms down here. In fact, Hughes was quite surprised that any of the rooms in the stable were locked."

"Excellent work, Redvers." I crossed to the next closed door and turned the handle. It opened easily and I put my head inside. It was a room similar to Simon's, but completely bare, the bed stripped clean. I closed the door again.

Redvers cocked a brow but did the same with the door nearest him and we worked our way down the hall. Only two of the doors were locked—I assumed one belonged to Martha, and the other to Sergeant Barlow. The rest were empty.

That task done, we bundled up and headed outside, Redvers remembering to grab an umbrella at the last moment as he had promised my aunt earlier.

"Aunt Millie isn't like Old Saint Nick, you know. She's not *always* watching."

"I'm not so sure," he said darkly, but shot me a wink.

We were halfway to the stables before I remembered why

Redvers hadn't been able to search the room the day before. "You couldn't get past the lock yesterday. Are you more prepared for breaking and entering than you were before?"

He cocked a brow at me. "Oh, ye of little faith." He patted his pocket where I assumed he had secured some tools. I wondered how easy it would be to get my own lock-picking kit—it was looking more and more like something that would come in handy.

As we walked I suddenly recalled his unexpected appearance that morning as Hammond and I headed out to the plane.

"What were you doing out so early this morning?"

"You don't believe I was out for a stroll?"

I snorted in response.

He sighed. I was about to give him another verbal prod when he spoke again. "I suppose you aren't going to let this go."

"You know me so well."

He shrugged. "I just wanted to check over the airplane. Before you went up."

"Oh." I nearly stopped in my tracks, but merely stutter-stepped and continued on. "I . . . well, thank you." Instead of arguing about my lessons, he had simply done his best to ensure my safety. I was deeply touched.

He cleared his throat. "You're welcome."

The stable was set back from the barn that housed the cars and airplane. Made of the same gray stone as that building and the manor, it was another large and somewhat imposing building. I was fairly certain my father's entire home back in Boston would fit inside it.

The downstairs area was still used to house the two horses that Lord Hughes kept, although they had already been turned out to the fields for the day. The floor was swept clean and both the tack room and stalls were tidy—Sergeant Barlow obviously spent quite a bit of time here as well as in the gardens.

We climbed the stone stairs to the second floor where I wrinkled my nose at the musty smell that hung in the air. This level had a forgotten feeling—and smell—to it. A hallway ran along the north wall, with rooms off to the left. The first three doors hung open.

"You searched these yesterday?" I gestured to the open doors. Redvers nodded and we continued to the very end of the hall where we were greeted by the locked door. He and I both stood still for several moments, barely breathing, listening for the slightest sound within.

Nothing.

"If someone is in there, they certainly heard us coming," I whispered.

"But they would have nowhere to escape."

I shrugged one shoulder and hoped that no one would attack us once we did get inside.

Redvers knelt down so he was eye level with the lock, pulled out his small tool kit, and went to work. I watched his nimble fingers carefully work the thin metal rods in the lock, trying to pick up as much technique as I could for the future. You never knew when you might need to open an inconveniently locked door.

But this one seemed especially resistant. As the minutes stretched, I continued peering over his shoulder. "It doesn't look any more complicated than the door locks in the house. What makes it so difficult to open? It seems you're really having some trouble there."

Redvers paused in his work to shoot me a dark look.

I smothered a grin.

Several more minutes passed before we heard the quiet click. Redvers ran a hand through his dark hair before putting the kit back in his pocket. "It was rather gummed up—I suspect it hadn't been used in a long time before now. I'm surprised the key still works." His voice was low and quiet and vibrated in my chest as he stood near. Then he motioned for me to stand behind him as he pushed the silent wooden door open with one hand, peering cautiously into the room. I tried to peek around him, but I couldn't see much.

"What's in there?" I whispered, even though our presence had been announced long before.

Redvers poked his head in the room and looked both ways, one arm still corralling me behind him, before he relaxed and dropped his arm. He entered the room, still cautious, and I followed close behind.

It was immediately obvious there were very few hiding places. Weak light filtered through the filthy window, illuminating a table in the corner that held some wax wrappings and scraps of food. A mouse munching happily behind a table leg squeaked and went scurrying at the sight of us. Redvers looked at me, but I shrugged.

A small cot was set up along the wall next to the door. I walked toward it, observing the rumpled sheets. I picked up an empty pack of cigarettes thrown carelessly to the side.

"I don't recognize this brand." I held up the box, and Redvers crossed the room to look at it.

"That's because they're foreign," he said.

"Interesting. Do you know where from?"

"Not off the top of my head."

I looked around and felt it necessary to state the obvious. "Someone has been staying here."

"And fairly recently, from the look of things." Redvers nodded toward the food scraps.

There wasn't much else to see. It was obvious that the person had cleared out, at least for the time being. It made me deeply uncomfortable that some unknown individual was hiding on the property. And while it was impossible to say whether they were responsible for the sabotage next door, they were surely up to no good. With a shiver I remembered how easily Redvers had slipped past the lock on my bedroom door—it was child's play compared to the one we had encountered here. Jamming a chair under my doorknob at night was feeling less silly and more like a necessity, and even that wasn't going to ensure my safety.

"If it's not someone at the house, how is it that they have a key?" I asked.

Redvers shook his head. "And where are they now?"

We walked back to the house in silence, each lost in our own thoughts. A light mist had begun, gathering in tiny droplets on the shoulders of Redvers' wool overcoat. Just before we reached the house, Redvers stopped and put a hand on my arm.

"Jane, I want you to be careful. We don't know who this is." He was mirroring exactly what had occupied my own thoughts. "Maybe we can look at some way to reinforce the door to your room."

"I don't think I'm a target this time, Redvers." Although his concern was touching.

"We don't know that, though." His eyes met mine, and my breath caught in anticipation of what he might say. "Jane . . ."

"I thought you said you would have an umbrella." Millie's voice carried loudly from where she held open the back door. "Neither of you needs to be standing out there inviting a cold."

Redvers heaved a sigh and waved the collapsed umbrella he carried in his hand at Millie.

"A lot of good that does if you aren't using it."

We trudged inside.

"Where is everyone today?" I asked Millie as we removed our damp overcoats and hung them up.

"Lord Hughes is meeting with his lawyer over some business affairs." Millie's arms were crossed as she supervised us with her usual bossy demeanor, but I saw a flash of worry cross her stern features. Without asking, I knew it wasn't Redvers and I she was worried about, but Lord Hughes.

I wondered if it was actually business affairs that had called his lawyer to the estate or whether it was something more serious—like being framed for murder. I snuck a glance at Redvers, and from the thoughtful look on his face, I could tell his thoughts were traveling the same path. Lillian may have been concerned about suspicion falling on Millie, but it looked like it was her father she needed to worry about.

"And the others?"

"Alistair and the girls are practicing putting in the great hall."

At that, Redvers' eyebrows lifted straight up. I realized he wasn't yet acquainted with how serious this family was about golf.

Redvers gave a little cough. "Well, I need to see to some things myself." It was my turn to raise an eyebrow. "I should make a phone call to the inspector."

I nodded. He would need to report what we had found in the stable. I wouldn't be surprised if the inspector returned immediately to go over the area himself.

I hoped that would be the case. I had a few questions for the inspector.

CHAPTER 14

I spent the rest of the afternoon organizing my thoughts and mentally listing what I still needed to know. When the inspector arrived, I wanted to ask him about Simon's background since the police surely had looked into it by now. The most burning question was why Simon's previous employer was incarcerated—and whether Simon was truly innocent of whatever scheme had landed his boss there.

I sighed. If the inspector would even answer my questions. Despite his flirting, I suspected the man thought I would be better off minding my own business and letting the *men* do the investigating. Well, I'd never been good at embroidery—or whatever it was he thought women should be doing.

I shook off my irritation. Even if I was restricted to investigating suspects that were in residence at the estate, I would continue to do it. Although, given who those suspects were and my personal relationship with most of them, I did hope that the threat was coming from elsewhere.

Unless our culprit was the person lurking on the grounds. The hair on the back of my neck tickled at the thought and I shivered.

I turned my thoughts to the knife used to slice into the brake cables. It may have had Lord Hughes's initials on it, but like the police, I thought it was a pretty shoddy attempt to cast suspicion his way. From what I knew of him, Hughes appeared to be a genuinely good man. He loved his daughter unconditionally, and was kind to my aunt Millie—which wasn't the easiest of tasks. I was also impressed with his dedication to giving employment to needy veterans. It spoke highly of him.

But no man was completely without blame. Simon had supposedly learned something damning about Lord Hughes, and I made a note to do some more investigating in that direction. If Simon had been blackmailing the man, we needed to know why. Hughes may not have cared for the attention Simon showed to Lillian, but that was hardly worth killing a man over. Blackmail was a different story altogether.

Which also reminded me of Shaw's strange reaction to the question of what Simon knew about Lord Hughes—had I imagined it? Or was Shaw hiding something as well? He was another character that we knew very little about. Was he loyal to Lord Hughes or did he see this as some sort of opportunity for himself?

Alistair had only arrived the morning after, and had come from a distance. That put him out of the running. And by all accounts, Simon had driven the car multiple times since Alistair's last visit to the estate.

Who else had access? Group Captain Hammond had been here a few weeks, but he hadn't known Simon during the war. Why procure a job for someone only to kill them? Unless Hammond was some sort of hired assassin. I chuckled out loud at the thought.

Marie was unusually obsessed with Lillian. She truly hated sharing Lillian's time and attention with anyone else—even Lillian's own father, although Marie was at least more circumspect about that. I had noticed the same thing during our time in Egypt—Marie's devotion to Lillian bordered on the unusual. But was it enough to kill over? And did Marie know enough about mechanics to damage someone's brake cables with the precision that had been used? I would never discount a woman's ability to murder, but I simply didn't know if she was mechanically inclined. I knew the girl was an excellent horsewoman, but she had never expressed interest in much outside of that. Well, besides gossip and American movie stars. But I had never really talked with the girl at length before—perhaps it was time to remedy that.

I also needed to have a longer discussion with Sergeant Barlow. He had been pretty forthcoming about what he knew, but perhaps he knew something about Shaw or the others that hadn't come up. And since I'd forgotten to ask before, I could also find out if he had seen anyone who wasn't meant to be there. He spent time in the stables—did he truly not know that someone was staying up in that room?

About an hour before dinner I put on a navy silk dress and a string of venetian glass beads. I pulled on a pair of silver T-strap shoes and made my way down to the drawing room for our customary predinner cocktail.

Redvers was already there, standing near the bar cart with a neat dose of what I guessed to be Scotch. As soon as he saw me he lifted his glass in question. I smiled and nodded, and he set to work fixing my drink. A glance around the room told me that we were still alone.

"How was your chat with the inspector?"

"Informative. And he'll be stopping by later tonight to ask some more questions."

"And to take a look around the stables, I presume?" Perhaps I could catch the man and ask my questions about Simon's past.

"You presume correctly. I'll fill you in on the rest later." Redvers' eyes were watching the door as my Aunt Millie came bustling through, heading straight for us.

"Don't stop talking on my account." She pointed to the whiskey. "A highball, if you will, Mr. Redvers." Redvers looked bemused as he set about pouring Millie's drink. "I'm sure anything you have to say to Jane you can say with me here."

"Er, we were just discussing how the inspector will be joining us later."

Millie's lips pursed like she was eating a lemon, and she gave an indignant sniff. "Well, I don't see why he needs to. He should have gotten all he needed when he was here before."

I managed not to roll my eyes, and I changed the subject instead.

"Is Lord Hughes joining us?"

"He'll be along shortly." Millie flushed a bit and my eyes widened.

I looked at Redvers and he lifted one shoulder and gave his head a little shake.

Before I could probe any further, Alistair, Lillian, and Marie entered the room. Like me, the girls had changed into something slightly more formal. The gentlemen were still wearing their suits, although Alistair had added a tie instead of the scarf he'd worn earlier.

Conversation turned, as it often did, to golf and Lillian's training. She was determined to go semiprofessional and hoped to compete in the spring tournaments. I had already heard Millie and Lord Hughes discussing her chances—they were under the impression that she was more than ready to win.

Redvers offered the newcomers a drink, and everyone accepted. I tuned out the talk of sports and simply observed the party. There was definitely an air of competition between Alistair and Marie as they took turns bragging to Millie about Lillian's putting practice, although Alistair made sure to mention how well he had done also. Marie looked ready to sock the boy on the nose.

"Of course, sports are all well and good, but Lillian will have to quit golfing when she marries." Alistair had a distinctly proprietary air about him as he looked at Lillian. I could see he thought that her marriage would be to him.

The conversation came to a screeching halt.

"Excuse me?" Lillian said.

Even my aunt Millie looked shocked. Marie's hand balled into a fist and I wondered if she would actually take a swing. Glancing around, I noticed that Lord Hughes and Group Captain Hammond had joined us.

At the tone in Lillian's voice Alistair shifted uncomfortably. "Well, you'll have to take care of your husband's home. You can't be expected to do both." He looked around in genuine surprise at our reaction before turning to Lord Hughes. "Uncle?"

Lord Hughes grimaced. "We hadn't really discussed it." He looked at his daughter's reddening face. "It's not something you need to worry about now, of course, my dear. You can just concentrate on winning for the time being." He smiled around at our small crowd before turning to Chris. "Can I get you a drink, Group Captain Hammond?" The men moved away from the fireplace where we had all gathered, leaving a stilted silence behind them. Even Millie struggled to regain her conversational footing.

Drinks prepared and handed out, we went in to dinner, the chatter gradually rebuilding steam, although Lillian had yet to rejoin the fray. I wondered if this was the first time she had been presented with the topic, or if it was the reason she had insisted that she never wanted to marry at all. I suspected the latter.

We settled into our seats and started our meal. Martha had outdone herself with a pair of roast pheasants served with potatoes and root vegetables.

"Are these from your land, Lord Hughes?" Redvers asked.

"They are. I've never been fond of shooting for the sport of it, but since the war it's become something of a necessity. Luckily, we still have an abundance of fowl on the property."

"Do you go out yourself?"

"Well, sometimes Mr. Shaw does it in my stead . . ."

Alistair made a noise and Lord Hughes stopped midsentence to look at his nephew.

"Is there a problem, Alistair?"

"No." Alistair paused, taking a deep breath. "I just think you give these people entirely too much freedom. They'll take advantage, Uncle." He stuck his chin out stubbornly.

Hughes studied his nephew for a moment. "Perhaps this is something we can discuss later, Alistair. It seems we have quite a bit to talk about," Hughes said quietly. Alistair flushed and turned back to his meal. The young man had really stirred things up for the evening—if he had set out to cause trouble, he couldn't have done a better job.

The rest of the meal passed quietly and afterward we retreated to the drawing room, but everyone was restless and out of sorts. Lillian excused herself immediately and Millie's attempts to get a game of cards going fell flat, as no one could be persuaded to sit and concentrate. A debate on whether to raid the bar cart once more was interrupted when Shaw appeared and informed Redvers that he had a phone call. Redvers returned and quietly informed me that Inspector Greyson wouldn't be coming out until the following morning.

"Is everything all right, Mr. Redvers?" Millie demanded from her chair at the game table, hands absently shuffling a deck of cards. Lord Hughes had joined her there, but neither looked likely to start an actual game.

"Yes, everything is quite well." Redvers smiled at my aunt, but didn't elaborate, and Millie's answering glower would have sent a lesser man scurrying. Redvers just maintained his pleasant smile and gave her a nod before turning back to Hammond and me.

* * *

We all retired to our rooms not long after that. I found that mine was slightly stuffy, so I went to the window and opened it. The moon had broken through the clouds and cast silvery light on the gardens below my window where Martha grew herbs for the kitchen. I leaned for a moment against the sill, gazing out into the darkness and breathing in the cold night air. I pondered the wisdom of leaving the window cracked during the night—I loved a cold room while I slept.

A movement to the left caught my eye, and I squinted at it, before realizing I was illuminated by the light behind me and ducked behind the curtain. Whoever it was didn't need to see me watching them, and my room was lit up like a beacon on the second floor. I could easily be seen from below. From behind the heavy curtain I kept an eye on where I had seen the movement and was rewarded with the sight of a figure moving away from the kitchen entrance. They moved through the garden and out onto the grounds in the direction of the barn and stable.

Perhaps it was simply Sergeant Barlow. The grounds and the stables were his domain, after all. The figure turned slightly and the moon clearly illuminated the tall thin frame, reaching up to adjust the brim of his cap, before it disappeared into the shadow of the tree line.

A man with two hands.

Not Sergeant Barlow, then. And the figure looked too tall to be Hammond, nor did it match Mr. Shaw's tall but sturdy build. I closed and locked the window, regretting the loss of the crisp night air. But I was feeling none too comfortable about what I had just seen, and it wasn't worth taking the risk of leaving the window open. Even on the second floor. Whoever our prowler was, it looked like they were bold enough to stick around despite the police presence on the estate. The constables had been crawling all over the outbuildings, searching Simon's workspace—it seemed unlikely that the mysterious figure could have missed that.

I knew that I wasn't in any danger, but I still felt unsettled. Especially after my recent exploits where I had become the target of a murderous plot. I surveyed the room and remembered my conversation with Redvers about the flimsy locks on the bedroom doors. I went to the desk, grabbed the wooden chair, and stuffed it squarely beneath the doorknob.

Better safe than sorry.

Chapter 15

I tossed and turned all night. Without a cool breeze, the room had quickly become an oven. I hadn't been able to find the valve on the radiator to turn the heat off, and instead I lay on top of my covers and stared at the ceiling, listening for sounds at either the door or the window. It was something of an overreaction, but once my mind had latched on to the idea of an intruder, it couldn't seem to let it go. I must have dropped off at some point because when I awoke, I was twisted in the sweaty sheets with the quilt tossed to the floor. I felt wrung out, but the chair was still firmly in place and the windows were still tightly locked. It was a small consolation.

My first order of business today would be learning how to shut off the newly installed radiator. Otherwise there would be no reason for another pheasant shoot—they could serve me. Roasted, with a side of potatoes and some lovely asparagus.

I padded into the small bathroom attached to my room and ran myself a quick bath; I needed to scrub off the effects of my sleepless night. Tempted though I was to soak for as long as possible in the smooth claw-foot tub, I finished quickly and went to the wardrobe where I eyed up my meager assortment of warm clothing. I recalled our outdoor exploits the day before and the chill that had seeped through my coat. Figuring I might find myself investigating out-of-doors again, I pulled on a dark green sweater coat and paired it with a woolen skirt and thick tights.

It was still early, but Redvers was already seated in the breakfast room when I came down, and the inspector had joined him. Martha saw me moving down the hall and hurried after me with my pot of coffee. I could have kissed her—coffee was the only thing I wanted after my sleepless night. I settled into a chair next to Redvers and set about pouring myself a cup. I would get a plate of food in a moment; I needed to prop myself up with caffeine first.

"Mrs. Wunderly. Are you quite all right this morning?" From across the table Inspector Greyson was studying my face with a pinched look of concern. Redvers looked back and forth between us, brows low.

"Quite all right. Just a restless night."

"I'm sure you have nothing to worry about, Mrs. Wunderly." He gave me an encouraging smile. I felt certain that if I had been sitting near him he would have patted my arm.

"Well, that may be true. But I did see someone out on the grounds last night, walking toward the stables. So, I locked my windows instead of letting the breeze through. And then my room became entirely too warm and I didn't get much sleep."

The men had stopped listening after "someone on the grounds." I could tell by the sputtering that started almost immediately. I sighed and went to make myself that plate of food—I would need some sustenance to get me through the argument that was coming.

"Why didn't you call someone?" The inspector's face was an interesting shade of fuchsia. Almost a magenta. Redvers was practically out of his seat.

I filled my plate before answering. Then I sat back down and picked up my fork before addressing the men. "Because by the time I dressed, came downstairs, called the police, or even Mr. Redvers for that matter, there would be no one to find. These grounds are enormous, and if it was our prowler, he obviously knows we are looking for him. I doubt he would have stuck around to be captured."

There was some indignant silence as I quietly ate a few forkfuls of eggs. I could tell Redvers knew I was right. I glanced up at him while I took a sip from my cup and he was regarding me thoughtfully.

The inspector frowned. "I'll call in more men. We'll sweep the grounds again. We have to search all the rooms in the house, anyway." The inspector's face was regaining a normal color. I thought it looked much healthier.

"You have to search the house?" I asked mildly.

The inspector nodded. "The knife we found had damage to the blade, but our technicians don't think the thing was sharp enough to make the incisions we found. They were pretty clean cuts, and sliced just enough that the brakes would work initially but come apart pretty quickly after that. There was some precision involved."

"So, someone deliberately damaged a knife with Hughes's initials engraved on it and left it to be found." I nodded to myself. This just confirmed what I had suspected. "Someone is trying to frame Lord Hughes."

"It certainly looks that way." Greyson's tone was mild.

I cocked my head. "Why hasn't Lord Hughes been arrested? Don't you have enough evidence with the knife?" I wasn't suggesting that I hoped he would be, I was simply curious.

The inspector shifted uncomfortably in his seat. "Well, Lord Hughes . . . being a baron." He cleared his throat. "He would be tried in the House of Lords, and we simply have to be very certain before arresting a peer of the realm."

I nodded again and turned back to my breakfast. That explained why Lord Hughes was still free. The inspector was reluctant to arrest a peer.

I pushed my empty plate away and wondered at my own

reactions this morning. I couldn't work up any anxiety about the prowler, or about the search of the house, which was unusual for me. I really was quite tired. "Go ahead and search my room first. Then I can take a nap while you do the rest of the house."

Both men regarded me with some concern.

"Well . . . we can do that." The inspector didn't sound as sure as his words.

I rewarded the inspector with a dazzling smile and passed him my room key. A little color crept onto his high cheekbones. When I cocked my head at him, he shrugged. "I've never had a woman pass me her room key before. Even if it is just to search for a murder weapon." He gave me a crooked smile then left the room to direct the few men he had brought along to conduct the search. I gave my head a little shake. The inspector was charming in his own way, despite his old-fashioned ideas.

"He's flirting with you," Redvers leaned in and whispered.

I looked at him. "Do you think Martha has more coffee for me?"

When the inspector returned to the breakfast room I remembered to ask him whether they had yet learned anything interesting about Simon Marshall's background.

"Oh, I'm sure that's nothing you need to concern yourself with, Mrs. Wunderly." He was standing near my seat, and this time he did reach over and pat my arm while I shot mental daggers at him. Redvers grinned at me from across the table, and I slung a couple his way as well.

Irritated with the inspector, I decided to meander through the bit of woods edging the greens instead of returning to my room for a nap. There was a lovely stream that ran through the property, and along the path was a tiny wooden bridge leading over it. I stopped on the bridge for a moment, resting my arms on the wooden rails and enjoying the gentle burble of the water and the earthy scent of decaying leaves that hung in the air. I looked down and watched the water sluice over the stones, and my eyes caught on a sparkle. I squinted but couldn't make out what I was seeing. I moved to the bank of the stream and walked a few yards until I was level with the object. Now that I was closer, I could only just make out that it was metal and relatively shiny. A knife perhaps? Could it be the knife that sliced the brake cables—the knife the police were searching for even now? The water would most likely have washed away any evidence, but it was still worth retrieving. It might serve as proof that Lord Hughes was in fact being set up.

I got close to the water's edge, and realized the stream was just wide enough here that I wouldn't be able to reach the item without getting wet; I would have to return with some wading boots to retrieve it. The item could be nothing, but when it came to potential evidence, I would rather be safe than sorry.

I hefted a large rock from among the trees and hauled it down to the water's edge where I carefully marked the spot. Satisfied that I would be able to find the location again, I stood, brushing my hands together to remove the dirt and bits of rotting leaves. Then I went in search of Martha to see about finding a pair of boots for wading into the stream.

I found her where I usually found her—in the kitchen, preparing lunch.

"Lunch is not for several hours yet, Mrs. Wunderly," Martha told me, barely looking up from her work at the chopping block.

"I was actually wondering if there was a pair of wading boots about."

She gave me a quizzical look but didn't ask the question I knew she was thinking. "Check in the hall, Mrs. Wunderly.

There should be a pair of Wellingtons there. They should do for wading if you are not going too deep."

I thanked her and went to look. I found a pair of newer-looking boots that obviously belonged to a man, most likely Lord Hughes. They would be enormous on me, but I could make them work—I would only need to walk a few steps into the ankle-deep water to retrieve what I had seen. And since the police were busy with their searching, no one would miss my presence.

I paused for only a moment, considering whether I should simply tell the police about the potential evidence, but dismissed the idea. I had time on my hands, and if the shiny object was nothing special, I would merely be wasting an officer's time, which was better spent searching the house.

And if I was honest with myself, I didn't like being left out of the police investigation. This was my chance to actually do something instead of merely asking questions. Questions that wouldn't even be answered if Greyson had anything to do with it.

Nearing the bridge, I heard a rustle in the underbrush and paused, the large boots clutched to my chest. I was still a little jumpy from all the time I had spent worrying about the prowler on the grounds. When a rabbit scurried past I breathed out the air that had caught in my lungs. It was broad daylight, and the police were in the house. I was perfectly safe and behaving foolishly about the mysterious figure I had seen.

I moved forward, retracing my steps along the bank of the stream until I located the large rock I had placed there earlier. I peered into the water and didn't see the shiny object that I had earlier. I moved slightly to the left, and the bright sunlight caught a sparkle. It looked as though the object had shifted slightly in the current. I was lucky it was still there.

I kept my eye on the general area of the item and sat down

on the dying grass to pull on the olive green Wellingtons. Once they were on, I pushed myself up and tottered to the edge of the stream in the overlarge galoshes. I was about to step into the water when I heard the fast crunch of leaves behind me, and before I could turn in the sloppy boots, I felt two hands on my back, giving me a firm shove.

Chapter 16

The water was freezing cold, and I felt rocks cutting into my legs where I landed on them. The stream wasn't deep, but there was enough water that I was nearly completely submerged. If I hadn't been wearing the large boots, I might have been able to keep from getting completely soaked, but I had no balance in these Wellingtons, so I had toppled in easily. I pushed myself up, sharp rocks pressing uncomfortably into the palms of both hands. Once I shoved the wet hair out of my face, I turned to see who had pushed me, but all I could make out was a vague figure crashing away through the trees. The only thing I could say for certain was that they seemed tall and male—but they were already too far away to see them clearly.

I gingerly picked myself out of the water, rivulets streaming from my clothes and down my face. I immediately began shivering, my teeth chattering uncontrollably. It had been an unseasonably warm day, but the water hadn't benefited from that in the slightest. I glanced down, and a foot away I could see sunlight glinting off my mystery item nestled against a rock. I was already wet, so hugging my arms to my body, I picked my way over and thrust my hand back into the freezing water. I fumbled for a few seconds before coming up with the shiny object that had led me to this moment.

It was a fork.

I muttered an unladylike curse before I clamped my chattering teeth together and picked my way across the rocks, slipping once and almost going back into the water. I flopped onto the bank and clutched the fork to my chest. All this for a ridiculous piece of silverware.

Shivering with real enthusiasm now, I pulled off the boots, emptying them of several inches of water and put my own sensible brogues back on. My numb fingers couldn't hold on to the boots, so I left them by the stream bank—someone could go back for them later. I marched myself back to the house and practically fell through the door into the back hallway.

Martha heard my commotion and bustled into the hall, her face falling at the sight of me.

"Oh, Mrs. Wunderly. Your lips are blue! We need to get you out of those clothes."

"You may as well call me Jane now," I said through chattering teeth. "Especially if you're going to help me undress."

Martha's lips twitched as she pulled my sodden wool coat off me. She threw it into a pile on the floor. "I will deal with this later," she muttered to herself.

Mr. Shaw chose that moment to appear, and Martha shooed him off with instructions to go ahead and keep everyone, including the police, away from the kitchen while she dealt with me.

Once she was sure Shaw had gone to do her bidding, Martha turned back to me. I helped her as much as I could, but my fingers were too numb to work properly, and Martha did most of the work getting me out my clothes—for such a thin woman, she was surprisingly strong. As she removed each piece, she tossed it onto the sodden heap, and pulled one of Lord Hughes's greatcoats from a hook and wrapped me in it. I was still in my underthings, so I started to complain that I would get the coat wet, but she shushed me then bustled me up a back staircase to my room.

Martha ran a warm bath and helped me get into it. I lowered myself into the tub with my underclothes still on—they were already ruined and I could maintain at least some modesty.

"This is not hot," Martha said, testing the temperature with her hand. "We will raise the temperature gradually. We do not want any more shock to your system." I nodded and hoped that my teeth would quit chattering soon.

Martha stayed with me until I had regained something of a normal color. She continued to run the taps until the water in the bath was quite warm and my shivering had stopped. Only then did she leave me with a towel and go to add some hot water bottles to my bed. I was feeling better, but still had a bit of a chill I couldn't seem to shake, even after the hot bath. I blamed the fifteen-minute walk back to the house in the soaking wet clothes.

"You get into bed and keep warm so you do not get sick," Martha pulled the covers back and kept her back turned while I changed into a nightdress. I crawled into the bed that she had warmed up for me.

"I will add extra blankets. And bring you a tray for lunch. You need to eat something."

"I don't want you to go to any more trouble, Martha."

She glared at me. "It is no trouble."

"Thank you, Martha." I was no longer shivering and was able to speak more normally.

"You are welcome, Jane. But you should not go swimming this time of year." Her eyes had a gleam in them.

I smiled at her joke, but my face quickly fell. "I didn't mean to. I was pushed."

Martha was quiet for a moment, looking at me with dark eyes. "You need to be careful." She looked at the door. "Make sure you lock this door tonight."

I nodded. "I will. Thank you again."

She nodded and was back in no time with a thick warm stew and fresh bread laden with butter. I wondered if it was what the rest of the family had eaten for lunch, or if it was something she had warmed up especially for me. The woman was a treasure—Lord Hughes was right to do whatever it took to keep her on.

Martha fussed over me a bit more, but finally let me be. I finished my lunch and was just closing my tired eyes when I heard a knock at my door. I called for them to come in, pulling the thick robe I had donned closer around me, and Martha bustled in once again.

"Good. You are wearing a thick robe. Are you warm enough?" I nodded and she did the same. "You need to keep warm so you do not get sick." She turned her head to the left and mocked spitting three times over her shoulder. "I ward off the devil."

There wasn't much to say to that, so I nodded. "Thank you. But I'm sure I don't need to stay the whole day in bed . . ."

Martha gave me a dark look, and I stopped talking. I pulled up the heavy covers I had just smoothed out and closed my eyes briefly. I wasn't feeling ill, but I was exhausted from my lack of sleep the night before and more than a bit sore where my various limbs had made contact with stones and rocks.

"Now, I found the inspector for you. He was not so hard to find."

I looked up in surprise. "Why?"

"Because you were pushed. You need to tell him. He will find out who did this."

I smiled at Martha. She seemed rather austere and remote at times, but underneath she was a deeply caring person. I could tell she was worried for me, so instead of arguing, I agreed to meet with the inspector.

"I can hardly meet with him here though." I gestured to my bed and my robe.

Martha pursed her lips. "We will think of something."

But in the end that was exactly what we did. Martha wouldn't hear of my getting out of bed, so she escorted both the inspector and Redvers into my room and then stayed to chaperone. She planted herself in a chair at my side, crossed her arms, and settled in. Martha was taking her job as nursemaid very seriously.

The three of us looked at her and then at each other. I shrugged.

"Good afternoon, gentlemen. I apologize for my appearance."

"It's quite all right, Mrs. Wunderly." Both the inspector's and Redvers' faces were creased in concern.

Greyson continued. "Can you tell me what happened? Miss Fedec told me you were pushed."

I nodded, and tugged the lapels of my robe even closer together, then recounted the events of my going into the water. It had only been several hours since I had seen the men at the breakfast table, but it already felt like an eternity had passed.

The men were quiet for a moment when I had finished, but then Redvers spoke up. "What was it that you ended up retrieving? I assume you still fetched it out of the water."

I lifted my chin. "It might have been a very important clue."

Redvers' lips twitched. "And was it?"

I struggled with whether to make something up, but quickly gave up the idea. "Very well. It was a fork."

Redvers looked at me for a moment before he burst out laughing. It was a loud belly laugh, and I couldn't help but smile at the sight of him, head thrown back, laughing for all he was worth. I had heard Redvers chuckle on occasion, but

I think I had only ever heard a laugh like this from him one other time. It was a rather glorious sight, and more than a little infectious. I wondered if there were many people who could say they had seen Redvers let go like this. I suspected not—it felt like a gift.

He wiped tears from his eyes, and I pursed my lips to hide the smile lurking there. The inspector looked quite shocked at his reaction, and Martha's glare could have dropped a man in his tracks, but truth be told I thought Redvers' reaction was appropriate. It *was* rather funny that I had taken a dunk for nothing more than a fork.

"You could have been hurt, Mrs. Wunderly. This is why you should have told us immediately and left it to the police," the inspector said, and Martha nodded vehemently.

"You were busy with your search."

Redvers sobered a bit and turned to the inspector. "She would never be able to do that. And I wouldn't be laughing if she had been hurt." He turned back to me. "But you're fine, aren't you? Not injured?"

"Just my pride," I muttered. Louder, I went on. "I wish I had gotten a decent look at whoever pushed me, but the boots I had on were too large and I went down quickly. I'm afraid I didn't see much. All I can say is that they were wearing trousers and were on the tall side." I bit my lip and recalled the figure darting through the trees. "And they moved quickly."

Greyson sighed and returned to the story at hand. "Why did you go in the water in the first place? What did you think you might find?"

"I was hoping it was the knife that was responsible for all the sabotage. I realize all the evidence would have been ruined by the water, but I thought it was at least worth retrieving. It might clear Lord Hughes of suspicion if we could prove he was being set up."

The inspector pursed his lips. "Again, Mrs. Wunderly. I wish you would leave those problems to the police. It isn't anything you should be troubling yourself with."

Redvers stepped in. "Tall and wearing trousers. That doesn't narrow it down much."

"It doesn't," I agreed, casting Redvers a grateful look. "The only person we can truly eliminate is Sergeant Barlow." There had been two hands on my back. "And my aunt Millie. She's a bit too . . . plump." I thought we could also eliminate Marie from suspicion since she was rather short and round as well, but I didn't feel the need to throw the girl's name into the ring.

Greyson raised his eyebrows. "I would hope your aunt isn't trying to kill you."

I shrugged. "I don't think they were trying to kill me." The water wasn't terribly deep in the stream, and even though it was possible to drown in only several inches of water, it was unlikely that I would have done so. If they had been seeking that outcome, they would have been better off striking me in the head and ensuring I was unconscious before I went into the water.

Redvers agreed. "More likely they were trying to scare you off."

The inspector huffed. "I would think this is enough to convince you that you should keep well clear of things, Mrs. Wunderly." His voice softened. "I would hate for anything more serious to happen to you. This was quite enough, don't you think? Please leave things to us from now on."

I forced myself to smile at the man, letting him believe that I agreed with him without actually doing so.

"Now, if you'll excuse me, I need to pull my men off their searching the house and send them out into the woods to take a look." The inspector gave a brief bow and hurried from the room.

Redvers smirked. "I notice you didn't actually agree to keep out of things."

I gave him a full-on smile. "Never. Anyway, they won't find anything out there. Whoever pushed me is long gone."

"You read my mind."

"Have you learned anything interesting about anyone else on the estate? Or have the police?"

Redvers glanced over at Martha, who crossed her arms and stared him down.

"Could you give us a moment, Martha? It will be entirely appropriate, I promise."

Martha grumbled, but eventually agreed to step outside, but only after assuring me that she would be right outside the door.

"Did you learn something?" I asked eagerly, leaning forward, then grasping the edges of my robe and pulling them tight again.

"Not really." Redvers moved around to the side of the bed and perched on the edge. "Simon was let go from the mechanic's shop where he worked after the war just before the boss was arrested."

"What was he arrested for?"

"Dealing on the black market. And since Simon was let go, it looks like he wasn't involved, although they'll keep digging to make certain that's true."

I was disappointed. It would have been a simpler solution to Simon's death than worrying that someone on the estate was responsible.

"Is that it? You hardly needed to send Martha from the room for that."

Redvers smiled. "I just wanted to make sure you were really okay. Are you?" His warm eyes crinkled slightly at the corners, and I read his concern there, despite his laughing fit earlier.

I nodded, suddenly feeling slightly warm. "I really am. Just cold."

Redvers looked amused. "You don't look cold now."

We both stopped talking and he was gazing down at me. I realized just how close he was sitting when his dark eyes flitted to my lips. I felt them part, all thoughts of my swim in the creek and Lord Hughes's problems fleeing my mind. Like a magnet pulled by its opposite half, I found myself leaning toward Redvers ever so slightly.

Then the door burst open.

Chapter 17

A series of questions rained down upon me. "Why on earth are you still in bed? And Mr. Redvers, why are you in her room? Alone! It's most inappropriate."

Aunt Millie.

I almost groaned out loud at the interruption. Redvers and I shared a look before I faced my aunt. "I'm not feeling very well today. Martha thinks I should take it easy."

"Martha thinks—that young woman. Well, I should be the judge of that." By Millie's standards, I supposed Martha was quite young. I squeezed my eyes shut and I could feel Millie inspecting me. Finally, she sniffed. "I suppose you do look unwell. I've seen you looking worse, of course, but not by much."

You could always count on Millie for the unvarnished truth. Whether you wanted to hear it or not.

Redvers took that as his cue to leave.

"I see you are well in hand now, Mrs. Wunderly. I will leave you to your rest." I shot him a dark look as he grinned and slipped out the door. I could have cursed my aunt for interrupting when she did, even though I knew kissing Redvers again was a terrible idea. Despite the fact that the man was attractive, kind, and thoughtful. And spent an awful lot of time defending me to the inspector.

I sighed.

"And I hear the inspector was here, too? What was he doing here? Were you alone with him as well?"

"Just checking in on me. And giving me an update about their investigation." I didn't feel the need to fill Millie in on the fact that someone had pushed me into the stream. It would only lead to . . . well, heaven only knew what. More lectures, certainly.

"Well, I suppose we should be grateful for that at least." I heard her settle into the chair Martha had vacated and make herself comfortable. I wished someone had thought to remove it. Now there was little chance of my resting.

Well, now was as good a time as any to ask some questions about our host. "How well do you know Lord Hughes?" I asked.

Millie pursed her lips at that. "Fairly well, Jane." Millie's tone was meant to shut down my line of questions, but I had few reservations about annoying my aunt. Turnabout was fair play after all.

"Do you know anything about his past? And what exactly is his title?" It was something I hadn't been comfortable asking Lord Hughes directly, not wanting to prove my ignorance about the British aristocracy. But I was curious about the man and his family.

"Lord Hughes is a baron." She stressed the title as if it held great importance, but it still didn't mean anything to me. "He inherited his father's title when the old Lord Hughes died some twenty years ago." Millie thought for a moment. "It might have been even longer than that, actually. Regardless, his father had lost their estate and most of their fortune." I raised my eyebrows, and Millie dropped her voice. "Gambling."

I almost smiled at her serious whisper, but I controlled my face.

"Edward is a very savvy investor, and managed to make

back the family money, and he purchased this estate. Named it Wedgefield, and I'm sure you can guess why."

My face was a blank and Millie huffed in frustration. "Wedge, as in a golf wedge. Field, for the many acres of the estate. Keep up, Jane."

I rolled my eyes. I wasn't going to even try keeping up with the golf references.

"I believe Edward's younger brother has had some problems though." Millie frowned. "Same trouble as the father, I think."

"Gambling?"

Millie nodded.

"What is his name? I haven't heard anything about him."

"James Hughes. And I'm not surprised you haven't heard anything about the man. They don't really discuss him. The brothers have never gotten on well, especially given James's gambling habits."

I was quiet for a moment. Could Lord Hughes's brother be the person we were looking for? If there was enough animosity between the two men, it might provide James with the motive to want to see his brother destroyed. Was it possible that he was the figure we had seen lurking about, causing mayhem on his brother's property? But was a gambling problem enough to cause two brothers to stop speaking?

"How do you know all this?" I finally asked. "We've only been here a few weeks."

Millie pinned me with a glare. "I listen, Jane. If you want to be helpful, you'll need to learn to do the same."

I ignored that. She was just being difficult.

Just being herself, really. It was going to be a long afternoon.

Chapter 18

I stayed in bed at both Martha's and my aunt's insistence until the following morning. By that time, I couldn't stand to stay in bed for a moment longer—my body ached from inactivity and I was anxious to see what might have been discovered in my absence. Neither of the men had bothered to stop by again to update me, and I was keen to learn what was happening outside my room.

I was also curious—and a bit nervous—to see if Redvers would acknowledge what had almost happened between us the day before. And I wasn't at all sure whether I wanted him to or not.

No one was to be found in any of the common rooms and the door to Lord Hughes's study was firmly shut. I headed to the one place where I knew I could find at least one person—the kitchen.

I prowled through the doorway and found Hammond seated at the table while Martha frantically chopped vegetables across from him. She didn't even look up when I came in, but shot me a question anyway.

"Are you sure you should be out of bed, Jane?"

"Very sure. I'm feeling quite well. I think all your work yesterday meant that I won't be catching any sort of illness."

She glanced up, taking me in all at once, and gave a brief nod before returning to her work.

I turned to Chris, who gave me a strained smile. Since I had been out of commission and Lord Hughes was closed up in his study, it looked like he wasn't taking the Moth out. The knowledge that I wasn't being left behind made me feel slightly better, but I was hoping to get back in the cockpit as soon as possible.

"Maybe tomorrow morning we can head up?"

"Of course," Chris said. "If you're feeling up to it." He was gazing intently at Martha while he said it. I looked back and forth between the two of them, but Martha was focused on her task.

"Where is everyone?"

Martha didn't even pause in her chopping. "The girls are outside with your aunt. His Lordship, the inspector, and Mr. Redvers are in the study."

"Ah," I said. "And Mr. Shaw? Or Sergeant Barlow?"

"I think Shaw ran into town to pick up something for Lord Hughes," the group captain said. "And last I saw Barlow, he was out in the stables."

"I see." So, Shaw had been sent into town. "Did Shaw leave long ago?"

"Probably only a half hour or so. He took the Bentley."

I nodded and thanked him for the update. We silently watched Martha for a moment.

"It is just going to be cold sandwiches for lunch today. Too many interruptions . . ." Martha was muttering.

Hammond and I shared a glance before I jumped in. "I'm sure that will be fine, Martha. You're doing the best you can with all these police about. And all the extra people besides."

She looked up and shot me a grateful look, her gaze pausing for a moment as it passed over Hammond. "Thank you, Jane." But she immediately went back to chopping and tossing things into the pot on the stove.

I excused myself, and Chris gave me a distracted wave. I stepped into the hall and briefly wondered about the cozy scene between the two, but then shrugged. It was likely Chris was just trying to scrounge a snack. The man was always hungry.

I wandered toward the back stairwell and down to the servants' quarters. If Mr. Shaw was running an errand, that meant his quarters were unoccupied. The police had searched all the rooms in the house only the day before, but perhaps there was something that would give me an indication of what the man was up to. I couldn't stop thinking about the sly look on his face when I had mentioned Lord Hughes's secrets. I hurried down the hallway, shoes tapping on the unforgiving concrete floor, and I winced at the loud noise in the quiet. When I reached Mr. Shaw's door, I glanced back down the row of closed rooms, and seeing no one, I reached for the doorknob.

It turned easily in my hand. It seemed strange that Shaw would leave it unlocked while he was out, but perhaps the man had been in a hurry. The room looked much as it had the day Redvers and I visited Shaw, but it showed all the signs of the police search—and it was obvious the officers had searched with much less care than abovestairs. Stacks of newspapers had been rifled and carelessly tossed on the floor, and the small oak desk in the corner had been thoroughly gone over, papers strewn all about. I walked over and picked up a stack of racing sheets that had been tossed aside and shuffled through them. Then I frowned and shuffled through again.

The forms appeared to have been written by two different people. One set of sheets was sloppily marked up, the writing almost illegible where notations had been made. The other set of sheets was marked with precise little marks and a practiced hand. The sloppy set was obviously Shaw's—the writing matched other records I had seen written by the man. But the neat and tidy set . . . could it be Lord Hughes's writing?

But why would Shaw have Lord Hughes's racing forms? I selected one of each dated earlier in the month and stowed them in my pocket.

Everything else seemed typical of a butler's desk: expense records for the wine cellar and bar carts alongside a book of accounts tracking the local vendors that Lord Hughes did business with. Nothing seemed out of the ordinary, although I didn't have time to examine whether all the numbers added up. But I doubted that skimming some money off the accounts was what had put the crafty look in Shaw's eye. That had more to do with Lord Hughes's secrets than Shaw's own.

I poked my head into Mr. Shaw's room, where I could see that the police had rifled through his belongings here, too, tossing them into a heap on his bed. I shook my head. It would take the man some time to put things right. I stepped forward, but then stopped. It wasn't worth the bother of going through his clothes myself—it was obvious the police had been thorough. I would ask Redvers if anything of note had been found.

Irritation sliced through me. Whatever they had found was probably being discussed right this moment, yet I had been left out of the meeting. I had half a mind to barge in and demand to be included, but it wouldn't accomplish anything. Greyson was unlikely to include me in the discussion, and frankly, we needed the inspector on our side, especially if Lord Hughes was still their prime suspect in Simon's death.

After a final poke around, I left Shaw's rooms and headed back upstairs. There was nothing else of interest to find, and the man could return at any moment. I paused in the back hallway before deciding to head outside. I put on my gray tweed wool coat, belted it up snugly, and added my favorite wine-colored cloche. I wrapped a scarf around my neck, an ivory wool one, and headed out onto the grounds. The wind reddened my cheeks in moments, but at least I felt sufficiently warm today. I was glad for my thick tights and the long sweater layered underneath the rest.

I crunched out across the lawn toward the stable and barn to see if Mr. Shaw had returned Lord Hughes's car yet—and finished whatever errand he had been sent out on.

Chapter 19

As I neared the barn, I could see the tall wooden door had been pushed aside and men's voices came from within. I considered creeping close and listening from the other side of the door, but the voices stopped as I neared. I looked down and cursed the broken stick that had heralded my appearance. It was probably one of Rascal's.

I strolled inside, grateful to be out of the wind, and saw that Mr. Shaw had indeed returned and was conversing with Sergeant Barlow. I sent up a brief thanks that I had left the man's quarters when I did—it would have been very uncomfortable to be caught searching his rooms, especially by myself. I liked Shaw fine, but I didn't want to find out what sort of temper he had. The man had at least six inches and a hundred pounds advantage over me.

"Gentlemen," I said. Both men nodded to me in greeting but didn't resume their conversation. Shaw's arms were crossed over his chest and Barlow shifted uneasily on his hay bale, his eyes studying the hammer he twirled in his right hand. His fingers were remarkably nimble.

I let the silence stretch uncomfortably until Shaw finally cleared his throat. "Can we 'elp you, ma'am?"

I smiled. "I hope so."

Barlow stood. "I'll leave you to it."

"Oh, please do stay, Sergeant Barlow. I have questions for you as well."

The man sat back down, but slowly.

"Mr. Shaw, what errand did Lord Hughes have you run this morning?"

Shaw's eyes narrowed at me. "I'm not sure that's your business, all due respect."

"That may be true, but I'm curious just the same. And I'm here to help Lord Hughes in any way I can."

The men said nothing, so I slid the racing sheets out of my pocket and held them up. "Well, then, how about these? What can you tell me about these forms?"

Shaw's face turned a mottled red and he took a step toward me, but I was ready for him, and stopped his advance with an upheld hand and a quick story.

"Oh, no, Mr. Shaw. I won't be giving these up easily. Besides, Mr. Redvers already knows all about them, so there isn't any sense in you doing whatever you were thinking of just now." It wasn't true, but he didn't need to know that. I just needed to stop him from snatching them away from me and destroying the rest.

Barlow had watched this entire exchange with something close to amusement. "She's got you there, Shaw. Might as well tell the lady."

Shaw looked between the two of us before throwing up his hands. "Fine. If ye must know, 'is Lordship likes to put a little money on the ponies 'isself. And I place the bets with Charlie down at the pub. There. 'appy now?"

I was pleased that I'd been right about the owners of the penmanship. But I had other questions. "But why all the secrecy? Why doesn't Lord Hughes just do it himself?"

Shaw shrugged. "The man doesn't want anyone to know. Something to do with 'is family. And 'e doesn't bet much, just a few bob now and then. What's the date on those sheets? They ain't from yesterday, are they?"

I shook my head. "They're from last month or so."

Shaw visibly relaxed. "Well, that's fine then."

Hughes's secret hobby would explain the sheets written in two different hands and why Shaw had looked as though he knew something about Lord Hughes. But was it too convenient an explanation? And it certainly couldn't be the thing that Simon Marshall knew about His Lordship—placing a few bets on horse races was nothing worth blackmailing a man over. Although I did have to wonder why Lord Hughes would bother with all the secrecy over placing a few innocent bets.

I would take some time to think it over later; right now, I still had a few questions for the men. "Very well." I turned to include Sergeant Barlow. "But I have another question. Have either of you seen someone prowling around on the grounds that didn't belong?"

"Like the police?" Shaw's eyebrow had pulled toward the middle, creating a thicker forest than usual above his hawk-like nose.

"No, like someone living in one of the rooms above the stables." I looked over and watched Barlow's expression alternate between surprise and worry. "I know you spend quite a bit of time with the horses; have you seen anything out of the ordinary, Sergeant Barlow?"

"No, ma'am. I haven't seen anyone around that doesn't belong." I looked hard at the sergeant, but he appeared to be telling the truth. His face had settled into a pinched look of concern. "Are you sure there's someone staying up there? I don't like that there's someone sleeping in the same building as the horses."

"I'm afraid so. I saw the evidence myself. You never venture upstairs?"

Barlow shook his head. "No reason, ma'am. There's nothing up there. At least, there wasn't." His grip on the hammer tightened. "One forgotten candle or a cigarette, and the whole place could go up in flame. I don't like it. There would be no one to let the poor creatures out."

I agreed somberly and turned back to Shaw. "You haven't seen anything?"

Shaw shook his head. "Not a thing. But I'm not out on the grounds much." That was probably true. My guess was that when he wasn't immediately needed by Lord Hughes, the man was closeted away with his radio. And his racing sheets.

With a sigh I asked both men to be on the lookout, then left them to their own devices and returned to the house. It seemed that both Shaw and Barlow were telling the truth. Whoever our prowler was, they had been very careful to remain unnoticed.

CHAPTER 20

I went looking for Redvers, but the door to the study was closed and I assumed that he was still sealed in there with Lord Hughes and the inspector. Frustration bubbled up again, but I tamped it down. I was making the most of my time, and I could talk to Redvers later.

The downstairs rooms normally occupied by the family were abandoned, so I sat down in the library for a moment to think. There were still too many questions and I didn't have any answers. I considered what I did have—the possibility of blackmail, an unknown intruder, a frame-up job, and murder. There was no apparent connection between them, but someone was nervous enough about my asking questions to shove me into the stream.

It was still worth looking into Shaw's background, but everything he told me lined up. I considered tossing the racing sheets, but decided to turn them over to Redvers instead. One of us should double-check the story with Lord Hughes later. But for now, it looked like a dead end.

As for the identity of our nighttime prowler, I was convinced both Shaw and Barlow were telling the truth—neither of them had any idea someone was lurking about the grounds. Shaw seemed perplexed by the whole idea, and Barlow was worried for the safety of the horses. Neither of those reactions was faked.

With a grunt of frustration, I pushed up out of the comfortable chair and wandered back into the kitchen. Martha seemed to be the heartbeat of the house, knowing where everyone was at all times, and I might as well continue asking questions.

Martha was alone now, standing at the kitchen sink, her hands gripping the edge as she gazed out the large window overlooking the back gardens. My room offered a similar view, and I realized my room must be directly overhead.

"Martha?" I kept my voice low to keep from startling her, but I wasn't successful. Wherever Martha's mind was, she hadn't heard me come in, and she jumped before whirling around.

"Jane! You scared me out of my skin." She crossed herself then made the motion of spitting over her left shoulder.

I was becoming accustomed to her strange superstitions, so the spitting hardly had me raising an eyebrow, but I wondered where her beliefs came from. Her home country? Not for the first time, I recognized that Martha had a hint of an accent, but not of the British variety. It seemed Eastern European.

"I'm very sorry, Martha. I really didn't mean to scare you. Are you all right?"

Martha wiped her hands on her apron and avoided my eyes. "Yes, yes, I am fine. I did not expect you back so soon." She started bustling around the room, moving pans about and pulling containers of sugar and flour from the large wooden pantry.

"Have the girls or my aunt returned? No one seems to be about."

She paused in her movements for a moment, eyes on the flour in her hand. "The last time I saw the ladies, they were following Lillian outside. With her clubs."

"As usual, then."

Martha's eyes met mine and she smiled. "That girl loves her sport."

I returned her smile. "She does. Even in this cold weather." I regarded her for a moment as she broke eye contact and went back to work. "Are you sure you're okay?"

She gave a stilted laugh. "Of course. Just busy with extra bodies in the house." She opened another drawer and then paused. "You do not think the police inspector will be staying also?"

"I'm sure he won't, Martha. He'll look for whatever he needs and then be on his way."

Martha nodded. All I could see was the side of her face, but the tight lines around her mouth eased a bit.

"Martha, I'm trying to figure out who might have pushed me." Or whether she had seen the prowler. "Have you seen anyone suspicious lately? Outside the kitchen perhaps?"

The tight lines returned, Martha's mouth now flattening into a narrow line. "No, I have not seen any strangers on the property. Other than the police. Why do you ask?" Martha wouldn't quite look at me as she continued pulling ingredients and utensils onto the table. I couldn't tell if it was simply stress causing her to avoid meeting my eyes, or something else entirely.

"I saw someone the other night. They seemed to be coming from the kitchen door, but I didn't recognize who it was."

"Well, that is nerve-making. Especially after you were pushed into the water." I nodded and she continued on in her matter-of-fact way, measuring out ingredients as she spoke. "But one does not mean the other. Perhaps it was Sergeant Barlow that you saw. He likes to come in for a bite to eat before he goes out to take care of the horses."

I nodded. "Yes, perhaps it was him that I saw." I knew with certainty that it wasn't, but it didn't seem worth arguing the point. She had been terribly concerned about my safety after my dunk, so I thought it was strange that she was so matter-of-fact about the possibility of a stranger on the grounds. But perhaps she wanted to keep her head firmly in the sand about the possibility of danger. I couldn't really blame her—I would have preferred not to worry about it myself.

"Or perhaps it was Marie."

I raised my eyebrows.

Martha glanced up and with a shrug went back to what she was doing. "The girl is strange. And she is fond of the horses."

"But does she wander outside after dark?"

"Who can say with that girl?"

The figure wasn't tall enough to be Marie, but it was interesting that Martha thought the girl to be so odd. I would have to explore what the others thought of the girl—and what she might be capable of.

Martha was obviously done with our conversation, but I settled myself on a stool, unwilling to let her off the hook just yet. I was curious about Lillian's cousin, even though he hadn't been here when Simon's car was sabotaged. "How well do you know Alistair, Martha?"

Martha shrugged and began creaming butter in a large bowl. "The boy and his sister, Poppy, come by fairly regularly. It is good for them to spend time with Lord Hughes."

"Alistair and Lord Hughes are close?"

"Well, Lord Hughes has . . . what is expression?" Her eyebrows knitted, then smoothed out. "Taken Alistair under his wing. Which is good thing, since Alistair's father is . . . not well. But we should not gossip about family."

"Is Alistair's father ill?" Millie hadn't mentioned anything about that to me during our discussion.

Martha glanced up and eyed me. "In a manner of speaking." Her eyes narrowed shrewdly, and I could see her weighing the wisdom of elaborating. But she finally nodded once before continuing on with her mixing. "It is the alcohol."

So, Alistair's father was a drunk in addition to having a gambling problem. It didn't entirely surprise me, but again I wondered where Lord Hughes's brother was now. He was already on my list of suspects for framing Lord Hughes—could I add him to the list of suspects for my push as well? But if he was Alistair's father, why would he sneak around the estate and stay in a dank room above the stables?

James Hughes or not, we needed to discover our intruder's identity. I didn't think we would be able to make any headway with finding the person responsible for Simon's death until we knew who it was.

Chapter 21

Leaving Martha in peace, I decided to head back outside, and armed myself with my thick wool coat, scarf, and felt cloche yet again. I hoped that Lillian would be alone for once, although I doubted she would be. I had rarely seen the girl without Marie trailing close behind.

But today I was in luck.

As I crested a hill, I saw a single figure striding across the lawn toward a small red flag fluttering in the distance. I hurried to catch up, finally coming close when she stopped on the small putting green, the once-distant flag cheerfully marking its target, a small hole a few yards from where I now stood. I was out of breath, my gasps blowing white clouds into the crisp fall air.

"Lillian!" I held a gloved hand to my side where a slight stitch had made its presence known by shooting little darts of pain all about. I had practically run across the lawn to catch the athletic girl.

At the sound of my voice, Lillian turned, obviously startled to see me. "Jane! What are you doing out here?"

I was surprised she hadn't heard my wheezing approach, but from the distracted look on her face, I suspected she might not have heard a steam train. "I've come to talk to you. Where's Marie?"

Lillian grunted and turned back toward her ball, lining up her club with the little white projectile. "I told her I didn't want her out here with me."

That seemed unnecessarily cruel. "Lillian."

She sighed and turned back to me, the shot untaken. "I just don't want her to get hurt, and the way things are going . . ." Lillian sighed again. "I tried to send her home, but she said she has nowhere to go." Lillian and I both frowned at that. She clicked the club a few times against her sturdy brogue.

"Doesn't she have a family of her own?"

"They're . . . estranged."

I processed that bit of information. I didn't know much about Marie, and had never managed to draw her out into conversation. It was something I was going to have to remedy immediately, especially given Martha's comments about the girl.

"So, she just lives here?"

"Pretty much. Ever since we left school."

"And your father doesn't mind?"

Lillian shook her head. "Since I don't have any siblings, he's happy for me to have the company."

This didn't surprise me. Lord Hughes was nothing but generous and thoughtful when it came to his daughter. And everyone else on his estate, frankly.

"Do you ever find Marie . . . acting strangely?"

Lillian narrowed her eyes. "In what way?"

"I'm not sure. Martha seemed to think that she might go out after dark." It wasn't exactly what Martha had said, but I wasn't sure how else to ask if her friend had been doing anything strange on the grounds.

"I can't see it." Lillian's voice was firm. "Marie is a bit odd at times, and she's difficult to get to know, but she is a loyal friend."

"She didn't seem to care for Simon much."

Lillian waved that away. "Marie is just protective of me."

That seemed to be an understatement, but Lillian was obviously convinced of Marie's loyalty. And I doubted Lillian had ever considered whether her friend was capable of causing Simon's demise. I was beginning to wonder if I had misstepped in overlooking Marie, although it was difficult to see the girl trying to frame Lord Hughes for murder after he had taken her in.

I looked over the rolling landscape for a moment to collect my thoughts. I needed to delicately ask Lillian about her relationship with her cousin Alistair and I wasn't sure how best to approach the topic. But before I could figure out how to make the transition, Lillian beat me to the punch.

"I suppose you want to ask me about Alistair." She went back to lining up her shot.

"I do, actually." It wasn't why I had come looking for Lillian, but I was curious about how attentive Alistair was to her. Especially after his announcement the other night, I suspected the boy had designs on Lillian.

Lillian nodded and gave the ball a gentle bump, sending it to within a foot of the hole marked by the fluttering red flag. I looked around and wondered how many of these holes Lord Hughes had set up for Lillian to practice on.

"He's my cousin, and I enjoy having him around." I nodded encouragingly, although Lillian was completely focused on the ball as she lined up another shot. "But I don't have feelings for him in a . . . well, in a romantic sense."

But then, Lillian didn't seem the type to have romantic feelings in any sense of the word. She was a lovely young woman, but single-minded in her obsession with golf. And she was not at all given to emotional outbursts—the ones we had seen when Simon died were quite the anomaly, but she had more or less admitted to the reason for that.

"And do you think Alistair has romantic feelings toward you?" I asked.

"I think he would like to marry into our family. But I don't really have any interest in that." Lillian sank her ball. "Especially not after what he said the other night," she muttered.

"I can see how that would be the case." Lillian's reaction had not been favorable toward the young man. Nor had anyone's really. "So, you're not interested in ever getting married? Or just not interested in marrying Alistair?"

"Either," she said firmly. Lillian sank the ball, bent down to scoop it up, and started walking, glancing back to make sure I would follow. She picked up her bag of clubs lying at the edge of the green as she passed and slung it over her shoulder. "I would never give up my career to 'take care of someone's home.'" She said the last in a singsong voice.

"I see." I did actually. Lillian wasn't a typical young woman in any sense of the word. Learning that she wasn't interested in trading her beloved golf for a traditional marriage wasn't exactly surprising information. "And what about Simon?"

"Oh, lovely Simon. He was a delight to have around. Always so cheerful and full of fun. Sometimes it gets a bit stuffy around here and it was nice to have him around for a laugh." Lillian slowed down. "Except of course when he got upset and had to go for his drives." She sighed. "Like I told you and Mr. Redvers, I did feel dreadfully for him. He was still having a hard time—his experiences in the war, and all."

"But you weren't interested in him, either?"

She sighed, and gazed out over the green for a moment before refocusing. "I guess I can't exactly say that. I did . . . care for him. But I never gave it serious consideration." Lillian stopped and gave me a direct look. "And if you're wondering whether I prefer women, I don't feel romantically toward them either." I raised both eyebrows. I had begun to wonder, but it was certainly not something that was discussed in polite society. Lillian had no compunctions, though, and I couldn't help but give her a grin. I liked her straightforward approach.

"Well. I hope you go far with golf, Lillian." It was the truth. I may not want to discuss it ad nauseum, but I did wish her every success.

"Thank you." She shrugged and continued walking. "What I really want is to win the amateur tournament in London next spring. Then I could go on to the semi-pros." Her face twisted. "Not that they let women go any further than that."

My face soured as well. "Maybe someday that will change."

She gave me a sideways smile. "We can only hope."

We walked along companionably for a few minutes, Lillian carrying the leather bag of clubs on her strong shoulder with ease. We stopped on the crest of another small hill and I could see a tiny flag waving in the distance. Lillian set her ball up and pulled a sturdy club out of the bag. Watching her gave me a moment to remember what else I had wanted to ask her about.

She took a swing and the ball sailed out of sight. This was the first time I had actually seen the girl golf, and she was obviously in her element.

We started moving toward where Lillian had seen the ball drop from the sky. I'd lost sight of the thing immediately.

"I'm worried about my father. I'm certain he wouldn't have done anything to that car," Lillian said.

I wasn't sure how she knew about the knife with Lord Hughes's initials, since neither the inspector nor Redvers had discussed it with anyone in the family besides Lord Hughes himself, but again, Lillian was a rather astute observer. Or she had an eavesdropping habit I wasn't aware of.

"It is a bit of a mess right now, but hopefully we can get it sorted out." I cocked my head and gazed out across the gently rolling hills. "It seems Simon might have learned something about your father. Do you know what that could be?"

Lillian thought for a moment. “It could have to do with how he made his latest fortune.” My head snapped around to look at her. “During the war. I think he feels guilty about something, and that’s why he hires so many veterans to work for us. I’m sure we would have a veteran cooking for us as well if Martha hadn’t been with us for so long.”

I was right that I had underestimated this girl. “How do you know this?”

“People always underestimate women, don’t they, Jane?” I was forced to agree—wholeheartedly. “I’ve heard things around the house—Father talking on the phone and meetings in his office. I don’t know much more than that, though.”

“It’s a good guess though. Thank you, Lillian.” I would have Redvers follow up on that line of inquiry. Sometimes it seemed he could just make a mysterious phone call and return with information. In my imagination there was a file room of secrets somewhere that he could just tap into at will.

Lillian stopped and put her hand on my arm. “But my father is a good man.”

I nodded. My gut told me that he was, and I was hoping that whatever he had done during the war wasn’t as bad as it sounded.

We stood quietly for a moment before I remembered to ask her about the other members of the staff. “Do you happen to know anything about Mr. Shaw? Or Sergeant Barlow?”

Lillian started walking again. “I don’t really.” She paused and her voice filled with horror. “You don’t think either of them had anything to do with Simon’s . . . death, do you?”

“I’m just wondering if perhaps they know something they aren’t telling us. Maybe something about Simon, or your father.”

Lillian shook her head. “Sergeant Barlow really keeps to himself. So does Mr. Shaw for that matter. I can’t see either of them having a quarrel with Simon or my father.”

We were quiet for a moment. I didn't agree with her assessment, but I didn't want to argue with the girl. It was hard enough that someone she cared about had died and her father was being framed for it. I contemplated the wisdom of asking about the prowler on the grounds, but decided there was no need to give Lillian one more thing to worry about.

"What about your uncle James?"

Lillian looked startled for a moment, then thoughtful. "I don't know him well, really. We don't see him here at the estate that often, and Alistair doesn't like to talk about him." We walked a bit farther before stopping again. "I think there's bad blood between him and father, but I'm not sure I can see him doing something like this." I nodded. I was tempted to ask further questions, but I wasn't sure how much Lillian knew about her uncle and his problems.

Before I could decide whether to tell her what I knew about James, Lillian looked at me and seemed to make up her mind about something. "Is Lord Hughes really my father?"

Lillian truly had a gift for speaking her mind. Few people at home in Boston would speak so directly, and it was even more startling to have it come from a proper young British woman. Lillian really was her own person and I admired her for it.

"Yes, he is."

"And you would tell me the truth, wouldn't you?"

I gentled my voice and gave her arm a squeeze. "I would, Lillian. Lord Hughes is your natural father."

"And Millie is my mother." Lillian mused as she began walking again. We were close to her ball and she started hunting around for it.

"She is." I looked about as well, seeing nothing but fading grass and fallen leaves.

She looked up. "So, that would make us cousins."

I smiled and nodded. Lillian suddenly dropped her club and grabbed me in a tight hug. Surprised, I took a step back to catch her momentum but quickly hugged her back. I felt moisture gathering in my eyes at her effusive display.

She released me, stepped back, and smiled. "I'm glad."

"Me, too, Lillian."

Chapter 22

I left Lillian to her practice and wandered slowly back to the house, hands tucked into my pockets. As I drew closer to the house, I saw a cherry red convertible parked out front. I wondered who on earth it could belong to—it certainly wasn't a police car.

I slipped around to the kitchen entrance and took off my warm things, hanging them neatly before stopping into the kitchen.

"Is someone new here?"

Martha looked up from the dough she was kneading. "Miss Poppy. Alistair's sister. She came not even an hour ago."

"Oh, Martha! Not another person for you to cook for." I felt terrible that we kept adding to the number of people Martha was expected to take care of without any notice.

But Martha's face creased into a smile. "She is no trouble, Jane. Poppy barely eats enough for mouse to live on. I will not have to do anything extra."

I cocked an eyebrow and left Martha to her baking.

It was time to meet Poppy Hughes.

It wasn't difficult to find the girl. I simply had to follow the sounds of giggling and the occasional squeal. I found her cocooned on a love seat with Marie in the drawing room. Millie was seated nearby with such a look of horror on her face that it was difficult to stop a small smile from creeping onto mine.

The girls were poring over a stack of magazines. *Photoplay* and some others, by the look of things.

"Isn't he just dreamy?" Poppy cooed, pointing to something in the magazine Marie was holding. Marie agreed and grinned at the girl next to her. The girls had obviously met before, since they were leaning close together and seemed quite comfortable with each other.

As soon as she saw me, Poppy burst from the couch and came trotting over. "You must be Jane!" Her thin arms wrapped around me in an effusive hug as my eyes widened. Millie's mouth now mirrored the smug smile that had just been wiped off mine.

"It's . . . a pleasure to meet you. Poppy?"

She flung herself back and gazed up into my face. "Yes! I was bored at home by myself so I came to see everyone! Join us!" Her voice was high and girlish, with just the slightest hint of a lisp. She trotted back to her seat and rejoined Marie.

Martha hadn't been exaggerating. The girl was fine-boned, but painfully thin. In fact, she was small all around—the only exception being her large round eyes that were done up dramatically. I could see her resemblance to Alistair in their fine features, but she was much shorter than he, so on her they looked elfin. Her blond hair was carefully bobbed and pressed into marcel waves. She wore a long-sleeve jersey knit dress with a drop waist in forest green with a yellow sash tied around her straight hips.

I thought it was an odd time for the girl to join the household, what with there being a murder investigation going on, but I didn't have a chance to reflect on it for long before Poppy began chattering at me.

"We were just talking about our favorite American movie stars!" Poppy said.

I took a seat next to my aunt and tried to look interested, although I was mostly bemused.

"How many of them have you met?" Poppy fixed her wide eyes on me.

I looked at her for a moment in confusion. "Well, I haven't met any."

Poppy's golden eyebrows pulled together. "Really? Why not? You should be friends with them!"

I tried to explain to the girl that America was a large place and we didn't live anywhere near where the movies were made, but her nose merely wrinkled up. It only took me a moment to realize nothing in my explanation was getting through and I trailed off midsentence.

"Okay!" she said cheerfully, and went back to looking at pictures with Marie.

Wide-eyed, I turned to Millie, but she just shrugged.

Our stay at Wedgefield just got a lot more . . . interesting.

I excused myself and went in search of Redvers. The girls didn't even look up, but Millie gave me a dark look that said I would pay later for abandoning her. I couldn't even pretend to be apologetic, but I did wonder how long Millie would wait before she hit up the bar cart.

Probably no time at all.

My search didn't take me far—I wandered into the library, the murmur of male voices in one corner. The library was otherwise peaceful, and I took a moment to soak in the relative quiet. Dark wood shelves lined any wall that was absent a window, and there were several small seating arrangements scattered about the room. There was also a long dark wood table with finely carved legs and matching chairs that sat before a bay of windows, the dim light illuminating an atlas that lay open on one end. I trailed my fingers over it as I passed, reflecting on the many places I had yet to travel to but would love to explore.

I wandered over to find Redvers and Hammond tucked into a quiet corner with their backs to the room. It almost appeared that these grown men were attempting to hide. They stood when I approached them.

"How long have you two been in here?"

"Have you met Poppy?" Hammond asked me. I nodded.

"That long."

I smothered a laugh. So, they were hiding, and from a mere slip of a girl.

"She's very . . . effusive," Redvers said, and Hammond nodded enthusiastically.

"That's a good word for it." I noticed that the men had glasses of what appeared to be whiskey. I eyed the liquid, wondering if I should have one as well.

Hammond tossed the rest of his drink back and motioned for me to take his chair in their cozy twosome. "I need to make some calls." He turned to Redvers. "Thanks for the drink, old man."

Redvers lifted his glass in salute as Hammond left us alone. I took his seat, which was still warm, and Redvers sat back down.

"Did you have a nice chat?"

"We were discussing what the plans were for Flight Lieutenant Marshall's body."

I sobered immediately. "And what are the plans?"

"His old unit is going to have a memorial service down near London. He'll be buried in a military cemetery there."

I nodded. "Not much chance of us attending then."

Redvers raised an eyebrow.

"In case we need to investigate anyone from Simon's past."

"I'm sure the police have that well in hand. And I'm fairly certain it's someone much closer to home." Redvers raised his glass. "I'm sorry, did you want one of these?"

I shook my head and smiled. We were quiet for a moment

before I was compelled to tell Redvers everything I had learned from my conversation with Lillian.

"Do you think you can find out about Lord Hughes's . . . involvement in the war? Lillian seemed to think that Hughes feels guilty about something and that's why he hires all these veterans to work for him." I gave a small shrug. "Whatever it is, I'm wondering if it's the thing that Simon learned."

"I agree. I'll make some phone calls."

"To your magical file room of secrets, I suppose."

Redvers looked amused. "If we had one of those, I think it would be more like a warehouse."

I wished there was such a thing. My fingers itched to dig through those imaginary files.

I gave myself a moment to fantasize about all the secrets I could learn, before I brought myself back to reality and told Redvers about my discussion with Lillian. Redvers was as unsurprised as I was about the girl's utter lack of interest in marriage with Alistair—or anyone. Especially if it meant giving up her golf career.

"What did you learn from the inspector?" They had been closeted in Hughes's study for hours. It occurred to me that despite all my frustration at being left out, I might have been better off—I'd been able to cover much more ground on my own.

"Obviously we need to know the identity of whoever is prowling around the grounds before we can make any further progress. It's simply too likely that they had something to do with Simon's death." Redvers had one ankle propped on his opposite knee and looked completely at ease.

I bounced my leg a few times. "I would feel better as well. It's more than a little disconcerting to have someone roaming the grounds and possibly the house. The chair under my doorknob isn't going to do much if someone is determined to get in."

Redvers nodded but didn't say anything else.

I eyed him up. There was no way the police didn't have a strategy laid out already. "What's the plan, Redvers? Don't think you can keep me from finding out."

"I know better than that." He sighed. "They're going to conduct a stakeout."

I sat up in excitement. "Excellent! Where will we be hiding?"

Redvers groaned. "I knew this would be your reaction."

"Well, of course. You're not going to have all the fun without me."

He looked at me for a long moment and I could see him weighing the wisdom of arguing with me. He shrugged. "I couldn't keep you away even if I tried." I rewarded him with a smile. He was catching on. "We'll be staking out the stable tomorrow night. And since you'll be joining me, I'll make sure we have someplace comfortable to sit."

"I don't need the Taj Mahal, you know. But I appreciate the thought." I tapped one finger to my lip. "I had better make some preparations, too. Find my darkest warm clothing." I started making a mental list of what I would need to spend the evening outside trying to catch the prowler. Definitely some long underwear and woolen . . . well, everything. I would also try to dig up a blanket in case it was cold. The weather was crisp during the day and was positively chilly at night. Even in the safety of the stable I knew the cold would creep in and sink beneath my clothes.

I thought about what time the prowler had been spotted before, and decided he wouldn't be on the move any too early. Perhaps we could close this case as soon as the next day—my blood sang at the possibility of having answers so soon.

I added a thermos of coffee to my mental list of necessities.

"We can't do it tonight?" I asked hopefully.

Redvers shook his dark head. "We need time for news to

get out among the staff and in the village that the police have gone. I don't think our intruder will come back until he's sure they're off the property."

I sighed with longing. I really wanted something to break free and get this case moving. Then I thought about how the gentlemen spent the morning; more than a stakeout had to have been discussed. "You were in there an awfully long time. Did you learn anything else?"

"Greyson questioned Hughes extensively, but there wasn't much we didn't already know. Nothing about the war, but of course, we didn't know to ask. Greyson did cover Hughes's alibi and his relationship with his nephew, since Alistair conveniently turned up to comfort Lillian."

"Anything interesting there?"

"Just that Lord Hughes and Alistair seem quite fond of each other. And Hughes insists the lad isn't as unlikable as he seems. Just young and confused."

I gave a little snort, then turned my mind to Hughes's brother. "Do you know anything about James Hughes?"

Redvers shook his head. "He came up, but only in passing."

I filled him in on what I had heard about the man.

Redvers looked interested. "It could just be gossip, but it's worth looking into. Did you learn anything else today?"

I grinned and passed Redvers the racing forms while I shared what Mr. Shaw had to say about them.

"It's unlikely that this is what Simon was blackmailing Lord Hughes over." Redvers looked the sheets over before tucking them into his pocket.

I agreed. "And neither he nor Barlow knew anything about the prowler on the grounds. I'm certain they were telling the truth on that." I blew out a puff of air. "I think the only thing we can do is figure out who the person is. I don't think we'll make any progress on Simon's death until we know."

We slipped into a comfortable silence. I listened to the pop and crack of the burning log in the fireplace and watched the low flames dance for a while before turning back to him.

"Do you think Hughes could have anything to do with Simon's death?"

Redvers met my eyes. "I really don't. I think he's being set up."

Of course, Lord Hughes wasn't completely blameless. There was something unsavory in his past that he wasn't being forthcoming about. Some kind of scheme he was involved in that made him feel guilty—and for whatever reason, hiring veterans assuaged that guilt.

But guilt didn't necessarily lead to murder, did it?

Chapter 23

Before long, it was time to go in to dinner. Redvers tried to convince me that we could head into the village and eat at the local pub instead. My position was that we should eat with the family.

"I don't want to miss anything!"

"What do you think we'll miss? Someone being bludgeoned over the soup?"

"No, but . . ."

He sighed. "Wouldn't it be nice to have a quiet dinner, just the two of us?" The idea gave me pause. I could feel myself giving in to how much I enjoyed his company, forgetting all my arguments about keeping him at a distance the more time I spent with him. And there was something he wanted to say to me, but the interruptions had stopped him so far. Perhaps if we were away from the family, he would bring it up again.

"Without having to deal with . . ." Redvers gestured at the drawing room, where the rest of the family had gathered before the meal. I poked my head around the doorframe to make sure no one could hear him, but everyone inside the room was occupied far from where we stood.

Then his words sunk in. It would have been nicer if he wanted to be alone with *me* instead of merely avoiding Poppy Hughes and the rest of the family. I felt my eyes narrowing at him.

Redvers saw where my thoughts were headed and threw his hands up. "Very well. In we go."

We joined the family and went in to dinner.

"Where's Simon?" Poppy chirped. "He usually joins us."

There was an uncomfortable silence as we either studied our plates or stared in horror at the girl. Lillian's face had drained of all color whereas Alistair's had turned a shade of pink, as if the blood poured out of one and into the other.

Lord Hughes cleared his throat. "Poppy, dear, Simon was killed a few days ago. In a motorcar accident."

I was gratified to see Poppy respond appropriately. I'd only known the girl a few hours, but it was long enough to be concerned with how she might react. "Oh, I'm so sorry. I didn't know." Poppy turned to Lillian, her normally exuberant face filled with sorrow. "Lilli, dear, I'm very sorry. I know you were fond of him."

Lillian nodded and thanked her cousin.

Millie strong-armed the conversation in another direction entirely and there was a palpable sense of relief from everyone at the table. No one wanted to dwell on the tragedies that had plagued the house of late.

At another break in the conversation, I turned to our host. "Where's Sergeant Barlow, Lord Hughes? He never joins us for dinner."

Lord Hughes looked up from his plate in some surprise. "The sergeant prefers to keep his own company, Jane. Although I hope he knows he's always welcome to join us. The same with Mr. Shaw, although I believe he and Martha like to have their own meal in the kitchen."

I glanced over and saw a little crease develop between Alistair's brows, and he stabbed a bit of broccoli with unnecessary vigor. Interesting. It seemed Alistair didn't care for the idea of the servants joining us as members of the family. Well, if that was the case, he could learn from his uncle's generous spirit. No matter the reason for Hughes hiring the men, he treated them as part of the family.

"Yes, I imagine that must be the case for many of the men. After what they've been through."

Group Captain Hammond entered the conversation with a shrug, not quite disagreeing with me. "It varies from person to person, of course. Some miss the feeling of camaraderie once they're out of the service and can't stand to be alone with their own thoughts. Others find the presence of people intolerable."

Millie was glaring at me farther down the table. It appeared she didn't appreciate my choice of dinner conversation either. But I was at a bit of a loss for something she would deem more appropriate. Murder? I didn't think she would be thrilled with that either, and I knew it was the thing foremost on everyone's mind, even though we were all trying to avoid the topic.

"Lillian, how was your practice today?" Millie asked, giving me a direct look. I barely managed to keep from rolling my eyes.

Redvers had watched the exchange with amusement. He leaned over. "And you didn't want to go to the village pub." I pulled a face at him and he chuckled.

Talk over dessert eventually did turn to the investigation, although I noticed that Redvers skillfully led the discussion that way.

"When do you think the police will finally be clearing out? I can't see that having them here has done any good." Millie was leaning in to her indignation. "And they've gotten nowhere with this investigation."

"They'll be leaving this evening, actually," Redvers informed her.

"That's news to me." Lord Hughes looked surprised.

"I believe they decided this afternoon, just as the inspector was leaving. I happened to be with him."

Lord Hughes regarded Redvers for a moment, then nodded. The men had been closed up in the study together for hours—I was surprised the topic hadn't come up, unless they were purposely keeping Lord Hughes in the dark. I casually glanced around the table, but no one else appeared interested in the police's activities. It didn't mean that the news wouldn't quickly spread though the occupants of the estate though.

Lillian sighed. "I just hope they figure out who wanted to hurt poor Simon." We were all quiet for a moment.

Poppy suddenly burst out. "Maybe it's a ghost!" We sat blinking at her like a parliament of owls.

"What was a ghost?" Alistair finally asked.

"The person who killed Simon, silly!" She frowned. "This house is old! It must have a ghost. Have you seen one, Lillian?"

"Ahm, no. I haven't."

"Well! It couldn't be anyone here, so I say it was a ghost!" She gave one nod and went back to her chocolate trifle.

No one bothered to argue with the girl that a ghost would lack the ability to slice a brake cable. Or whether they even existed. We all just sat in stunned silence, the scrape of Poppy's fork on the plate the only sound in the room.

So much for reasonable responses from Poppy Hughes.

"Can't prove it wasn't, I suppose." Alistair said kindly. He shrugged to the rest of us, a little defensive of his sister, and we went back to our own desserts.

Chapter 24

The next morning, I was up bright and early, ready for another go at the skies in the Moth. I hurried through breakfast and Group Captain Hammond and I headed out to the barn. I found myself hoping that even with a few days in between lessons I wouldn't have forgotten what I already learned.

"You disappeared early last night, Chris."

Hammond reddened slightly, and I looked at him in surprise. I had only been making conversation, but perhaps there was a reason he had excused himself immediately after dinner.

"Yes, well . . . I was quite tired. Decided to call it an early night."

I let it go since I didn't want to make things awkward right before we went up in the plane. But it didn't mean I could forget about it completely, especially since his response was anything but casual. I wondered why he would react so strongly to an innocent question. Could Hammond have something to hide? The idea left me somewhat dispirited.

"You're feeling up to this?" the group captain asked solicitously, effectively changing the subject.

"Of course. I'm feeling right as rain."

Hammond smiled, but I could see him inspecting my face closely, looking for any signs of illness. I ignored him.

"Has Lord Hughes been continuing his lessons?"

Hammond shook his head ruefully. "With everything that's going on, His Lordship has decided to take a bit of a hiatus. At least until things have been cleared up."

We reached the barn and Chris pushed back the large sliding door, a raspy creak greeting his effort, and we moved toward the little yellow plane, dust motes floating before us in the dim light. Almost immediately, we noticed a large wet patch on the ground beneath the engine compartment.

"Oh, no." I did not have a good feeling about this. The weather had been dry overnight, and it was unlikely the liquid came from anywhere but the plane.

We both bent down, and Chris put his finger in the liquid, bringing it up to his nose. I already suspected what he was going to say—the sweet smell of gasoline lingered in the air.

"Damn. It's fuel."

I nodded, a sinking feeling in the pit of my stomach. I watched as Chris opened the maintenance panel and peered inside.

"Looks like the fuel line has been cut." He reached inside, plucked at something I couldn't see, and nodded at his prognosis.

"Blast it all!" I felt like kicking something—or someone—but I scuffed my shoe on the stone floor instead. Another cut line. "Who would do this?"

"I don't know. But it's not the end of the world. I have to go over to London in the next day or so anyway and I'll pick up what I need to repair this." He smiled, although his cheerfulness looked forced. "You'll be back in the sky in no time."

I gave him a wan smile in return.

"In the meantime, we should try to find some sawdust or something to soak up this mess."

We hunted around the barn until we finally found a pile of old flannel rags. Hammond decided they would do until he could return with some sawdust to absorb the rest.

* * *

I returned to the house alone. Hammond stayed behind to try to repair what he could and make a list of what he needed to install the new line. I half wondered if he would start sleeping in the barn in order to guard the little biplane—he was very protective of his charge. Selfishly, I had to admit feeling nervous that Hammond would decide it wasn't worth staying at Wedgefield if the Moth was in danger, but so far, the group captain seemed willing to stay on and continue giving lessons to both Lord Hughes and myself. I found myself profoundly grateful the damage wasn't any worse than it was.

But I couldn't decide whether or not the sabotage had anything to do with Simon's murder. It was possible that it was unrelated, but it did seem to be quite the coincidence. And I wasn't sure I believed in coincidences. Not one like this, at any rate.

I joined the early risers in the breakfast room. So far, it appeared only Lillian, Millie, and Redvers were up and moving around.

Millie eyed me as I entered and took the seat next to Redvers. "You're back early. And your hair isn't the usual disgrace. What happened?"

"Someone cut the fuel line on the plane." I wondered if I looked as glum as I sounded.

Redvers' head whipped up to look at me. I shrugged.

Millie made a satisfied noise. "Well, it was a bit extreme, but it seems that you discovered the issue right away." When I nodded, she beamed down the table. "Well done, Mr. Redvers."

Redvers and I both looked at her. "I beg your pardon?" Redvers' dark eyes were wide.

"Taking matters into your own hands to stop Jane from this foolishness. I approve of your methods. Very direct." Millie gave Redvers a smile and went back to buttering her toast.

Despite the circumstances, and my disappointment in the morning, I stifled a giggle at the look on Redvers' face. He seemed torn between disbelief and horror.

"I'm afraid I can't take credit for this one, Mrs. Stanley." Redvers was shaking his head firmly.

"Nonsense. No need to be so modest. And it's Millie."

I smothered another giggle, hiding behind my cup of coffee, and Redvers shot me a dirty look. I winked in response.

I knew full well that Redvers hadn't sabotaged the airplane. Not when he had gotten up early to simply check it over for me—frankly, he could have cut the line then. But he would never do something to put me in harm's way. That much I knew for certain.

Which begged the question: Who would?

Chapter 25

The day passed slowly. Without my morning flying lessons I was quite at loose ends. Group Captain Hammond had gone first thing in the morning, Marie and Poppy were inseparable so I couldn't get Marie alone for a chat, and both Shaw and Sergeant Barlow had made themselves scarce. There was no one to talk to and nothing to investigate. Lord Hughes had taken Redvers out fishing, something I wasn't even aware Redvers was interested in. They had kindly invited me to join them, but sitting still and waiting for fish to bite was hardly going to help my anxiety. I was almost twitchy with anticipation for the night's stakeout.

After pulling together an outfit to change into after dinner, I lay down for a nap—if I was going to be up all night, I needed to bank some extra sleep. Just when I started to believe I was too excited for the evening's adventure to nap at all, I drifted off. I awoke several hours later and, checking the clock, hurried to freshen up before heading downstairs.

Upon entering the drawing room, I found that I was the last to arrive. I was also surprised to see that Sergeant Barlow had decided to join us. He and Redvers were chatting in a corner. Well, it looked like Redvers was doing most of the chatting, but Sergeant Barlow looked engaged in the conversation.

Millie had set herself up in the seating arrangement nearest the bar cart. She and Lord Hughes were turned toward each other, my aunt's face lit with delight at whatever anecdote Hughes was relating. She reached out and put a hand on his forearm, letting it linger for far longer than was proper for two unmarried people. Hughes didn't seem to mind.

Giving them their privacy, I helped myself to a drink and wandered over to where the three girls were sitting with Alistair. Before I could even get the gist of what was being discussed, Martha appeared in the doorway and announced dinner. We dutifully filed into the dining room.

After supper festivities were starting to resume their normal shape and color—the girls and Alistair put on music while my aunt and Lord Hughes sat down to a card game, Rascal curled beneath the table at their feet. The evenings were slowly losing the somber tone they had taken on after Simon's death.

Redvers and I excused ourselves from the drawing room early. Sergeant Barlow had begged off directly after supper—he seemed anxious to return to the quiet solitude of the outdoors, but I appreciated that he had joined us in the first place, especially since Hammond had gone over to London. It was pleasant having another body at dinner to round out the group, even if he didn't have much to add to the conversation. I had waited all through dinner for Alistair to make some remark about the man dining with us, but he had been nothing but pleasant to Barlow. I wondered if Lord Hughes had had a talk with the young man—it certainly seemed as if Alistair was making an effort to be polite.

Redvers and I had agreed to meet downstairs after everyone else had retired. I changed into a pair of dark woolen trousers that I found in the armoire. They were thicker than anything I had with me, so I decided they were my best bet, and the easiest to layer over my thick wool tights. The pants were a little big on me, so I belted them tight and added several layers on top as well, hoping everything would fit beneath my jacket. I then sat and bounced my leg while trying to read a book and waited for everyone to drift off to bed.

After an hour I had removed all my layers but the last one, a long sweater and my tights. The family was taking entirely too long downstairs and even with the window open I had begun to roast. I'd asked Martha to have the radiator in my room turned off, but she had obviously forgotten, and the thing was going full steam ahead. I stuck my head out of the window for a few minutes, trying to cool down my reddened cheeks, before taking up my post on the bed once again. I flopped back in frustration and studied the ceiling again.

I finally heard footsteps heading down the hall, followed by another set and a faint "good night," so I reassembled my outfit and prepared to sneak downstairs to meet Redvers. When the last set of footsteps had echoed down the hall and I heard the door shut, I doused my lights and peered out of my room. I came into the hall and locked the door firmly behind me, before moving quietly down the stairs.

I found Redvers waiting for me in the back hall. "What are you wearing?" he whispered, one eyebrow raised.

I looked down at my baggy trousers. "I found them. I thought they would be warm for tonight." Seeing them through his eyes, I had to admit they looked a little ridiculous. But I hadn't anything nearly as warm, and trousers would make chasing down criminals that much easier. Unless I got lost in them. There was an awful lot of spare fabric.

He gave his head a little shake, but a ghost of a smile played at his lips. We donned our coats, scarves, and gloves before slipping out into the inky night. My layers were so thick beneath the coat that I had a hard time putting my arms down completely.

We were halfway to the barn and entirely alone when I whispered, "What time is it? I didn't look at a clock."

"It's just after eleven."

"Where are the police? I haven't seen the slightest sign of them."

Redvers smiled. "Then they're doing their jobs."

I could only hope so. As much as I wanted to be a part of this stakeout, I didn't want Redvers and I out here alone without backup.

We made our way into the stable, closing the door firmly behind us, and went up the stairs into the first room on the left. Redvers had brought a pile of blankets with him and set them against the wall that adjoined the hallway. The half-open door would block us from view if someone came down the hall. If they came all the way into the room, they would of course see us, but at that point we should be able to apprehend them.

I settled onto the pile of blankets and rested my back against the wall. I set the basket of supplies I had brought with me next to me on the floor and cracked open the thermos of coffee.

"Don't drink too much of that." Redvers was eyeing the thermos.

"Why not? I need to stay awake."

"There aren't any . . . facilities . . . out here."

I sighed and rescrewed the top after taking only a sip. I hadn't thought of that.

It was dark in the room, moonlight filtering through the grimy windows across from us. Redvers settled himself onto the blankets next to me—close, but not too close. Minutes stretched into the half hour as we waited and I grew more and more restless.

I changed my position. Again. My backside seemed to be falling asleep.

"How do you know Lord Hughes?" I whispered. "When you first arrived, you greeted him as though you had already met."

I could see Redvers turn slightly toward me as he returned the whisper. "He knows my father."

It seemed Redvers would say nothing more. "You never talk about your family."

He was quiet for so long I thought he wouldn't respond. "No, I don't."

"Why is that?"

We listened to the sounds of the horses shifting around downstairs until even they seemed to be dropping off to sleep. But I was wide awake with the possibility of learning something new about the mysterious Redvers.

He was still staring straight ahead at the windows when his answer finally came. "Because of my brother." I didn't say anything, I just watched him as he worked out his words. "Percival was an officer during the war. He was killed by his own men." I gasped, but in the pale light I could see his jaw clench and he shook his head. "He had it coming. He would have been executed anyway for treason." I reached out and took his hand, saying nothing.

"My parents were devastated. Perhaps no more so because it ruined my father's chance to be knighted. It had looked like a possibility before that. My father was a stern man, but very popular at court. He was, anyway."

"How is it that you're still working for the government? They still trust you?"

"I had distanced myself from my family long before any of this happened. And because of my work during the war, none of my family's . . . troubles . . . came down on me."

I had approximately hundreds of follow-up questions, and there were many more stories tucked into the folds of what he had just told me, but I could sense that was as much as Redvers was willing to reveal tonight. So, instead of trying to satiate my curiosity, I simply squeezed his hand. I could feel a little of the tension that had been building in his body release as he settled back against the wall once more.

I released his hand and reached for my coffee.

I could feel Redvers looking at me, so I replaced the cap without taking a drink and started to chat. Quietly, of course. "I've been thinking about Alistair and Poppy. Both of them are flirting with people who aren't entirely appropriate for them. I wonder if it runs in the family." I imagined that Redvers' eyebrow was raised—it was hard to see in the dark. I couldn't make out much besides the moonlight glittering off his dark eyes as they regarded me.

"I suppose it's fine for Alistair to flirt with his cousin, but I hope he isn't actually interested." I continued my whispered rant in an effort to put Redvers further at ease. It was difficult for him to open up, and I appreciated that he had finally made the effort to talk about his family.

He cocked his head as though he was trying to listen to something, but I kept whispering. "And Marie and Poppy seem quite close, which makes me wonder . . ."

He grasped me by the shoulders and pulled me to him, his lips finding mine even in the darkness. He slanted his mouth, and I leaned in to him, electricity singing in my veins. It had been like this when I kissed the man in Egypt, and if anything, the sizzle had intensified. I reached one hand up and ran it through his thick dark hair, my other hand grasping his broad shoulder as I started to drown in sensation.

And then the door downstairs opened.

Chapter 26

We pulled apart, both of us trying to control our breathing and listen instead. Neither of us dared move as we heard light footsteps moving cautiously up the stairs.

Everyone on the estate had terrible timing. Even the prowler.

Redvers leaned carefully away, disentangling himself from me while making as little sound as possible. He came to his feet, one hand on my shoulder to keep me where I was. For once, I was fine with this. I needed a minute to recover from what had just passed between us. He could tackle the intruder alone while I learned how to breathe again.

The footsteps continued down the hall, and I could hear metal against metal as someone tried to insert a key into a lock, fumbling in the darkness. Redvers moved to the doorway without a sound and I was once again struck by how quietly the man could move. He turned into the hallway, and I rose to my feet, careful not to make a sound, bracing one shaky hand against the wall behind me.

The lock clicked over and Redvers spoke into the quiet. "Hello."

A hoarse shout was followed by the sounds of scuffling. I rushed into the hall just as I heard a loud thump. Then silence.

"Turn on a light, will you, Jane?"

I shuffled back into the room where we had been hiding

and located the flashlight Redvers had brought along. I switched it on and made my way back into the hallway, shining it into the faces of the men at the end of the hall. Redvers had already turned his head away, and the light caught the man he was nearly lying on full in the face. The prowler blinked rapidly and closed his eyes, craning away from the bright light. The face below the flat tweed cap was long and slightly dirty, as though he had been sleeping rough for quite some time; a flick of the light downward showed that his clothes were in equally rough shape.

A familiar picnic basket lay on its side at his feet. I stared at it for a moment, eyebrows raised before turning my attention back to Redvers.

"Shall we tie him up?" I could see that Redvers had the man's arms held tightly behind his back.

"Perhaps just fetch a few constables." The man's face twisted at that.

I trotted downstairs and stuck my head out the door and let loose a few shouts. Before long I heard replies from several different directions as men began sprinting across the lawn toward the stables. I hoped one of them would be wise enough to bring a lantern. The stable hadn't been fitted out with electricity.

By the time a few young constables arrived, Redvers had manhandled the intruder down the stairs to the first floor and he passed his charge off to the men. Inspector Greyson had followed at a sedate pace, a lantern at his side.

"Mrs. Wunderly." The inspector looked over at Redvers. "I thought you had talked her out of joining you."

Redvers barely glanced up from where he stood brushing straw and dirt from his trousers, and didn't bother to respond.

"Lovely to see you as well, Inspector. I'm glad to see you brought some light with you." I said.

The inspector spluttered a bit. "That's not . . . I just think it's too dangerous for a woman to be involved . . . and it's not comfortable out here . . ." He trailed off as he held the lantern aloft. As his gray eyes took in my unusual outfit, he shook his head and turned toward the intruder, now held between two husky constables, their dark uniforms blending with the night. The man's face was sullen, his eyes glittering and angry. Greyson regarded him for a moment, then addressed the group.

"Let's head back to the station, shall we? I think we'll be more comfortable there." He looked over at me. "Won't you be more comfortable going back to the house, Mrs. Wunderly? It's awfully late and you must be quite tired."

I simply smiled and followed the man to his car before settling myself into the front passenger seat. Redvers climbed into the car without a word as well, although I did notice a slight smile on his lips as the inspector got in and started the engine. Suddenly, I was grateful for the inspector's presence as a buffer between Redvers and I, despite my irritation with the man. While I had come down from the initial shock of our kiss, I needed some time to decide how to handle things—and how I felt—before I was left alone with Redvers again.

We rolled past darkened hills that I knew were spotted with grazing sheep during the day, but now looked like a blanket of moon-soaked moss. Our procession of cars twisted slowly through the landscape, and I was struck by just how far from the village Lord Hughes actually lived. It was at least a twenty-minute ride, and we didn't see another house or human until we reached the village. We truly were isolated out at Wedgefield Manor.

I hadn't come close to ordering my thoughts by the time we reached the village, the dark stone houses standing sentinel along the narrow roads, so I gave them up and concentrated on the scenery instead. The police station was the only building that showed any signs of life this late at night—I noticed that even the village pub had closed down for the evening. As we pulled up, I could see two constables escorting our mystery man into the building. His head was bowed, and he didn't struggle.

The little gray stone building looked as though it had been here as long as the village itself. When we entered, I saw the long, scarred wood counter that separated the rest of the station from the small waiting room just beyond the front door. We walked through a small swinging gate in the counter, waist height, and continued past several desks covered in paperwork with the odd typewriter scattered here and there.

The men had taken our prisoner down a short hall and through a door, which they now stood guard in front of. They were obviously waiting for the inspector to conduct his interview. I wondered what the odds were that I would be allowed to attend.

"We'll let him stew for a moment, shall we?" the inspector said. "Can I offer you both some tea?"

"Do you have any coffee, actually?" The adrenaline rush from the evening had started to wear off on the drive and I now felt incredibly tired. A caffeine boost would be welcome, but in the excitement, I had forgotten my thermos in the stable.

"I'm sure we can find some for you." He barked an order at the nearest policeman who scrambled through some overhead cabinets before he located a tin of instant coffee. I shrugged to myself. It would have to do, especially since the inspector wasn't overjoyed at having me there in the first place.

Minutes later I had my hands wrapped around a warm mug. Redvers had refused the offer of a refreshment, but then he looked more alert than I did.

There were the sounds of a scuffle outside and someone shouting. We all turned toward the door as Martha burst in.

"You have my brother! He did nothing. You must believe me."

Chapter 27

There was shocked silence as we all stared at Martha.

"Your brother?" Inspector Greyson moved toward Martha where she now stood pressed against the counter, coat unbuttoned, hair in disarray. I could see her nightshirt beneath the open coat—she had left the house in a hurry.

"Yes. My baby brother, Sergei. Please. You must let me see him."

The inspector and Redvers shared a look.

"Are you quite certain it's your brother that we have?" Greyson asked. But I already knew the answer to that question. They shared the same red hair, and the same long, lanky build. In retrospect, the similarities were unmistakable.

And the picnic basket. It explained why Martha acted so strangely when I mentioned the wicker basket—it was the same one we had found with Sergei when we caught him in the stable. She must have been passing food to her brother with it. Most likely the same food we had seen scraps of in the room above the stable.

That our prowler was Martha's brother also explained why Martha had been so nervous about the police presence. I'd assumed it was the extra work she had been forced to pick up that made her so twitchy—and I mentally kicked myself for not seeing the truth sooner.

"Yes, yes. I saw you take him away." Martha's face was

pinched with fear and worry, but she was holding her back ramrod straight. I could see how much control it was taking for her to hold her fear at bay.

The inspector opened the swinging gate for her, and she passed through, coming straight to my side. I gave her hand a squeeze, and she gave me a tiny smile in thanks.

"I suppose you'll want Mrs. Wunderly with you, then, won't you?" It was more of a statement than a question, and the inspector sounded resigned. I was grateful that I wouldn't have to argue my way into the room or sit in the waiting room while the men learned everything worth knowing.

Martha nodded firmly.

"Well, let's get started, shall we?"

I fell into line behind Redvers and the inspector, Martha trailing close behind. As soon as we entered the room, Martha ran to her brother and put her arms around him, hugging him close. Then she gave him a not-so-gentle smack to the back of the head. He looked at her sheepishly.

"Stupid! Getting caught like this. I told you to stay in the woods and not go back to the stable until later."

"But I was cold."

I could see that both Redvers and the inspector were doing their best to hide smiles at Martha's sisterly demonstration. The inspector turned toward the door and shouted a request for a few more chairs. They were quickly delivered.

Martha took a seat next to her brother. Sergei's hands were handcuffed in front of him, and they rested on the small table he was seated behind. Redvers and the inspector sat on the other side of the table, and I pulled my chair to one side, between both parties. I crossed my legs and sipped my coffee. It tasted terrible.

"Your sister has already given us some of it, but what's your full name?" Inspector Greyson leaned forward on the table.

"Sergei Fedec." His head hung slightly. I had a feeling he

would be no trouble in this interview, especially now that his sister was here. He seemed slightly cowed by her.

"What kind of name is that?"

"Is Russian." Sergei's head came up a bit at that and a little of the fire returned to his eyes.

I had been correct then about Martha's accent originating in Eastern Europe.

"And what are you doing here in England?"

Here Martha interrupted and answered for her brother. "My grandfather, he was run out of his village years ago." Redvers raised an eyebrow and she nodded. "They thought he was a werewolf." My eyebrows shot straight up. This was a story that I definitely wanted to hear more details about, but she moved on. "He moved to the city after that. Then my father and our family, they come here when we are young. My father wanted a better life for us." She nodded her head at Sergei. "But this one, he is always so stubborn. He went back to Russia to fight."

"Fight whom?" the inspector asked.

"The White Russians."

It explained why his accent was somewhat stronger than his sister's. Martha had been away much longer than he had.

Martha continued with her brother's story. "And when they were defeated he came here looking for work. And like a fool, he got involved in the labor strike." Martha rolled her eyes, and I waited for her to smack her brother again, but she kept her hands in her lap. Just barely though—I had seen them twitch.

"The miners' strike?" Greyson asked. I was only vaguely aware of what they were referring to. I remembered reading something in the paper about how the miners were striking for better pay, but the large coal companies were unimpressed and had hired foreigners to replace them.

"The workers deserve to make living wage." Sergei finally spoke up.

"I'm sure they do." The inspector's voice was mild.

Sergei continued with his own story now. "But there was some trouble at the strikes. I got caught up in some fighting, and the police, they are going to arrest me so I come here."

"Why didn't you just tell Lord Hughes that your brother needed a place to stay?" I couldn't help interrupting at this point. Both Greyson and Redvers shot me a look, but I refused to acknowledge them. "Lord Hughes is a good man, and he's fond of you, Martha."

Martha looked pained. "That is true, but he is wealthy man. I did not think he would look so kindly on a Communist causing trouble for other wealthy men. He would not want such a man staying on his property, so I decided it was best to keep Sergei a secret."

I thought that was debatable. I didn't think Lord Hughes would have turned Sergei over to the police based on his beliefs, but I didn't argue with her. However, I did believe what Martha and Sergei were telling us. Both their stories had the ring of truth about them and fit the pieces of the puzzle regarding our mysterious intruder.

But that also meant it was very likely that Sergei had nothing to do with Simon's death or the cut fuel line on the Moth. I would reserve judgment until the interview was over, but that was what my instincts were telling me. This man wouldn't have a good motive to do either—which left us back at square one.

Inspector Greyson sighed. "I'll have to make some phone calls about all this." He looked at his watch. "But it's probably too late to make those calls now. No one who knows anything will be around until the morning."

Redvers was leaning back in his chair, arms crossed over his chest. He hadn't spoken a word during the interview, and I looked at him curiously, wondering what he was thinking.

He finally spoke. "I assume you had nothing to do with

slicing the brake cables on the car in the barn. Or the fuel line of the airplane."

Sergei shook his head violently. "No. Martha told me these things happened, but I had no part in them. I did not know anyone else there. Why would I want to hurt them? I just stayed in the room and kept quiet. Martha brought me food."

Redvers nodded. "Did you see anyone else? When you weren't in the room?" I thought it an excellent question.

Sergei tilted his head slightly. "I come out only when it is dark and everyone is asleep. I almost was caught by the man with one hand, but he did not see me." Sergei paused and thought for a moment. "There is one night I am supposed to meet Martha. I thought everyone is asleep, but I hear someone moving around in the building where the vehicles are."

Redvers uncrossed his arms. "Did you see the person?"

"No. I did not see face. I only see shadow as they leave. I hide behind building to make sure they go."

We all deflated a bit. It was too good to hope that he had seen our saboteur.

"Could it have been Sergeant Barlow?"

"Barlow?" Sergei asked.

"The man with one hand." Redvers explained.

"No, this person has two hands. Tall and thin. That I can tell."

It didn't give us much to go on. Lots of men were tall and thin.

"When was this?" Redvers asked.

Sergei thought for a moment. "I do not know exactly. The days, they run into each other when you hide. But definitely before that man took out the car and died."

I sighed. We had our prowler, but we didn't have our killer.

Light was beginning to creep through the station windows when we finally finished talking with the Fedec siblings. By that point, my eyes were so blurry I could barely see. Greyson was holding Sergei in a cell until he could determine if there were charges against him for the dust-up in the workers' strike down south, but other than that, it was up to Lord Hughes whether he wanted to press trespassing charges. I suspected that he wouldn't.

Martha's spine sagged a bit as we left the police station, and she dragged a hand down over her face—a face that still looked worried. I suspected that wouldn't change until her brother was completely free. Luckily for us, she had driven Lord Hughes's Bentley to the station the night before, so we could drive it back to the estate instead of begging a ride from the police. It was decided that Redvers would take the wheel since both Martha and I were completely wrung out.

On the ride back, I put my head back against the leather seat and closed my gritty eyes, letting my mind drift. Despite all our efforts, we were no closer to solving Simon's murder.

Chapter 28

The crunch of tires on the gravel drive woke me; I had fallen asleep at some point during the trip. Redvers stopped the Bentley, and Martha and I expended the last of our energy pushing ourselves out of the car. Her face was etched with exhaustion—the adrenaline and worry having finally leached from her system. I could barely keep my eyes open, and I longed to fall into my bed.

"I will head in. I have to be up in a few hours to start breakfast." Martha stood for a moment gazing at the house.

"I think we can fetch ourselves breakfast in the morning, Martha. Especially after the night we've all had."

She gave me a wan smile and shook her head. I started to follow her inside when I heard Redvers' voice at my back.

"A moment, Jane."

I stopped but didn't immediately turn around. I watched Martha make her way into the house and close the door behind her before turning slowly to face Redvers. He was leaning against the side of the car, arms crossed.

"Are we going to talk about what happened?"

I squeezed my tired eyes shut for a moment. "Not really. I think it's pretty self-explanatory. Sergei Fedec isn't our killer—we'll have to start from square one."

He gritted his teeth. "I'm not talking about the murder. I'm talking about the kiss." He blew out a puff of air. "I'm sorry if I startled you, but I couldn't think of any other way to stop you from talking."

"Really? No other way? And I was only talking to put you at ease after you poured your heart out."

"I didn't pour my heart out."

"Fine. Spilled it a little." I crossed my arms. "And is that the only reason you kissed me? To stop me from talking?" The answer to this suddenly seemed like the most important question I had ever asked.

"Of course not, but . . ."

I didn't hear the rest. I could only feel my heart unclench.

"Well, there's nothing else to discuss then." My voice was suddenly cheerful, and I dropped my arms to my side. Redvers narrowed his eyes at my abrupt change from combative to friendly. Then his face relaxed and he studied me.

"I hate it when you shut me out. I wish I knew how to stop it." His voice was quiet.

I opened my mouth to argue, but then I paused and thought about what he said. Did I shut down my emotions when things became too intense between us? I closed my mouth and realized that I couldn't argue the point. It was something I needed to think about—I just couldn't do it on so little sleep. I would have to work it out later.

"You might be right about that."

Redvers' eyes widened in shock.

I closed my eyes again briefly before opening them again and meeting Redvers' gaze directly. "I'll give it some thought. But right now, I have to sleep."

He pushed off the car and nodded. He was letting it go, but I wouldn't be able to avoid this discussion forever.

I passed out fully clothed on my bed. I didn't wake up until nearly noon, which felt shockingly late, even though I was still tired when I finally forced myself to get up. I took a quick bath and pulled on fresh clothes before heading downstairs. Given the hour, I knew my best bet for finding food and coffee was to head straight to the kitchen.

I found Martha there, stirring a large pot on the stove. I collapsed into the chair at the large table.

"I'll have some coffee for you in just a moment, Jane." She turned the heat down on her pot and bustled around, pulling together what she needed to make a pot of coffee, throwing some toast into a pan at the same time.

"I can help, Martha. You can't have gotten any sleep."

"No," she said firmly. "I have to keep busy or I fall asleep on my feet. And is no trouble now that Queenie is gone—I have twice as much to do."

I looked at her and raised an eyebrow. "Queenie?"

"The maid. She called here and quit. Would not even come do it in person. Said it was over a boy." Martha rolled her eyes and I laughed. Then she stopped moving and her tired face lit with a wide smile. "Lord Hughes has already hired a solicitor for Sergei. A good solicitor. So, I am not so worried as I was." She leaned over and knocked on the wood table three times.

"Oh, Martha, that's wonderful!" My instincts about Hughes had been correct.

"And I will not let the man down. I go to bed early tonight and catch up. Hopefully they release Sergei soon."

"Where will he go?"

"He will stay right here. But no more sneaking around. Lord Hughes said my brother can stay in that room he was using, but we fix it up nice. And he will find Sergei some work. Until then, Sergei can do some of Simon's jobs to pay for room and board."

I smiled at her. At least someone on the estate seemed to be getting a happy ending. Although it did seem awfully trusting on Lord Hughes's part to have a stranger come stay—even if he was Martha's brother—with the murder and sabotage happening on the estate. I felt certain that Sergei wasn't a part of it, but Lord Hughes had no way of knowing that. I would have to give that some thought.

After my coffee. All thinking would happen after coffee.

Martha handed me my cup and looked at me for a moment. "He's a good boy, my brother. But he does not use his head."

I nodded. "I could tell that he is."

She studied my face for a moment, then nodded and went back to her work.

After I finished my coffee and toast I went wandering through the house. It was dead silent and I wondered where everyone had taken themselves off to.

I wandered down the long hall on the ground floor, admiring the oil landscape paintings in the hall when I heard a whisper coming from behind the cracked library door.

"Shhh . . . we have to be quiet. We can't get caught."

This was followed by a high-pitched giggle. I got close to the wall and crept forward, praying my shoes wouldn't make a noise or the wood floors wouldn't choose that moment to creak.

But I needn't have worried. When I peered around the partially opened door, I could see Poppy and Marie mostly hidden behind a thick brocade curtain, tangled in what appeared to be a passionate embrace. I don't think they would have heard me if I had marched in banging pots and pans.

I crept backward and slipped into Lord Hughes's open study instead. I gave the girls their privacy, hoping they would be cleared out by the time Redvers returned from the barn.

I'd long suspected that Marie's feelings for Lillian were more than friendly, and it seemed I now had confirmation. It was a little shocking to see in person, but I reminded myself that it truly wasn't any of my business. My traditional marriage had been a disaster—who was I to judge another's personal choices? And when I thought about it, I was happy for Marie that she had found someone else. Lillian certainly wasn't interested, and it was healthier for Marie to move on. I just hoped the girl would be a little more circumspect in the future.

I looked around Lord Hughes's study. There were several dark wood bookcases, although not nearly the number that graced the walls of the library. A large round mahogany table stood in one corner, and from where I was, it appeared to be covered in maps. A matching heavy wood desk dominated the room, a worn leather chair pushed in behind it. I took a seat across from his desk, but near the windows, and gazed up at the sky. It was clear blue, a beautiful fall day—a perfect day for flying, if the plane were in working order. I sighed. I was incredibly disappointed that my flying lessons were on hiatus. I hoped Hammond returned soon so that we could get back to it.

"Wishing you were flying?" Lord Hughes's smooth voice interrupted my thoughts and I jumped.

"You caught me. It looks like such a perfect day for it." Rascal had followed Lord Hughes into the room and now bumped my hand with his head, seeking some scratches. I obliged and his tongue flapped happily.

"It is. Everyone else has escaped outdoors—it's unseasonably warm today. They wanted to take advantage."

I cocked my head at him. "Why didn't you join them?"

He gestured at the chair opposite me instead of his desk chair, a silent request to join me even though I had invaded his office. I nodded and he sat down. It was strange, but I realized that Lord Hughes and I had never been alone together before. Rascal left me and settled himself at Lord Hughes's feet.

"I was making arrangements for Martha's brother."

I smiled. "It's very kind of you to do so."

He gave a small laugh. "Well, I can't lose my best cook,

can I? Especially not after we lost the maid." I recognized the bluster for what it was—an attempt to downplay his good deed. "Truly though, Martha has been wonderful and it's no trouble to help out her brother."

"Even though he's a Communist?"

Lord Hughes shrugged. "We all have some strange beliefs when we're young."

I thought that was incredibly charitable of him, but I didn't press him on it.

"Do you have any ideas about what is happening here? I'm afraid someone is going to great lengths to make it look as though you are the culprit, Lord Hughes."

"Please, call me Edward. We're practically family, after all."

My eyebrows did raise at that, but he continued on, oblivious.

"I'm afraid I don't. I have a few enemies out there, but who doesn't? And I can't think that any of them would come here and set up such an elaborate scheme to frame me."

I thought about that for a moment. "It does seem rather personal. None of your enemies would fall into that category?"

He shook his head. "Strictly business."

"Someone from the village perhaps?" I was ashamed to admit it was an avenue that hadn't even occurred to me.

He thought for a moment. "I truly can't think of anyone. I try to give the local shops and tradesmen as much business as I can. It's the duty of the estate to help support the locals, and I take that very seriously."

This was not a surprise.

"What about Alistair and Poppy?" I finally asked. I hated to cast aspersions on his own family, but everyone was a suspect. In my mind, at least.

Lord Hughes shrugged. "Alistair and I have always been close. His relationship with his own father is somewhat . . . contentious, and I try to fill that role as much as possible."

I nodded.

"And dear Poppy." Hughes shook his head with a wry smile. "I'm afraid I don't think the girl is capable."

I was inclined to agree with him. If anything, Poppy seemed impulsive and not the sort to make a plan and carry it out. It was possible that we were underestimating the girl—like people underestimated most women—but with Poppy I didn't think that was the case. I briefly wondered if Hughes knew about the relationship between Poppy and Marie—or if he had seen them in the library—but given his traditional attitude toward marriage, I doubted that he had. He wouldn't be sitting here calmly with me if he'd seen the girls together.

Hughes gave me a questioning glance, and I shook my head. "Just thinking." I moved past the issue of Poppy Hughes. "What about your brother?"

Lord Hughes gave me a questioning glance and I expanded on my question. "Millie mentioned him earlier, and I had been meaning to ask you about him. How is your relationship with him?"

"With James?" Lord Hughes sighed and leaned farther back into his chair, resting his head on the back for a moment, before raising it to look at me. "James always resented the fact that I was the eldest and stood to inherit the title." His face twisted. "It's often the way in titled families, I fear." I wouldn't know, but I nodded for him to continue. "Although by the time we reached adulthood I would have thought we were beyond all that. Father had lost everything anyway, and we were both forced to make our own way. The only thing that came to me is the title and this sense of responsibility for everyone else. And I would be more than happy to hand over both."

I had no idea what to say to that. Luckily, he continued without waiting for a response.

"We haven't actually spoken in some time, but last I heard James was pretty heavily in debt." Hughes frowned. "I don't actually know where he is these days."

"He isn't at his home?"

"I'm afraid he doesn't have one any longer."

It sounded to me as though it would be worth doing some digging on James Hughes. I was an only child so I couldn't speak from experience, but it seemed to me that the felt injustices of childhood—real or imagined—could create lasting resentments well into adulthood. Although it didn't answer the question of why he would kill Lord Hughes's mechanic or cut the fuel line on the Moth. I released a quiet sigh. There were no easy answers here.

Unless the damaged brakes hadn't been meant for Simon. Could someone have intended for Lord Hughes to die in that crash instead?

Could Lord Hughes have been the target all along?

Chapter 29

I didn't mention it to Lord Hughes while he was sitting in front of me, but I wanted to discuss the possibility with Redvers. Perhaps we were looking at things all wrong. If someone off the estate was responsible, they would have no way of knowing that the car they sabotaged was one exclusively used by Simon. It was natural to assume that Lord Hughes was the one using his own vehicles. But once the plan fell apart, perhaps they decided to frame Lord Hughes instead.

I sighed. It was a reach, since that person would have to have been close enough to plant the evidence without being seen by anyone on the estate.

But it would also explain why the fuel line on the plane was cut if our killer knew Lord Hughes was taking lessons. Perhaps they hoped he would meet his end in a fiery plane crash. Of course, they should have known the plane would never get off the ground with that obvious of a leak, but could it have been a sloppy case of sabotage?

I was lost in my own thoughts, and jerked back to attention when Lord Hughes spoke again. "I'm worried about Lillian."

"I think she's taking this all rather well, considering."

"True enough, she's a strong girl. But what I mean is . . .

well, I'm worried something will happen to her next. I'm not sure I could survive it."

It was an extreme statement, but I couldn't argue the man's devotion to his daughter. I simply nodded. "Well, let's make sure that nothing does."

Lord Hughes excused himself to attend to some business that needed his attention, and I stayed where I was. I probably should have gone out to enjoy the weather, but I had too much to think over, so I stayed seated at the window, gazing out, lost in my own thoughts.

None of the pieces seemed to fit together in any neat and orderly way. Either we were missing larger pieces of the puzzle or they didn't fit together at all. Much like our midnight prowler—Martha's brother—didn't have anything to do with the murder and sabotage, perhaps not everything was connected. Although that everything should happen at once seemed entirely too coincidental.

I sighed again. I wanted to talk this over with Redvers and see what he could find out about James Hughes and any of Lord Hughes's enemies. Lord Hughes claimed that those enemies were strictly business, but the Great War had been personal to more than a few people. Could Lord Hughes's involvement have made a business enemy into a personal one? Or was this a case of sibling rivalry gone too far?

But talking these questions over with Redvers meant that we needed to be alone. And if we were alone, we would surely have to address . . . whatever . . . there was between us. I wasn't foolish enough to pretend that I didn't have some sort of feelings for the man, but they scared me.

No, *terrified* me.

I knew deep within my heart that Redvers was nothing like my deceased husband—thank the heavens for that. But I had rigidly clung to the safety of being single for so long, that it was terrifying to let go of that and jump into something less sure. I hadn't been safe for the entirety of my marriage—due to my husband's heavy fists and love for inflicting pain—and safety now felt as necessary as breath. With Grant's death on the front lines during the war, I had won my freedom back. Was I ready to give that away again?

And could I explain all this in a way that made sense to Redvers? As large and strong as Redvers was, he had proved himself to be remarkably sensitive and understanding. Why was I afraid he wouldn't be the same now?

Truly, Redvers had been nothing but supportive since his arrival. The man hadn't said a word about my taking flying lessons, he merely attempted to ensure that I would be safe. And he defended my investigating to the inspector at every turn. Redvers wasn't making any attempt to control me, completely unlike so many other people in my life. It was refreshing, and thinking about our easy back-and-forth combined with his unerring support warmed me toward him considerably.

I worried at my lip.

Did I want to take such a leap of faith with someone who kept so many secrets? They were necessary for his work, but still. Partnering with someone who kept so many secrets would prove to be torment in the long run—it was torment when he kept things from me now. And what would we be jumping into? A casual flirtation? Or something more?

There was much to think about.

In the end, Redvers found me there, still lost in thought. He wearily lowered himself into the opposite chair and I gave him a smile.

"You were up much earlier than I was."

"I couldn't sleep." He did look a little more rumpled than usual, the waves of his dark hair springing free from their normally tidy style.

"That's becoming a recurring theme." I studied him for a moment, but his face gave nothing away. I wondered what kept him up at night. Thoughts of his family? Work?

"I've been thinking." He raised an eyebrow, but I ignored him and forged on. "Perhaps Lord Hughes was the target all along."

"I've been wondering the same thing. We might be looking at this from the wrong angle."

I smiled. We were still on the same page. "And we need to look into Lord Hughes's brother."

"Once again, you've read my thoughts." He cleared his throat. "In fact, I'm going to head into London for just a day or two and check some things out."

I could feel my face fall with disappointment.

He held one hand up. "And before you say anything, I think you should stay here and keep the investigation going from this end. There's still plenty here to be learned, I'm certain."

Normally I would have argued with the man and insisted he take me along, but I couldn't help but worry that he needed to escape for a few days. From me. Had I been worried about something that wasn't even a possibility with this man? Suddenly I had no idea where I stood.

"All right." I forced cheerfulness into my tone. Then I convinced myself it was a very good idea. I could take the time to talk with Marie and see if she knew anything from her long stay on the estate. I could also talk to Poppy . . . and both those interviews would be much easier without Redvers around. I meant to mention to Redvers what I had seen between the girls, but on second thought decided to keep it to myself.

I could see Redvers' shoulders relax—he had obviously been expecting an argument. It was probably the first time I hadn't given him one.

"You're right. I have plenty of investigating to do here." I gave him a sideways smile. "And it will be easier to get done without you interfering."

Redvers rolled his eyes. "Don't do anything foolish while I'm gone." He considered me for a moment. "I'll be back before you know it."

"Of course, you will. Drive safely." I narrowed my eyes at him. "And be sure to give me a full report on what you find out when you get back. No leaving things out."

He gave a small smile. "I'll see you in a few days." He seemed to want to say something more, but shook his head and left.

Within minutes, I saw his car pass by the front windows as it left the estate.

His bag had already been packed.

Chapter 30

I grabbed a coat and headed outside to find the rest of the party. I told myself I was glad of the opportunity to get a little breathing room from Redvers' nearness. It would allow me to think with a clear head. I could also get some investigating done while he was gone, and that was precisely what I intended to do.

If I had any doubts when he announced his plan about why he was leaving, they were now firmly stowed away in a tiny box in the back of my mind. One that I placed heavy boulders on.

That mental tidying done, I forged ahead. I found Millie hiking back to the house as I crested the first hill.

"You certainly slept long enough this morning," Millie called to me.

"It was a late night, Aunt Millie. Out catching the prowler, and all."

"What you caught is Martha's brother." Millie huffed to a stop, hands on her hips. "Are you making any other progress?"

"Slowly but surely." I came to a stop in front of her. "Where are the girls?" I shaded my eyes and tried to find their figures in the distance.

"Lillian is practicing. Such dedication, really." Millie beamed for a moment before continuing. "Those other two girls are being very silly, prancing around and carrying on. It's a wonder Lillian can concentrate with such a distraction."

It sounded to me like girls being girls, but I wasn't going to argue the point with Millie. It was hard to imagine that she had ever been a young girl herself. I made a note to ask my father about their childhood and what Millie had been like.

"It was very kind of Lord Hughes to hire a lawyer for Martha's brother."

"They call them solicitors here." Millie's face softened. "Edward has a good heart. And I see no reason why not, since that boy likely had nothing to do with the other nonsense going on."

Murder was a lot more than nonsense, but I let it go. Truly, I found it surprising that Millie didn't disapprove of Hughes's generosity with Sergei, especially given her vocal disapproval of Hughes's hiring practices. Perhaps Lord Hughes was finally breaking through Millie's crust.

"Well, I think I'll try to find the girls."

"The fresh air will do you some good. You look a bit peaked." Millie turned. "And do try to make some actual progress, will you?" This she called over her shoulder as she continued toward the house. I gave a sigh and went on my way.

Millie's crust was intact and crispy.

It didn't take me long to find the girls once I moved out of the woods and back onto the wide fields that made up most of the estate. It seemed that Lillian was practicing her swings and sending a series of balls sailing down the green expanse while Marie and Poppy practiced the Charleston. I stood at a distance and watched them for a few minutes. Lillian didn't seem bothered by the girls; in fact, I could see her sending the pair an occasional smile. From what I had learned about Lillian, I suspected she knew what was happening between them and was happy for them to have found each other.

Marie stopped abruptly when she saw me, but Poppy

grabbed her arm and pulled her back into the dance. Marie laughed, but shook her head, and Poppy stopped, lip thrust out in a pout.

"Hello, girls! It's a lovely afternoon, isn't it?"

Lillian smiled at me, agreed, and went back to whacking golf balls into oblivion. Marie regarded me warily, and Poppy widened her heavily outlined eyes and nodded in earnest. "Do you want to practice the Charleston with us?" Poppy asked. "Or maybe you know another new dance!"

I grimaced and Marie shook her head. "I don't think Mrs. Wunderly is hoofin' at the clubs, Pops." She was right. In fact, I wasn't much for dancing at all. But it was a matter of rhythm, and my lack of it, not distaste for the activity.

"Really?" Poppy's eyebrows bunched together in confusion. Perhaps she didn't realize that I was quite a few years older than they were. Or more likely she simply hadn't thought about me at all.

"We were just heading back, anyway." Marie sent what was meant to be a meaningful look at Poppy. The girl missed it entirely.

"Excellent. I'll walk back with you." I looked at Lillian to see if she would join us. She shook her head.

"I'll stay out for a bit longer. There's still good light left and I want to make the most of it."

Marie looked resigned to the fact that I would be accompanying them. I needed to talk with her as well, but right now my purpose was to talk to Poppy and get some information from her. I had hoped to find her alone, but I realized that would be difficult to do—wherever Poppy went, Marie was likely to be close at hand. So, I decided I might as well take advantage of the opportunity to talk to her now.

But she spoke first. "Do you have a gasper? I'm dying for one after all that dancing!"

It took me a moment to realize what she was talking about. "Ah, no, Poppy. I'm afraid I don't smoke."

Before the girl could so much as stick her lip out for a pout, Marie was pulling two cigarettes out of a discreet silver case in her pocket. We stopped walking as she lit one for each of them, passing one over to Poppy.

"So, Poppy." I had maneuvered myself so that I was walking next to Poppy with Marie on the other side while keeping myself upwind of their smoke.

"Yes!" Poppy had such a spring to her step that I wondered if she was part rabbit.

"Where do you and your brother usually live? With your father?"

"Oh, no!" She giggled, and the sound was like tinkling bells. "We haven't lived with Papa for a while now. Not since he sold our house."

"Do you know why he sold it?" I looked at Poppy and I could see on her other side Marie was also looking at her with some concern. Marie knew what it was like to be without a home.

"He said he would get us a better one!" Poppy looked unconcerned by her father's actions. And his obvious lie—I knew that James Hughes didn't have any money left, so he certainly wouldn't be buying a new home.

"I see. So, where do you usually stay now?"

"We stay with my auntie now! She was my mother's sister. I like staying with her, she has dogs. And one of them, Barkley, he sleeps in my bed when I'm there. I think that's sweet, don't you?"

I smiled and told her that I did think that was sweet, and I asked her what type of dog it was.

"I'm not sure! He's brown! And quite fluffy." She exhaled some smoke. "And sometimes we stay here with Uncle Edward, too. I like it here too, even though Rascal doesn't sleep in my room."

I imagined that was true. Rascal was friendly, but absolutely devoted to Lord Hughes. If he and Millie were . . .

sharing a bedroom as Redvers had implied, I wonder how Millie dealt with Rascal's attachment to his master. And the dog hair. I nearly giggled at the thought.

"And where does your father stay? Does he live with your aunt?"

"Oh, no. I mean, sometimes he comes to stay! But he doesn't like the country. Or dogs. So, he mostly stays at his club in London!"

I wondered what club he belonged to and whether Redvers would be investigating that. I wished we had discussed more thoroughly what he was going to be looking into. Then I shrugged. We would compare notes when he returned.

Unless he was going to London for personal reasons. But that thought was unsettling and I tucked it back into its box.

We were all quiet for a moment, our footsteps crunching through fallen leaves as we passed near the edge of the woods. Then Poppy had another thought.

"Alistair likes to stay here more though. I think he wants to marry Lillian!"

Given how much attention Alistair paid Lillian and his awkward announcement about Lillian quitting her golf career once she married, I should not have found this announcement shocking. But the mention of marriage from someone as otherwise oblivious as Poppy startled me.

But the more I thought about it, the more I found it disconcerting that Alistair wanted to marry his first cousin. I thought the practice had fallen out of favor. Lillian was adopted; perhaps Alistair didn't realize that Lord Hughes was still in fact Lillian's natural father—the boy might be operating under the assumption they weren't blood related at all. And was Alistair in love with Lillian? He certainly did pay her a lot of attention. If that was the case, I felt a little bad for him. Lillian did not feel the same way about him, and it was even less likely a possibility after his comment about marriage the other night.

Neither Marie nor I had any response for Poppy, but I searched my mind for something appropriate to say.

"Why aren't you saying anything?" Poppy's dainty face twisted in frustration. "Lillian isn't too good for Alistair!"

"No! Not at all. That isn't what I was thinking." I rushed to reassure the girl. "If that's what they both want, I'd be very happy for them." Marie said something very similar, and Poppy went back to smiling.

But it was interesting that she immediately jumped to that conclusion. Was it something she thought on her own, or had someone put the idea in her head?

There was not much else to be learned from Poppy Hughes. I was grateful that Marie had let me ask the girl what I needed to without interruption. Although once we reached the manor house, the two girls disappeared for parts unknown.

That was unfortunate, because I still needed to talk with Marie.

CHAPTER 31

As soon as my foot hit the bottom stair on my way up to my room, Mr. Shaw found me.

"The inspector is 'ere to see you, miss."

"Oh. Well, thank you, Shaw. Where is he?"

"In the drawin' room."

I gave the man a nod and a smile and proceeded to the drawing room, wondering why the inspector would be seeking me out. He had made his feelings about my snooping into his case very clear.

"Mrs. Wunderly! You're looking well."

I couldn't stop my eyes from narrowing slightly at the compliment, but I managed to keep my smile and joined the inspector where he stood near the fireplace.

"Please, take a seat." He gestured to the stuffed chair, and once I was seated, he took the one opposite mine.

"What can I help you with, Inspector?"

He smiled again. "Please, call me Hugh."

I'm sure my face registered my surprise, but I tipped my head in assent, although I decided I wasn't comfortable with the man calling me by my given name.

After a slightly awkward pause, he cleared his throat. "Since Mr. Redvers has gone into Town, I thought I would stop by and make sure you're doing all right. There's been so much trouble here at the estate, I just want to reassure you that we have things well under control. There's no reason for you to worry."

I suspected he truly meant there was no reason for me to meddle. But since I had the man at my disposal, I may as well ask a few questions. Whether he would answer them remained to be seen, of course.

"Have you learned anything interesting about anyone else on the estate?"

The inspector tipped his head to the right, and I knew he was considering whether to tell me anything.

"Oh, come now, Hugh." I reminded myself to use the name he had asked me to. "If you tell me, I won't have to try to find out for myself."

His face soured slightly and he regarded me for a moment, then came to a decision. "Well, Jane." I bristled a bit but didn't interrupt him. "We've looked into the staff here at the estate. Sergeant Barlow checks out. And there's nothing in his past that would indicate anything suspicious. He lived the straight and narrow until the war, and he's been here since."

I nodded. I wasn't terribly surprised at that bit of information.

"We're still working on Mr. Shaw, but there's nothing to indicate anything other than his interest in horse racing."

I nodded encouragingly at him and gave him a bright smile. He smiled back and continued. "Alistair and his sister live with their aunt. And neither of them was here when the brake cables were damaged anyway." Greyson sat back. "Alistair has a bit of a reputation as a troublemaker."

"What sort of trouble?"

"Nothing too serious for a young man of his age. Drinking too much at nightclubs and getting into arguments. That sort of thing."

I nodded. That didn't sound like anything terribly out of the ordinary for a young man. I was about to ask another question when the inspector went ahead with one of his own.

"How well do you know Group Captain Hammond?"

I felt both of my eyebrows go up. "Well enough, I suppose. He's been giving me flying lessons. Why do you ask?"

"Because I'm not certain he is who he says he is."

"What do you mean?" I sat up a bit straighter against my chair.

"Well, he does fly with London's Royal Aero Club, we've found that much out."

I sagged back a little. Then at least the man knew what he was talking about when it came to flying. And selfishly, that had been my first concern.

"But we can't find any records of him with the RAF."

I stared at the inspector for a moment, uncertain what he meant. "No record at all?"

He shook his head. "As though he didn't exist. Or wasn't in the service."

"Well, that is . . . alarming." It was also surprising since Hammond was so well-connected with military officials, helping to place veterans with jobs.

"We'll keep digging, of course. It could be that he changed his name, but the question then is why."

I nodded.

"So, for the time being, I would suggest keeping your distance from the man." The inspector's face was grave.

I almost groaned out loud. I supposed that meant I shouldn't continue my flying lessons. I chewed on my lip, wondering if there was some way to get around that. As soon as the plane was fixed, I wanted to take that Moth up.

But instead I gave the inspector a weak smile. He nodded with satisfaction, obviously reading it as my agreement. Which of course it wasn't.

He cleared his throat again. "Are you available for dinner this evening? The pub in town makes a delicious steak pie."

I blinked at the man in shock. I had assumed his flirtation was nothing more than that; I certainly hadn't anticipated the man actually asking me to dinner. I floundered a moment for a way to respond, but quickly caught my footing. I already knew what my answer was—even if I was passing up an opportunity to learn more about the investigation, I didn't want to give him the wrong idea.

"I am very flattered that you ask, Hugh." His face fell a bit, and I sensed that he knew what was coming already. "But I don't want to give you the wrong idea. You're a lovely man, but I'll be heading back to the States soon, and I'm afraid I would . . . hate to start something that couldn't be finished." It wasn't precisely true, but I hoped that letting the man down easy wouldn't alienate him completely.

The inspector thought for a moment, then nodded. "I understand and I appreciate your honesty." He heaved a bit of a sigh. "I'm afraid I had hoped that your plans were to stay a bit more long-term."

I shook my head sadly. I didn't feel the need to elaborate on the fact that we also would have suited terribly—he wanted a docile wife who fit his traditional ideas of womanhood, and while I might be changing my mind on remaining unattached, I had no intention of changing my "eccentric" ways.

With a decisive nod, Greyson stood and took my hand. "Well, with that, I need to get back to work." I looked up into his gray eyes, realizing that his warm hand still held mine. It was pleasant, but there was no electricity. No spark. Without question, I'd made the correct decision in turning him down for dinner.

I smiled at him and gently squeezed his hand before pulling mine free. "Thank you for coming . . . Hugh. I appreciate it."

He smiled and moved to the door before turning back, his face serious once again. "Be careful, Jane. I would hate for something else to happen to you." His eyes studied mine.

I nodded, and he went out.

Chapter 32

The evening passed uneventfully and the next morning absolutely crawled by. I spent time walking the grounds and rehashing everything I knew as well as absorbing what Greyson had told me. I couldn't believe that Group Captain Hammond was dangerous, but I hadn't seriously considered him in any part of the mayhem until now. Unfortunately, I couldn't ask Redvers about it until he returned from London.

There were a number of things I needed to ask Redvers about when he returned.

Feeling out of sorts, I decided to return to my room for a bit. But when I turned the corner and entered the hallway, I came upon a scene. Alistair was at the far end of the hall, laughing so hard that tears were streaming down his face. In one hand he held a piece of wire.

At Poppy's door, Marie was consoling a sobbing Poppy. A few feet away a pile of what looked to be gauze lay in a lump on the floor.

Hammond stood outside his door in his stocking feet, although he was completely dressed otherwise. I wondered when he had returned and why he was standing in the hallway without his boots. I gave him a quick smile before I turned to the girls.

"What happened here?"

No one bothered to answer, but Marie walked over to Alistair, swung back, and punched him squarely in the stomach. The young man was caught midchuckle and I could hear all the wind go out of him before he crumpled to his knees, clutching his midsection. Marie shook out her fist and walked back to Poppy who was now hiccupping quietly with her eyes wide.

"You hit him!" Poppy said.

Marie simply nodded then guided Poppy into her room and shut the door firmly behind them.

Hammond and I were left staring at each other, mouths open, when Lord Hughes came up the stairs behind me.

"What's going on here?"

Alistair wheezed a bit, and I wondered at the power behind the punch Marie had served him. There had been quite a bit of force behind it.

"I'm sorry, Uncle. I played a little prank on the girls and I'm afraid it got out of hand." He gave a tug on the wire, and the mound of gauze came to life, shooting into the air. Looking up, I could see that he had rigged it up through a small hook discretely pushed into the ceiling.

"When Poppy said that she thought the manor was haunted, I thought it would be fun to give her a ghost." Alistair's face was sober now, and it looked as though he was genuinely contrite. "I rigged it up this afternoon. When they came into the hall, I just gave her a little scare."

"And why are you on the ground now?"

Alistair looked uncomfortable as he pushed himself to his feet, so I answered for him. "Marie didn't take kindly to Poppy's being frightened," I said.

A glimmer of a smile graced Lord Hughes's lips. "You managed to scare her with a ghost in broad daylight?" He shook his head. "Well, you should certainly apologize to the girls, Alistair."

"I will, Uncle Edward. It was a silly idea and I regret it

now. I was just having a bit of fun, but I can see it was a mistake."

Lord Hughes nodded absently and continued on to his quarters.

Alistair grimaced and gathered up his fake ghost before knocking on Marie's door. There was no response and he shrugged. "I'll apologize to them later." He went to his own room down the hall.

"Well," I said to Hammond.

The group captain shook his head. "That wasn't what I expected to see when I came out of my room."

"When did you get back? I thought you would be gone a few days at least. Did you manage to get what you needed to fix the plane?" I hoped it wasn't obvious that the plane was my first concern.

Hammond's face flushed and his eyes fixed on something behind my left shoulder. I sent a fast glance behind me but saw nothing of interest. "I just got back." Then he dragged his eyes back to mine. "I'll have the Moth up and running in no time. I was just heading out to the barn."

I looked down at his feet and back at his face. He pasted a smile on, excused himself, and hurriedly went into his room and closed the door.

I could not even begin to imagine what that was about. But it was obvious he was being evasive about something—he couldn't even look at me when he told me he'd just returned. And why would he feel the need to lie about that?

It certainly wasn't helping my suspicions about the man after my conversation with the inspector. I sighed. Was Inspector Greyson correct? Should I postpone any further flying lessons?

Was Group Captain Hammond not the man he claimed to be?

Chapter 33

An hour later, after restlessly pacing the various downstairs rooms, I finally found Marie alone in her bedroom. It used to be the quarters for the lady's maid and was attached to Lillian's bedroom with an adjoining door between the two. It was a lovely room, brightly decorated with cheerful floral wallpaper and a large woven rug with yellows and greens. At my knock, I heard a soft "Come in," and I pushed the door open to find Marie seated in an upholstered chair near the window with a magazine in her lap. She was ignoring the pages opened on her lap and gazing out the window.

"How's your hand?"

She still didn't look at me, but I could see her flex her fist once before setting it back in her lap.

"Not bad. I've had worse."

Her closed expression told me that asking about "worse" would get me nowhere, so I decided to start with a safer topic. I looked around the room and back at Marie. "This is a lovely room, but I'm sure they would have given you one of the larger guest rooms."

She turned her attention to me. "They offered, but I wanted to stick close to Lillian. Plus, this smaller room makes it feel more cozy. More like home."

"May I sit?" I asked. She nodded and I perched myself on the side of her neatly made single bed.

"And where is home, Marie?"

"Here, now." She looked down at the magazine in her lap, slowly folded it closed, and ran a finger over the glossy cover.

I watched her quietly, then pressed her on the issue. "And why is that?"

She looked up at me and then back out the window. "I'm not terribly . . . welcome in my old man's house anymore." A ghost of a smile graced her lips. "But Lillian and Lord Hughes have been swell enough to take me in."

I would have to come at this another way to get direct answers. "How long have you known Poppy?"

She glanced over at me, eyes narrowed slightly. "For a while. She and her brother come visit here pretty often."

"Did she go back to her room?"

Marie nodded but didn't say anything.

"She was pretty upset."

"Alistair is a heel."

I couldn't completely disagree with the girl, although I did think that Alistair had seemed contrite after his antics with the ghost.

"Are things serious between you two?"

Marie's jaw tightened. "I don't know what you mean."

I would have to be direct. "Marie. I saw you and Poppy in the library."

Marie flushed red, but met my eyes defiantly. I smiled gently at her. "I'm happy for you, Marie. That you have found someone . . . to spend time with."

Her shoulders relaxed a fraction. "Thank you," she whispered.

"Is that why you aren't welcome at home anymore?"

Marie nodded, fingers toying with the skirt in her lap. "My pops . . . well, he and Ma are missionaries." She looked out the window again, and the words came pouring out. "They found me and another girl, and decided to dump me off at a boarding school here in England instead of taking me with them."

"Where are they?"

"India."

"How did they afford the school?"

Marie shook her head. "I was a scholarship girl. Daughter of a missionary and all." The girl still wouldn't look at me. "My folks said not to bother contacting them again."

I was quiet for a moment. Marie really didn't have anywhere else to go. Even if she tried to return to America, her parents weren't there. "Does Lillian know all this?"

Marie cocked her head slightly and looked up at me. "She knows about my folks and . . . how I am." A worry line appeared between Marie's brows. "She's not that way. I carried a torch for her for a long time, but I've always known that Lillian and I wouldn't go anywhere." Her words tumbled out, as though she sought to reassure me. "I'm not sure if she knows about me and Poppy though. I don't want Lillian or her pops to find out. If they don't like it, they might tell me to beat it, too." For the first time since meeting the girl, I could tell she was absolutely without artifice. It made me wonder how many different masks Marie was forced to wear, and if anyone ever truly saw behind them.

My heart ached for her. Marie was probably terrified of being sent away from yet another place she called home. I hoped for her sake that Poppy could be discreet—the girls were taking a big risk fooling around in the house with the possibility of Marie being banished yet again. But I felt fairly certain that Lillian already knew what Marie was about, and wouldn't care. I wasn't so sure about Lord Hughes, but with his generous spirit, I hoped he wouldn't be quick to send Marie away. Especially if Lillian advocated for her.

"I don't think they'll send you away, and your secret is safe with me." I frowned. "As long as your secret is safe with Poppy." We exchanged a loaded look and I could tell Marie hoped the same. Poppy was a flighty young thing, and didn't seem terribly bright—frankly, I wouldn't trust her with my laundry.

"Are you and Poppy serious?" I asked again. I thought it might be the case since Marie had resorted to violence on Poppy's behalf. Of course, with Marie's past, it was possible she'd been forced to defend herself in the same way. She certainly had seemed practiced with her direct hit. I cocked my head and considered the girl in an entirely new light.

Marie glanced at me, then shrugged. From the gesture and the tightness in her normally baby-round face, I sensed that this topic was closed. That was unfortunate—I would have to come at the heart of my questions from another angle.

"Marie, can you think of any reason why Simon was killed?"

Marie thought for a second. "I've been thinking about it a lot. It looks like it has to do with Lillian, doesn't it?"

It was certainly one explanation for the thing, although it had never seemed the most likely. But could we have been wrong about that?

"And that would point at either me or Lord Hughes. I know that I had nothing to do with it." I studied her face but couldn't read anything beyond her surface sincerity. "And I can't imagine Lord Hughes having anything to do with it. He's on the level." Her dark eyes took on a deeper level of intensity, bordering on a fervor.

When it came to Lord Hughes, it seemed that was the general consensus from everyone concerned, myself included. I was forced to wonder if we were all blind to something about Lord Hughes—like the something that Simon had discovered. And now I had to wonder the same about Marie.

I had been wrong about people before, to my own detriment. It taught me the hard way to be suspicious of everyone, even when I didn't want to be. That was something I was going to have to take out and examine later.

"So, you haven't heard anything about Lord Hughes? Something to do with the war perhaps?"

Marie shook her head, but her face also took on an obstinate look. I sighed inwardly. Her fervent loyalty to Lord Hughes also meant she might not tell anyone even if she did know something. And I doubted I would be able to break it from her. Marie had opened up to me a bit just now, but she was a girl used to keeping secrets.

I stood, getting ready to leave Marie alone with her thoughts.

Marie pinned me with her brown eyes. "You'll figure this out, right? And keep Lillian and Lord Hughes from gettin' knocked off?"

The idea that Lord Hughes and Lillian might be in physical danger was a thought I did my best to keep tucked down deep—in a place where I didn't need to examine it. I nearly stumbled at the reminder. "I'll do my best."

It seemed everyone wanted me to find the answers and protect the Hughes family. I only hope their faith in me wasn't misplaced.

And that I hadn't overlooked a killer.

Chapter 34

I soon realized I was making a mental list of things that I wanted to discuss with Redvers when he returned. I didn't like to admit it, even to myself, but I already missed having him here after just over a day. He was good to bounce ideas back and forth with. And . . . well, I enjoyed having him around.

I sighed and forced my thoughts back to what I had learned. I would leave the Redvers issue for another time. A much later time.

According to Greyson, Hammond might not be what he seemed. The prospect depressed me greatly. I had always thought my instincts about people to be fairly good, but after the debacle in Egypt and now this, I was beginning to wonder if that was true. Perhaps I wasn't as good at reading people as I thought. Because my gut told me that Group Captain Hammond was a good man—kind and easygoing. Could that be a front for something more sinister? I hadn't even considered him for any part of what was happening on the estate. I certainly couldn't imagine him cutting the fuel line on his precious aircraft—his dismay had not been faked. However, his strange behavior the day before left me scratching my head. At the very least there was something he was hiding from me.

Yet again, I pondered whether it would be safe for me to

go up for more lessons with him. He could hardly sabotage the plane again without endangering himself—so perhaps it wouldn't hurt to continue my lessons. And by *not* going up, wouldn't I be signaling that I suspected him of something?

Deep down I knew that I was simply trying to justify my desire to fly.

I sighed and turned my thoughts to Alistair. He was immature, but that was not new information. I should have asked how long it had taken him to set up his "ghost," and do it without anyone noticing. The hook in the ceiling likely hadn't been there before last night. And after Alistair had championed his flighty sister at dinner the other night, I was surprised he would play such a prank on her. Poor Poppy had obviously been frightened out of her wits—I wondered how the girl was recovering from her scare.

On the other hand, Alistair had been better behaved since Lord Hughes's talk with the boy, and he'd seemed genuinely sorry about his prank. Of course, whether he was sorry he had scared Poppy or just sorry he had gotten punched remained to be seen.

And even after my chat with Marie, the girl remained an enigma. I had learned quite a bit about her past, but none of it cleared her of my newly aroused suspicion. If anything, what I learned—as well as her actions—only confirmed that she was capable of far more violence than I had ever suspected. Throwing a punch was a far cry from murder, but even still.

I decided to take a bath before dinner, and allowed myself a good long soak before readying myself to head downstairs. I put on a cap-sleeve knit dress and pulled a cream wool cardigan over the top. It was slightly chilly in the house; I realized the temperature must have dropped outside by a few degrees while I was soaking my cares away.

It was still a little early, but I made my way downstairs. There was probably an hour or so before everyone would start to gather for a predinner drink and I was looking forward to a little more time alone to think. My T-strap kitten heels clicked down the hall, but as I drew near the drawing room I heard voices. I paused outside the door, then decided I wasn't quite ready for the company of others, so I wandered into the solitude of the library.

Lord Hughes had an eclectic mix of books in his library and I enjoyed looking at them. Everything from Charles Dickens to Dorothy Sayers to the Management and Care of Barnyard Animals.

I didn't hear anything behind me, but I caught a whiff of pine and the clean smell of soap.

"I leave you alone for one day, and suddenly the house is haunted." Redvers' low voice rumbled through my chest, and I felt myself give a small sigh of relief that he was back. I paused in my perusal of the shelves, but I didn't turn around.

"It was more than a day." Only by a few hours, but still. It paid to be precise.

"Were you counting?" There was a smile in his voice and I turned to face him.

He was wearing a dark suit instead of the country tweeds he had been wearing during this visit, and it fit him perfectly. One might say he looked devastatingly handsome.

But I ignored his question. "You heard about Alistair's antics?"

"Lord Hughes mentioned it a few moments ago."

That would account for the voices I heard in the drawing room. "Did he also mention that Marie gut-punched him?"

Redvers nodded and gestured for me to take a seat. I sat and he took the chair angled across from me.

"The girl packs quite a wallop." I shared some of what Marie had told me about her background, but left out what I had seen between the girls. I wasn't ready to spill that secret, even to Redvers, mostly because I was unsure of what his reaction would be. I didn't want Marie to be evicted from yet another home if Redvers decided he needed to tell Lord Hughes. Redvers was forward-thinking, but I wasn't sure exactly how far that extended.

"Sounds like she might have a more violent nature than we suspected."

I nodded. "I wonder if she's had to defend herself in the past. She certainly looked like she could handle herself. I wouldn't have thought it of her, but I saw it firsthand."

We sat quietly for a moment, then I turned my thoughts to what had taken Redvers away in the first place. "Did you learn anything about James Hughes while you were away?"

Redvers nodded once. "I did. It's unlikely that he had anything to do with what's happening. I'm not sure he could sober up long enough to even get here, let alone plan these attacks."

"That bad?"

"That bad. They practically carry him up to his room every night at his private club. He barely leaves the place."

"Do you think Lord Hughes knows what kind of shape his brother is in?" I couldn't imagine that he would do nothing to help his own brother if he knew how serious the problem was.

"I'm not sure, but I'll meet with him about it."

"Did you learn anything else?"

"I did. And it doesn't paint Lord Hughes in a flattering light, I'm afraid."

"What is it?"

"It appears he's something of a war profiteer."

Chapter 35

I gasped. "A war profiteer? Lord Hughes? Are you sure?"

He nodded. "My sources are reliable. He made a great deal of money investing with the wrong side during the war."

It was hard to reconcile the down-to-earth reasonable man with someone who made money off the misery and death of that conflict. So many men had come back broken or never came back at all—like my husband, although that had been an unexpected gift. But I hardly knew anyone who hadn't been negatively affected in some way. Redvers had not been exaggerating about this painting Lord Hughes in an unflattering light. It was difficult to reconcile this information with what I knew about him. From all appearances he was an even-keel and reasonable man. How could he have invested with the enemy?

"What are you thinking about?"

"Lord Hughes. It just seems so unlike him. What are you going to do with this?"

"Talk to him. See if he has some kind of explanation."

"Is what he did even legal?"

Redvers looked grim. "Yes. But only just."

"Why wouldn't Hughes have brought this up before? These investments?"

"The fact that he has tried to hide them from Greyson doesn't look good for him, I'll admit. He should have been up-front about them, especially since it's an excellent reason for blackmail."

With this revelation, it occurred to me that we should be looking at anyone who knew about Hughes's role in the war. There were plenty of people who would want to kill him for it—including some of the veterans he employed on his own estate. I thought it was looking more and more like Lord Hughes was the intended target after all. The killer just wasn't very effective.

But it was also very telling that Lord Hughes had failed to mention the investments at all.

I recalled my visit from Inspector Greyson and his warnings about Hammond. I opened my mouth to ask Redvers about Hammond when we were interrupted by the very object of my thoughts.

"Ah, here you are."

Redvers and I both turned to see the group captain standing in the doorway.

"Millie is *requesting* your presence, Jane."

I rolled my eyes and stood. My question would have to wait.

Hammond came forward and shook Redvers' hand. "And glad to see you're back, old man."

I left the men discussing mechanical technicalities and Hammond's plan to work on the Moth while I went to see what Aunt Millie needed.

I entered the drawing room and glanced around. Lillian fidgeted in a chair near the empty fireplace. Marie sat across from her casually reading a copy of *Photoplay* and smoking a cigarette while Poppy peered over her shoulder. Alistair rounded out their group, also smoking and blowing rings at the ceiling. They all seemed rather quiet.

Millie and Lord Hughes were seated near the window chatting in undertones. I headed their way.

"Did you need to see me, Aunt Millie?"

Millie pierced me with a look. "I just wanted to know where you'd gone off to. And to tell you that Mr. Redvers has returned so at least you haven't managed to run the man off."

From behind me Redvers' cheerful voice answered. "No, she hasn't run me off."

I closed my eyes for a moment, then opened them and decided to pretend the entire exchange hadn't happened.

"Well, if you don't need anything, I'll just fix myself a drink."

Millie waved a careless hand and Redvers and I moved to the bar cart and got busy fixing our respective cocktails. Despite the temptation, I added only a splash of alcohol to mine—I needed to keep my wits about me until we had solved the remaining mysteries surrounding us.

I belatedly remembered that I was feeling awkward about Redvers and I—with all the excitement I'd nearly forgotten how we had parted ways and my fears that he was leaving because of me. Millie had struck close to the bone there. But he'd returned much sooner than I had expected. Perhaps his trip to London had been strictly business after all.

Lord Hughes stood and approached the bar cart. "Can I get anyone a drink?" he asked the room.

"Could you fix me one, Uncle?" Alistair called out.

Lord Hughes turned to smile at his nephew. "Of course, my dear boy. The usual?" Alistair nodded.

I thought it was unusual for the lord of the manor to be fetching drinks, but Hughes *was* more down-to-earth than I'd expected a titled aristocrat to be. Hughes delivered Alistair's drink and returned to where Millie sat. I was somewhat surprised Millie hadn't requested a top-up on her own drink.

Meanwhile, Hammond had joined Redvers and I at the bar cart, and I studied Hammond's face for a moment while he poured himself a neat Scotch. Despite what the inspector had told me, I had a hard time believing ill of Hammond. He looked up and smiled at me, his face open and friendly.

I returned the smile. "How was your trip to London, Chris?"

"Good! I managed to get the parts we need to get the Moth up and flying again. We'll have you back in the air in no time."

I nodded and gave him an enthusiastic response, despite the worry nibbling at the back of my mind. Redvers excused himself to go talk with Lord Hughes and Millie, leaving me to chat with Hammond alone.

"And everything else you needed to take care of there?" I was fishing to see if he might spill his other reasons for the trip. Or his mysterious return.

"All taken care of." He gave me a wide smile. "I shouldn't have to go back for a while. Should we join your aunt?" He nodded toward Millie. I could see that Redvers and Lord Hughes were engaged in conversation and my aunt looked more than a little bored with whatever the men were discussing.

I nodded, but I was surprised at Hammond's suggestion. He and Millie hadn't exactly hit it off, and Millie never failed to give him a hard time about my flying lessons. It was difficult to imagine why he would want to purposely strike up a conversation with her. Unless he was trying to avoid my asking further questions.

So much for my fishing expedition.

At Martha's announcement, we filed in to dinner, the girls and Alistair bringing up the rear. Redvers seated himself at my side, solicitously pulling out my chair for me. I thanked him quietly and ignored the gleam in Millie's eye.

Martha eyed me up. "How are you feeling, Jane?"

I smiled. "I'm very well, thank you, Martha."

She looked at me suspiciously before knocking on the dining table three times, then continuing to bustle about. It felt like an eternity since my dunk into the creek, even though it had only been a matter of days, but I appreciated her continued concern.

As well as the reminder that we still hadn't solved that mystery either.

Lord Hughes frowned at me. "Have you been feeling ill?"

"No, just . . . I thought perhaps I had the beginnings of a cold, but I'm feeling fine now. Thank you." I didn't want to discuss my misadventure in front of everyone at the table, and I was reasonably sure Lord Hughes would have heard about it from Redvers when it happened. I cocked my head at him, suddenly uncertain.

"Excellent. We can't have . . ." Lord Hughes trailed off as Alistair, pale and beginning to sweat, doubled over his bowl of soup.

"Are you choking?" Lillian moved to pound him on the back, but Alistair shook his head violently.

"No . . . my stomach . . ." Alistair gagged and ran from the room, hands clutched over his mouth. The rest of us looked at one another in alarm.

Millie calmly put her fork down. "I think we should call the doctor." She stood and went into the hall to make the phone call while Lord Hughes went after Alistair. Lillian stood as though she would follow after, but Redvers stopped her.

"We should all stay here. You, too, Lillian. I'm sure Lord Hughes has it well in hand."

I looked at Redvers, but his face was closed and impossible to read.

"Do you think it was something he ate?" Marie's voice broke the silence and we all looked down at our steaming bowls of vegetable soup. My mouth watered a bit at the smell.

"No, he hadn't started eating yet." Redvers gestured to Alistair's bowl, where we could all see that he hadn't yet touched his soup. Gamely, I picked up my spoon and started in. The rest eventually followed suit.

The meal was suitably somber after that, and we hurried to finish before moving back into the drawing room to await news about Alistair. I felt a twinge of remorse that Martha's delicious meal and hard work should be overshadowed by Alistair taking ill, especially since she was in no way at fault.

The others gathered around the fireplace, but Redvers and I stood together near the bar cart.

"What do you think that was?" I asked. "A sudden influenza?"

"No." Redvers looked thoughtful. "He was perfectly fine leading up to it. And it can't have been anything we ate since he didn't touch the food, and the rest of us are fine." We both looked down at the cart.

"What was he drinking?"

Redvers picked up the decanter filled with brown liquid and held it up at eye level, giving it a little swirl. "I believe this was one of them." Setting it down, he regarded the bottles and put two more of them next to the decanter. "Let's just set these aside for the police, shall we?"

I grimaced. "Do you really think it was poison?"

"Better safe than sorry."

Chapter 36

The doctor came and examined Alistair. He quietly confided to Lord Hughes that Alistair's symptoms looked like a case of arsenic poisoning. The dose was far from fatal, but Alistair would be uncomfortable for a day or so until the last of the poison had passed from his system. Most of it had already come up, so the doctor felt certain he would make a full recovery. Lord Hughes relayed the information to Redvers and myself before going over to the rest of the group and assuring them that Alistair was going to be fine in a day or so.

"It's interesting that a small dose would make him so sick." I would have thought it would take a much larger amount to cause such a violent reaction—and so quickly.

"Except he didn't eat anything."

"Hmm."

"If it was in his drink, how did it get in there?" Redvers and I looked at one another, before casually scouting around the bar cart. There was nothing out of the ordinary, and we moved over to where Alistair had been sitting before we went in to dinner. Nothing was evident, so I got down on my knees to look beneath the love seat.

"Jane!" my aunt Millie called from her seat near the window. "What on earth are you doing?"

I ignored her and spoke to Redvers. "There's a folded piece of paper under here."

Redvers made a noise and joined me on the floor to inspect it. "Let's leave it. We'll let Greyson collect it."

Redvers helped me to my feet and I found the girls watching us, mouths agape. I shrugged and herded them along with my aunt Millie and Hammond into the library to sit and wait for the police.

Inspector Greyson arrived in record time with a young constable at his heel, and Redvers and I turned over the various bottles we thought had been used, as well as Alistair's glass. Redvers was able to rescue the glass from the kitchen before Martha washed it—there was nothing left in it, but Redvers was hopeful that some traces of the poison remained.

I pointed the inspector to the paper we had found.

"Thank you, Jane." Greyson's eyes crinkled with his smile and his tone was still warm despite my rejection of his dinner invitation. I was thankful he wasn't holding it against me—and also thankful he hadn't bothered with his usual lecture of my staying out of things.

The mood back in the library was tense. There was no light banter, music, or playing games tonight. Everyone appeared lost in their own thoughts, and no one was touching anything from the bar cart in this room either—even Millie. All the liquor in the house would probably have to be replaced.

My thoughts drifted to Marie for a moment. Had she seemed truly surprised that Alistair had been poisoned? I thought it unlikely that she would continue to take revenge on the boy, but I studied her face regardless. She was gazing at Lillian, and all I could read there was concern. And with good reason—even from across the room I could see that Lillian looked gray despite the news that Alistair would make a full recovery. I walked over and crouched in front of her, sparing a quick glance at Marie.

"He'll be okay, Lillian. It wasn't enough to kill him. He'll recover."

She shook her head. "I know that, and I'm relieved. But . . ." She looked at me, her eyes anxious. "Why is it that people who care for me are being killed? Or nearly killed?"

I didn't have an answer for her, so I patted her hand and stood.

Lillian turned sharply to Marie. "You'd better stay away from me, too."

"Lillian, no . . ." Marie reached out a hand, but Lillian threw it off, turning damp eyes toward the windows, arms crossed tightly across her chest.

"Lillian, that isn't fair. I love you, too, and I'm not worried." Poppy got up from her chair and snuggled herself between the two girls on the love seat, wrapping an arm around them both. It didn't look comfortable, but it was also impossible to ignore her, wedged between them as she was. After a few moments, Lillian released her arms and leaned in to Poppy a bit. On the other side, Marie stayed quiet, but did the same.

After a few beats, Millie cleared her throat. "I think I'll call it a night."

From the doorway the inspector agreed. "That's probably a good idea for everyone." His clear gray eyes took in everyone in the room. "Constable Jones will stay here overnight and I'll return in the morning." He turned toward Redvers, standing beside him. "With reinforcements."

The next morning dawned sunny and bright—a perfect day for flying. Peering out my window, I sighed with frustration. I doubted that Hammond could have the Moth up and running yet, but I decided to walk out to the barn to make sure. I grabbed my leather helmet and goggles just in case.

I ran into Lord Hughes in the hall. "How is Alistair this morning?"

"He's much better, thank you. The doctor has assured us he'll make a full recovery."

"That's good to hear." I paused. "The doctor seemed pretty sure it was poison. Will the police be searching the house again?"

Lord Hughes gave me a tight smile. "Yes, they've already begun."

I hadn't seen anyone, but that didn't mean they weren't there. Lord Hughes patted my arm absently before excusing himself, faithful Rascal bounding along in his wake, oblivious to the human drama around him. Despite the doctor's assurances, I could tell Lord Hughes was still concerned about his nephew—his puffy eyes told me he had spent a sleepless night.

I continued on my way; Redvers caught up with me halfway to the barn.

"I thought I would find you out here." He slowed his hurried pace to match my own.

"Guilty as charged. I want to see how much progress Group Captain Hammond is making with the repairs."

Redvers raised an eyebrow at the helmet and goggles I carried in one hand. "Repairs, eh?"

I gave a wry smile. "Very well. I was feeling hopeful that Hammond is some kind of miracle worker and the Moth is ready to go."

I recalled that I wanted to talk to Redvers about Hammond's background and the inspector's allegations, but we had already arrived at our destination. The barn doors were wide open, sunlight illuminating the dusty space, and I could see the group captain hard at work. He wore an oil-stained flight suit; dark swathes of fabric on the shoulders and chest showed where patches had been sewn on and later removed.

"How's it coming?" I stood just inside the door, watching as Hammond climbed a small ladder, wrench in hand.

"Pretty well. It's a shame the weather is so gorgeous today, but I'm hoping we can get her up tomorrow." He bent inside the compartment.

"Is there anything we can do to help?"

Redvers turned to me with raised eyebrows. I shrugged and mouthed, "What?"

"Not really. I've got things well in hand, I think," came the muffled reply as Hammond worked inside the plane's gaping side. I hadn't really expected him to need help, but it was a legitimate offer. I didn't mind getting my hands dirty.

I was searching for a way to follow up on what Greyson had told me and ask Hammond about his experience in the war. I thought it would be best to lead into it gently instead of blurting out questions about his combat experience and whether he even had any.

"How did you become so interested in airplanes?"

Hammond's voice was muffled inside the compartment. "My father."

"I thought he was a solicitor."

"He is, but he's always been interested in airplanes. Any mode of transportation, actually." Hammond's head came out and he held one end of the shredded fuel line. This had not been cut as neatly as the brake cables on Simon's car had been. Hammond's hand was dark with grease and what I assumed was fuel.

"Is that entirely safe?" I was worried about the man going up in flames.

He grinned. "As long as you don't light a match."

"Anyway, your father?" I moved to sit on a bale of hay near the plane. As I sat, a puff of dust went up into the air. I patted the seat next to me for Redvers to join me, but he shook his head vigorously. At my questioning look, he mimed sneezing.

Hammond had gone back to what he was doing. "He was very interested in any advances in aviation, and he sort of passed it along to me. He was thrilled when I went into the RAF."

"I'm sure he's very proud."

"He was. He passed during the war though."

"Oh, I'm so sorry." And I was. It was always difficult to lose a parent—especially one you are close to, as it seemed the group captain was. But he had given me the perfect opening to ask about his time in the service. "Where were you stationed during the war? Were you able to make it home for the funeral?"

"I was. I was lucky that I was nearby."

He went quiet, working steadily inside the compartment, using rags to clean leaked fluids, and tossing them to the ground below. It seemed he wouldn't say anything else on the subject.

I looked over at Redvers hoping he would be of some assistance, but he was simply giving me a strange look that I couldn't read. Had I not been sympathetic enough about Hammond's father? I decided to give it another try.

"Did you see a lot overseas?" I asked.

Chris's head came out and he shot me a strange look. "I saw my fair share."

This was going nowhere.

Redvers gestured with his head for us to head outside. I shrugged.

"I'll check on you later, Chris," I told him. He waved a free hand.

We got a little distance before Redvers asked his question. "What was that about?"

I sighed. "Inspector Greyson hinted that Group Captain Hammond might not be his name. Or that he didn't serve." I related the full story of what Greyson had told me.

Redvers frowned. "I'll make another phone call, but I'm

fairly certain I know where Group Captain Hammond served. And that is in fact his name."

"Why would Greyson tell me that?"

"He might not have access to the file."

"More secret society stuff?"

He paused. "Not exactly, although I believe the missions he flew were top secret."

"And that would explain why the inspector doesn't have access to them?"

"That, and the military isn't always happy to share."

I glanced at him, and he looked uncomfortable. I stopped walking and faced him.

"Is there something you aren't telling me?"

Redvers shifted from one foot to the other, hands clasped tightly behind his back. It was making me increasingly nervous to watch him.

"What is it?"

He focused his gaze on something off to our right. "My former fiancée . . . I know her brother served with Group Captain Hammond, and that's how I'm certain he did serve."

I stopped listening pretty early on in that explanation.

"Your *what*?"

"We aren't engaged now." He paused and looked at me. "It's not what you think, Jane."

"Are . . . is . . ." I couldn't piece together any of the questions I wanted to ask. Suddenly our "talk" that we were supposed to have took on an entirely different meaning. Was he going to tell me that he was in love with someone else?

I suddenly felt ill.

I turned abruptly and resumed walking toward the house. He waited a few beats before I heard his feet start to move also. But he was moving more slowly, and I was now moving at quite a clip. Full steam ahead, the HMS Jane Wunderly was not stopping until she was safely behind a closed door.

Alone.

"Jane . . ."

"It's good!" I called, as cheerfully as I could manage. "I'm glad we sorted that out about Group Captain Hammond!" I was nearing the kitchen door. "I can keep taking my lessons!"

I went through, not even stopping to take off my walking brogues or my coat before heading straight to my room. I wasn't sure if Redvers followed me inside because not once did I look behind me—in fact, I didn't stop steaming forward until I reached my room and was safely on the other side of the locked door.

I knew I was behaving childishly and that I should have stayed to listen to Redvers' story. He had been kind enough to listen to the terrible saga of my marriage—the abbreviated version, anyway, while we were in Egypt. And I hadn't been friend enough to ask about his broken engagement and find out if he was still pining away after her.

While kissing me in a stable.

Could he have only kissed me to shut me up? The thought was more devastating than it had any right to be. I had no business wanting anything from Redvers, and yet, it seemed I very much wanted something from him. What, I wasn't sure. But it was obvious from my physical reaction to his news that I didn't want him engaged to someone else.

And even if that engagement had been broken, I was terrified of learning about his feelings toward the woman. And even more frightening, what his feelings toward me were—or weren't.

I curled into a ball on my bed and squeezed a pillow to my chest.

I let myself stew for an hour, and then decided I needed to stop behaving foolishly by hiding in my room. I should make use of my afternoon, and while I wasn't brave enough to face anyone downstairs just yet, I could talk to Alistair and see how he was feeling. I cautiously let myself out of my room, ensuring there was no one about before I ventured into the mercifully deserted hallway. As I approached Alistair's door, a tall sober man in a dark suit carrying a black medical bag came out and pulled the door closed behind him.

"Is he awake? May I see him?"

The doctor regarded me for a moment then gave a slight nod. "Just for a moment. He's better, but he still needs to rest."

I quietly called a thank-you to the man's fast-retreating back before turning to Alistair's door. When I entered, Alistair was reclining on several pillows in the mahogany four-poster bed that dominated the room. His suitcase was open on the small chest of drawers—I thought it was interesting that he hadn't bothered to unpack, since he'd already been at the estate for quite a few days. Had he not intended to stay much longer?

"How are you feeling, Alistair?" I came near the bed. His skin was pale and wan, and he cracked bloodshot eyes to look at me.

"Better. I think most of it's out of my system. I didn't get much sleep though, and the doctor says I should rest now." He closed his eyes again.

I nodded, although if that was a hint for me to leave, I wasn't going to be taking him up on it just yet. "Have they told you what it was?"

Alistair opened his eyes more fully. "Arsenic! I can't believe it. Although, given how badly I feel, I guess that makes sense. I'm just lucky it wasn't enough to kill me."

"Do you have any idea who might have given it to you?" My voice was gentle in the quiet room.

"I overheard the constables beating their gums. They suspect it was Uncle Edward, but I can't believe that. I really can't . . ." Alistair's voice trailed off.

I was shocked to hear that the police suspected Lord Hughes for this. If anything, Marie would have been my first suspect, especially after the altercation between the two. Unless, of course, the police hadn't heard about it yet. I winced, thinking that I had yet another person to be concerned about.

He paused. "Uncle did make me that Between the Sheets last night, but he wouldn't want to harm me. My guess is it was one of the servants." His lean face twisted. "I mean, who knows where he's getting these people from. One of them is a bloody colored man and a foreigner!"

I regarded him for a moment. I'd thought that Lord Hughes had talked with the young man about his classist views, but apparently the lecture hadn't taken root. "Well, most of the men served in the war. They're veterans. Even Sergeant Barlow made sacrifices for this country."

"And look where that's got them. As for Barlow, he should just go back where he came from."

I couldn't even begin to address the ridiculousness of that statement. "And why would any of them want to poison you?"

"Jealousy, of course."

I couldn't stop my eyebrows from shooting up, but I walked to the window and composed myself before changing the subject. My arguing with the boy wouldn't change his views—perhaps I would mention to Lord Hughes that he had further work to do with the young man.

"Or maybe it was that girl Marie. Heaven knows why Lillian keeps her around."

I turned to look at him, but he didn't seem terribly riled—not as riled as I expected he would be if he knew Poppy and Marie were an item.

I decided to change the subject. "I've never heard of a 'Between the Sheets' before. What goes into it?"

"Rum, cognac, triple sec, and a little lemon. Everyone is drinking them."

Apparently, I wasn't "everyone," and that was fine with me. With a small shake of my head I turned my mind to those liquors. The poison might have been in any of them—none of the rest of the party took drinks that used those particular spirits. I was curious whether the poison had been added to his glass or to one of the liquor containers—it would make a significant difference when trying to determine when it was added. And by whom.

"Anyway. The police should be looking at anyone besides Uncle Hughes." I looked back at Alistair and saw that his eyes were closed. His voice sounded fairly vigorous at times, but he was obviously still feeling poorly. I decided to let him rest.

For now.

I would have more questions for the young man later. Especially about his feelings toward the help, and what precisely he had told the police. I didn't want to see the investigation focused on the staff simply because the young man appeared to have it in for those he deemed *inferior* to himself. It would be easy to railroad a man for a crime he didn't commit. Especially one who had several prejudicial strikes against him already, like Sergeant Barlow.

I hoped Greyson was better than that.

Chapter 37

I left Alistair's room and moved slowly down the hall, thinking. A theory had struck me about Alistair's poisoning, but it was unorthodox at best. At worst it was completely mad. I needed to think it over more before I mentioned it to anyone.

And the one person I really wanted to discuss it with was the one person I wasn't ready to face just yet. I was embarrassed that I had run from him. Even as a friend I should have stopped and given him the opportunity to explain, but I hadn't. Redvers had been correct when he had accused me of running from my feelings—it was something I did regularly, especially when it came to him. It was past time to admit that to the both of us.

But it was also a shock to realize just how strongly I felt about Redvers. I was a little surprised by my reaction—I'd convinced myself that I would never again have interest in romantic entanglements, but now I had to admit that wasn't entirely true. If my gut reaction was any indication, I hadn't been successful at rationalizing my feelings away after all—they'd somehow snuck past my walls and burrowed in.

I considered heading downstairs and meeting things head-on. But at the top of the stairs I met Mr. Shaw coming up.

"Can I 'elp you, Mrs. W.? Ye look like ye need something."

He looked at me speculatively. I couldn't even imagine what he saw.

"No, no, I'm fine, thank you, Mr. Shaw. I . . . forgot something in my room." I did an about-face and returned to that room. I wasn't ready to meet people head-on after all. Perhaps thinking things over for a few more hours would be a better idea.

When I was finally emerged from my cocoon and headed back downstairs, it was already time for predinner cocktails. By that time, I had convinced myself that I was fine with whatever Redvers' personal situation was, and I would try to be a good friend to him and listen to his story. I could handle a purely friendly relationship with the man.

I was quite the liar.

I headed straight for the bar cart on entering the drawing room before remembering Alistair's poisoning the night before. Hammond was already there, one hand holding an etched crystal highball glass and the open Scotch decanter in the other.

I eyed his drink warily. "Is this the same liquor?"

"Don't worry. Lord Hughes had fresh bottles of everything brought in first thing this morning."

"That's a relief." I grabbed a glass of my own, poured a shot of brandy, and knocked it straight back. The warmth flooded my stomach and moved north, leaving me feeling more prepared to face the evening. I realized Hammond was watching me with his mouth slightly open.

"Rough day?" he finally asked.

"Nothing out of the ordinary at this point." I went about making myself an actual cocktail this time, heavy on the alcohol. It wasn't my usual style, but for once I was going to take a cue from my aunt Millie. Fortify with alcohol. From what I could tell, it was how she got through her own scandals in the past. The same plan could get me through one uncomfortable evening.

I had already registered that Redvers was not in the room, but my shoulders were still tight. I knew he could enter at any moment, and the thought caused my stomach to pinch. No matter, I told myself as I took a big gulp of my drink. Another flood of warmth washed through me.

Hammond was still watching me with some concern as he sipped his drink. "Did you have lunch today? I didn't see you downstairs."

I thought back and realized that I hadn't left my room all afternoon except to visit Alistair and had missed the noon meal. "No, I was . . . busy."

The group captain regarded my drink. "You might want to take it a little easier."

I gave him what I imagined to be a dazzling smile. "I will be sure to." I took another drink, then went ahead and refilled my glass.

"Let's sit down." Hammond gently took my elbow and guided me to a seat on the opposite side of the room from the bar cart.

"How are your repairs coming along?" I was suddenly glad to be sitting. It was good he had thought of it. "I would love to be able to go up again. Maybe tomorrow if the weather is good."

Hammond eyed my drink and looked skeptical. "Sure. If the weather is good, we should be able to go up. I took her out for a test flight this afternoon just to make sure she's running okay, and she's going like a dream."

I was disappointed that I had missed the chance for even a quick flight while I was hiding in my room like a coward. No more hiding, I told myself. I took another sip. My whole body felt pleasantly warm now and my limbs felt loose; even my shoulders had found a way to relax. This was good.

"Did you do secret stuff during the war, Chris? You can tell me."

Hammond's lips twitched. "I did. But I'm not supposed to tell anyone."

I nodded somberly. "That makes sense." I cocked my head at him. "I'm glad you came back. With all your pieces and parts."

"Thank you. I am, too, Jane."

My glass had somehow become empty. I stood, somewhat unsteadily, and Hammond gestured for me to stay sitting.

"I'll get one for you. You just stay there." He took my glass and went to the cart. I leaned over the side of the chair and beamed at him.

"You're a real gentleman." His back was to me, blocking my view of what he was doing. "Be sure to put enough gin in there."

He nodded and came back just as Lord Hughes and Millie entered the room. Soon the others trickled in, Redvers last. He casually made himself a drink before coming over to where Hammond and I were sitting. Hammond tipped his head at me and Redvers' brows pulled together. I looked from one to the other, eyes narrowed.

"What are you saying?" At the sound of my slightly slurring words, Redvers' brows shot up.

Hammond leaned over and patted my arm. "Nothing, Jane." He turned back to Redvers. "How was your afternoon?"

"Eventful." Redvers' voice was dry, but I refused to look at him. Instead, I took a large swallow of the drink Chris had given me, frowning at it. I could barely taste any alcohol. I had asked him nicely to add a lot of gin though, so I must be mistaken.

Chatter went on around me as I nursed my drink and stared into the fire. I couldn't quite follow what was being said around me, and for once I was fine with that. The fire was making me slightly drowsy and I felt a bit muddled. I closed my eyes for just a second, and I heard my aunt's voice behind me.

"What is going on with her?"

"She's just not feeling well, Mrs. Stanley. I'll make sure she gets upstairs okay."

My aunt's dry voice replied. "I've seen this type of 'not feeling well' before, Mr. Redvers."

But then my aunt's voice faded and I was relieved. I didn't want to hear Millie anymore. My head was lying on the cushioned back of the high-backed chair and I thought it was quite pleasant here next to the fire.

The voices in the room started to fade entirely. I opened my eyes, but the room spun a bit, and so I slammed them closed again. Just as well. I was quite comfortable where I was.

"Should we get her to her room?" That sounded like Chris. He was a nice young man. I was sorry Inspector Greyson had said unkind things about him. I decided I should tell him that, but my tongue felt sticky.

"I've got her. You go in. Perhaps you could have Martha make her up a tray . . . we need to get her to eat something." That sounded like Redvers. I was mad at him, even though his voice was lovely to listen to.

"She missed lunch."

I tried to mumble that I wasn't hungry, but either the words were wrong or my mouth was. It was hard to tell.

I felt myself being effortlessly lifted up into strong arms, and I fell against a hard chest. I tried to open my eyes.

"No, keep your eyes closed." The familiar voice rumbled through my chest.

I nodded and snuggled closer to the source of that voice. Redvers carried me up the stairs, leaning forward slightly to turn my doorknob and push my door open.

He gently deposited me on my bed, and I heard my aunt's voice as I curled onto my side.

"I'll be right back. Keep her awake for a little while and leave this door open."

With my eyes closed, I heard brisk footsteps carry down the hall and I let myself drift.

"You can't go to sleep yet. You need to eat something. And drink some water." I felt arms pulling me into a sitting position and putting pillows behind me. "Your aunt will be here in a moment with a tray." I still hadn't opened my eyes. "Jane, this isn't the best time to tell you, but I never loved her."

"Who." I forced through my lips.

"The woman I was engaged to. It was arranged between our families." He sighed and I finally forced my eyes open. He was perched on the edge of the bed next to me, and he reached forward and gently brushed hair out of my eyes. "We'll talk about this later, though." Then he muttered to himself. "I don't know if you'll even remember any of this."

I tried to mount a protest, but Millie came through with a tray just then. Between the two of them they managed to get me to eat a bowl of soup with crackers and drink several glasses of water. Then they finally let me go to sleep.

I awoke several hours later to find that my room was dark, my stomach was queasy, and my head was pounding. I squeezed my eyes closed and wondered if I would die. I rather hoped I would. Then I reached over and fumbled for the light. Once I managed to pry my eyes back open I saw that there was a bottle of pain tablets and a glass of water next to my bed. I threw a couple of the pills back along with a few of the crackers that had been thoughtfully left on a plate. I leaned back and waited for my stomach to settle, chewed a few more crackers, and sipped some water. I realized I was fully dressed except for my shoes.

The house was quiet while I waited for the medicine to kick in and ease the pounding in my head. I had only a vague recollection of what had happened. Had I embarrassed myself? Had Redvers been here? I remembered that he had told me something important, but it was just beyond my reach.

I eased back against the pillows and flicked the light out. I would have to work on remembering what he said in the morning.

And then I heard a muffled scream.

Chapter 38

The scream wasn't loud, but it was enough to be concerning. I carefully pushed out of bed, stumbling for a moment before I found my footing. One hand to my head, I found my slippers, then pulled on my robe before heading into the hall.

I realized it must be quite late because no one else seemed to have heard the noise. I shuffled down the hall, stopping before Marie's door. I put my ear to the oak door and could hear muffled sounds behind it, as though someone was choking back sobs. I knocked quietly and pushed the door open without waiting for an answer.

Marie stood in the center of the room, her hands covering her mouth. The room was covered in feathers—it looked as though a goose had exploded. I took in her bed where the thickest of the mess was. Blankets had been pulled over a series of full pillows, but there were now huge gashes down the line of them, white feathers spilling like blood over the covers and floor. A straight razor stuck straight up out of the foot of the bed.

I moved to Marie's side, and gently pushed her to a corner. "Stay here," I said firmly, ignoring the evil elves smashing my brain with hammers. "Don't touch anything." I gave her a small shake, and she finally nodded through her shock.

I went out of her room, closing the door behind me, and moved down the hall to Redvers' room. Closing my eyes for a moment against the pain still banging about in my head, I knocked quietly. Nothing. I knocked again, more firmly this time, and finally heard movements from within. In less than a minute the door opened and Redvers peered out at me, hair rumpled by sleep and a plaid bathrobe belted firmly at his waist.

"Jane, are you all right?" He looked concerned.

I nodded, one hand moving to my temple at the movement. I needed to never do that again. "Come with me."

I was grateful that Redvers trusted me enough to follow without argument or question. He looked surprised when we stopped at Marie's room, and for a brief moment I wondered where he thought I was taking him. I pushed open the door, and found Marie where I had left her, although Lillian was now standing beside the trembling girl.

Redvers took in the room for a moment before commenting. "I'm guessing this is exactly what it looks like."

I thought about nodding, but I had learned my lesson there. "I believe so." I took a breath. "These pillows have been murdered."

"Let's head downstairs where we can talk. Marie, where is your key?"

As we filed out of the room, Marie passed Redvers her room key. Once the room was empty, Redvers locked the door behind us and pocketed the key.

"These rooms are connected." Redvers gestured to Lillian's door. "Is your door locked as well, Lillian?" At her nod, we headed downstairs and into the drawing room. My stomach turned when I saw the bar cart, and I almost groaned out loud. But I settled into a chair and closed my eyes, regaining my shaky equilibrium. A moment later I felt a cool glass being pressed into my hand. Before I could even ask, Redvers answered my question.

"It's water."

"Thank you," I said quietly. I took a long drink and reflected that the ache in my head was finally starting to subside from the tablets I had taken.

Redvers took the chair next to mine, facing the girls on a small love seat where they huddled together.

"Now, Marie. Tell me exactly what happened."

"I came back into my room, and just found it like that. I tried not to scream, but I must have a little, because Mrs. Wunderly came into the room just after me."

Redvers glanced at me and I nodded, then grimaced. My head was getting better, but it still wasn't ready to move. He gave a tiny shake of his head then turned back to the girls.

"And where were you, Marie? Since you weren't in your room?"

Marie twisted the edge of her dressing gown, shooting a quick sideways look at Lillian beside her.

Lillian patted Marie's arm. "It's okay, Marie. I know about you and Poppy."

Remembering that I hadn't filled him in on what I had seen between the two girls, I shot a quick glance at Redvers, but he seemed unsurprised.

Marie's eyes filled with tears, as she gave Lillian a watery smile. "You do? And you won't send me away?"

Lillian gave a little laugh and pulled Marie into a hug. "Silly goose. Of course not."

When they pulled away I could see several of the tears had escaped down Marie's full cheeks. She swiped at them and after giving Lillian a grateful smile, she turned to Redvers. Taking a deep breath, she answered him. "I was in Poppy's room."

"Why the pillows under your covers?"

Marie looked down at her hands. "I didn't want Lillian to know that her cousin and I . . . well. And our rooms connect, and if she came in and found me gone . . ." Marie stopped for a moment. "So, I tried to make it look like I was sleeping in the bed."

"Does anyone else know about you and Poppy?" Redvers asked gently. I was impressed at how considerately he was treating the girl. Perhaps I had been wrong in not trusting him with the girls' secret.

"Alistair does." Marie's face twisted. "He and Poppy have been arguing about it. I'm not sure if anyone else does."

Redvers nodded, thinking. I was embarrassed that I wasn't able to completely process what was happening, so I left the questioning to him.

"You'll have to sleep somewhere else tonight. And not go back into that room." Marie looked surprised. "We'll have to call the police. They'll want to process everything."

Lillian and Marie looked at each other. "You don't think it was a silly prank?" Lillian asked hopefully.

Redvers shook his head. "I think it's very likely someone wanted you dead."

The girls both gasped and clasped their hands together. "Marie can stay with me." Marie gave her a searching look, and Lillian nodded again, determined.

"I think that's a good idea." Redvers thought for a second. "Why didn't Poppy come out of her room when you screamed?"

"She was asleep when I left her." Marie's faced burned crimson.

"And everyone else is asleep." I looked at the clock on the mantel. It read half past two.

"Okay, girls. Go back to Lillian's room, and lock the door behind you. Don't go into Marie's room. Not for anything, do you understand?" Both girls nodded, and then went upstairs.

Redvers looked at me. "Come on."

"Come where?"

"To the kitchen. You need to eat something."

I sat at the small scarred table while Redvers pulled bread

from the drawer, and a brick of cheese and a slab of ham from the refrigerator. He cut a few slices of ham and cheese with a large knife and started assembling me a sandwich. I eyed it warily, since I didn't feel particularly hungry.

He caught my eye. "Trust me. You'll feel better tomorrow if you eat this." He set the plate in front of me, adding another glass of water, and sat in the opposite chair.

"How did you hear Marie scream?" He was distractingly handsome with his mussed hair and the dark line of whiskers lining his square jaw.

I took a tentative bite, chewed, swallowed, and drank some water before answering him. He was right, drat him. The sandwich did taste good and my stomach growled in appreciation. He waited patiently for my answer.

"I had just woken up and took some of the pills that were on my bedside table." I squinted at my hazy memory. "Was that you?"

Redvers nodded. "Thank you," I said quietly, and turned back to my sandwich. I knew that I should be embarrassed, and I most certainly would be the following morning, but for now I was simply trying to survive.

I chewed another bite. "It didn't seem like anyone else was awake."

Redvers shook his head. "Whoever did it would be pretending to be asleep now anyway. No one else came into the hall—they probably waited to see if everyone heard the scream or not, and when no one did, they stayed where they were."

"It wouldn't do any good to check on everyone."

Redvers shook his head, then considered me. "How long have you known about Poppy and Marie?"

I flushed a bit. "I saw them in the library . . . together."

Redvers nodded as though he somehow knew what I had seen. "And why didn't you want to share that with me?"

I considered him. "I like Marie. I didn't want her to get

evicted from yet another home. It is rather shocking, finding two women together." At his careless shrug I continued. "I wasn't sure how you would react."

"I've seen plenty." My curiosity was sparked, but the blasted man left it at that.

I focused on my water, finishing the first glass, and Redvers stood and refilled it for me. I continued working on the sandwich.

"Well, I had been considering Marie as a suspect since her incident with Alistair. Now it looks like that's out. Unless none of these things are connected and just a series of terrible coincidences."

"I don't believe in coincidence. Not this many, at any rate."

I agreed. "Did the police find anything this morning?" I recalled that the police had searched the house yet again while I hid from Redvers in my room.

Redvers looked grim. "They did. They found an arsenic bottle in Lord Hughes's room."

I groaned. With that sort of evidence, the police had little choice but to place Lord Hughes at the top of the suspect list.

"What about that paper we found? Was there poison in it?"

Redvers nodded. "It looks like it was used to carry the poison and put it in Alistair's glass. Then it was dropped on the floor and kicked beneath the love seat. It was probably dropped by accident."

"Are there any fingerprints?"

Redvers shook his head.

"How is that even possible?"

He shrugged. "Anything that was there was smudged. And the poisoner probably made sure to hold the edges." Redvers was thoughtfully regarding the woodwork on the table.

"What are you thinking?"

He looked up at me. "I'm thinking that Lord Hughes is being set up."

"I agree." I didn't think that Hughes would be so foolish as to leave the bottle amongst his things if he had poisoned Alistair. And what motive could he possibly have for poisoning his own nephew? "Do you think they'll arrest him?"

"Greyson might be forced to. With the knife, the arsenic bottle, and now this, I think even Hughes's position as a peer might not be able to protect him."

"It has to be someone in the house. Doesn't it?" I had finally finished my sandwich and I pushed around a few crumbs with my finger.

"I'm not sure. But with what happened tonight . . ."

"It would appear that way." I stopped toying with my food and wiped my hands on a napkin. "I can't imagine Lord Hughes had anything to do with what happened in Marie's room, though."

"I agree."

"But the police might not see things the same way." I sighed. "If we agree that Hughes had nothing to do with either incident, how did the poison bottle manage to get into his room? It would have had to have happened overnight, after they poisoned Alistair but before the police conducted their search. How could they have gone into Hughes's room with him sleeping in it?"

"Unless Lord Hughes wasn't in his room."

"Where on earth would he have been? We all retired early for the night."

Redvers cocked an eyebrow and waited. It took me several moments, but of course my brain was moving slower than normal. When I realized what he was insinuating, I gave a little shudder. I didn't want to think about my aunt's exploits, then or now.

Redvers just tilted his head and I sighed. "Well, if that's true, anyone could have planted that bottle. And that still doesn't explain how the poison got into Alistair's glass to begin with. Or why someone attacked Marie's pillow tonight."

We were both quiet for a moment, and I could feel Redvers' gaze as he regarded me. "You really did yourself an injury."

My face reddened and I opened my mouth, but he put up a hand with a tiny smile playing at his lips. "Happens to the best of us. And we can talk about all that later." I nodded, relieved, and felt the heat in my cheeks subsiding.

"What about the police?" I asked.

"I'll call them in the morning."

"Do you really think someone was trying to kill Marie?"

"It might have just been an attempt to scare her." Redvers looked thoughtful. "And yet . . ."

Chapter 39

I woke late the next morning, but the pounding in my head was gone. My mouth was still dry and my eyes felt puffy, but my stomach was no longer roiling with nausea. Redvers had been right about the sandwich.

After getting ready, I peeked into the hall and found that the police had already begun processing Marie's room. Redvers must have risen early and called Inspector Greyson. I considered poking my head into the room to see what progress they had made, but decided against it. I headed down to the breakfast room instead.

Millie was still seated at the table and raised an eyebrow when I entered. She put down the newspaper she was holding. "I'll have Martha bring you your coffee."

I gave her a weak smile. "Thank you, Aunt Millie."

She stood, and then paused. "You'll want to have lots of eggs this morning. Maybe with some cheese on them. And bread. It will help soak things up." I gave her a grateful smile, wider this time. She came around and patted my shoulder before leaving the room. I thanked the Fates that she had decided against the lecture I'd expected from her, fixed a plate as she recommended, and set into it. I couldn't imagine why Millie would do this to herself regularly.

Martha bustled in with a pot of coffee and a glass of orange juice moments later. "Fresh squeezed, Jane." She shook her head at me. "You'll need it."

I ducked my head. I had predicted correctly—I was now terribly embarrassed that everyone in the manor knew about my overindulgence the night before. I briefly contemplated retreating back to my room, but decided I was finished hiding.

I changed the subject instead. "How is Sergei doing?" I was curious how Martha's brother was settling in on the estate. With everything going on, I hadn't had a chance to check in about him.

Martha frowned. "He's doing well, although he's a bit nervous with the police back and forth all the time."

I nodded sympathetically, grateful that I could even make the motion again.

"Do you know why they're back again? And in Miss Marie's room?"

I was surprised that Martha would ask, since she didn't seem one to gossip. But perhaps she just wanted to be able to reassure her brother that he was safe. "It has nothing to do with Sergei. I'm certain of that."

Martha nodded, knocked on the wood dining table three times, and left.

I paused in my eating for a moment to contemplate what I had just told Martha. Was I sure that Sergei had nothing to do with anything? Fortunately, Redvers chose that moment to join me.

"Looks like you're thinking hard."

"It's more difficult than usual, I must admit." I continued on before he could make a comment. "Sergei is in the clear for suspicion, correct?"

Redvers nodded. "No motive. And the attacker had to be someone in the house for both last night and the poisoning."

"How are you so sure of that?"

"I checked the doors and windows downstairs after you

went to bed. Everything was locked up tight, and Sergei has been installed out in the stables."

I wondered again whether Redvers ever slept, and what it was that kept him up at night. And if he didn't sleep, why it didn't seem to affect him.

I poured myself another cup of coffee.

Lord Hughes entered, and went to where Millie had been seated earlier. He retrieved the newspaper that Millie had left behind and stopped when he realized both Redvers and I were looking at him strangely. Lord Hughes was normally clean-shaven and impeccable. Yet this morning he had obvious gray stubble lining his cheeks and chin.

He smiled ruefully and rubbed his chin. "I couldn't find my straight razor this morning. It's days like this when I wish I still had a valet. But personal servants are scarce on the ground these days."

Redvers and I exchanged a look. "What?" Lord Hughes asked.

Redvers cleared his throat. "The, um, trouble in Marie's room last night?"

Lord Hughes pulled out the chair and took a seat. He looked resigned to what was coming next.

"It was done with a straight razor."

"Of course it was." Lord Hughes sighed. "I should probably call my solicitor."

Redvers looked grim. "I think it's a good idea." As reluctant as Inspector Greyson was to arrest a peer, he would no doubt be forced to do so if the razor was traced back to Hughes. And at this point I thought it was a likely possibility.

Hughes nodded and stood, excusing himself to make his phone call. I chewed on some bacon and thought about Lord Hughes. A week ago, I would have never believed the man capable of violence, but after the revelation of his affairs during the war and the mounting evidence against him, I could no longer say that I was entirely convinced of the man's innocence.

It was as if Redvers could read my mind. "I still think someone is trying to set him up."

I worried at my lip and looked at him. "Are they? Or are we overlooking the obvious?"

Redvers shook his head. "I can't see Hughes being foolish enough to use items so closely linked to himself. His own straight razor?"

"A double blind perhaps?"

He thought that over, but quickly dismissed the idea. "I still don't think so. It feels too much like another attempt to cast him as the villain."

"Regardless, I would be willing to wager money that the inspector will find that the razor in Marie's room belongs to Lord Hughes. And the inspector will be back for Hughes with a pair of handcuffs."

"I wouldn't take that bet," Redvers agreed. "But even if they arrest him, I don't think they'll be able to make a case without more solid proof."

I hoped he was right. For everyone's sake.

Inspector Greyson came to arrest Lord Hughes that afternoon.

"I should set up shop with a crystal ball," I muttered. Redvers and I stood on the gravel driveway in front of the manor house. The others were still inside, ignorant of the scene unfolding before us. I dreaded telling Millie and Lillian that Lord Hughes had been arrested—neither of them would take the news well, although in entirely different ways.

"Pardon?" Redvers glanced at me as we watched the inspector lead Lord Hughes from the house and put him in the back of the inspector's black car. Hughes wasn't handcuffed, but it was still obvious he was being arrested.

I shook my head. "Nothing."

"Shall we join them?" Redvers was already moving toward his vehicle.

I was only a step behind. "Let's."

Lord Hughes's solicitor, a stout man by the name of Paulson, was waiting for us at the police station. It was handy that Hughes had called him earlier in the day and had him standing by. Greyson took Lord Hughes and Paulson into the interview room; this time we were not invited to attend. We were, however, invited to wait in the inspector's office.

I spent the time pacing back and forth in the small room, which was no small feat given the lack of space—it was a very short path that I was wearing in the cracked linoleum. Conversely, Redvers had folded himself elegantly into an uncomfortable chair and waited with his leg crossed and his hands patiently folded. He watched me pace for a few minutes before closing his eyes. I wondered how he could be so self-contained and calm when I felt ready to crawl out of my skin with nerves. At some point a young constable knocked on the door and offered us refreshments, but recalling the quality of the coffee the last time we visited, I declined his offer. Redvers echoed my polite refusal.

It seemed an eternity before Greyson returned to speak with us, and when he pushed through the door, I finally settled into the chair next to Redvers. Greyson rubbed a hand over his weary face, taking a seat behind his small wooden desk. He looked at me and opened his mouth, most likely to voice an objection to my presence, before he shook his head and said, "We'll have to hold him, at least overnight. Hopefully we can release him tomorrow based on his reputation."

I almost smiled since it appeared I was beginning to wear the man down—he had stopped arguing about whether I should be present. I still had some points to make in favor of Lord Hughes being released immediately, but the inspector cut me off before I could even start.

"There's nothing I can do. I'm receiving pressure from above to make the arrest. There's too much evidence stacked against him at this point."

"The razor?" Redvers asked.

"His prints were on the blade. Not on the handle, we weren't able to get anything from that. Anything there was smudged beyond recognition. Much like the paper you found." Greyson glanced at me. "With the arsenic bottle found in his room, the knife with his initials, and his background during the war, I'm afraid we have no choice."

I turned my glare to Redvers. "You told him."

Redvers cocked a brow. "Of course, I did. We're working *with* the police, Mrs. Wunderly."

I bristled at his formality. Greyson seemed amused, and I swung my glare back to him. His face quickly became serious again.

"Did you learn anything from him?" Redvers asked.

Greyson shook his head. "His solicitor would only let him answer the most basic questions. He did admit that the razor was his. And he obviously hasn't shaved today."

"I'm sure Paulson wasn't thrilled he admitted it."

Greyson gave a small smile. "He was not."

"Can we speak with him?" Perhaps we could learn something useful that the police did not. Or at the very least we could see if he needed us to do anything for him.

"That can be arranged. We've taken him back to the holding cell. Paulson has gone to start working on his release."

The holding cell was small, with just a hard wooden bench within it. Lord Hughes stood with his back against the wall, pushing off and coming forward to the heavy iron bars when he saw us. The constable who escorted us went back down the hallway and through the door, leaving us our privacy.

"It's a good thing I had the foresight to call Paulson,"

Hughes said. "With any luck, I should be out of here by tomorrow morning." He looked at me. "Will you assure Lillian and Millie that I'm fine? I don't want them to worry."

I nodded. "Of course." Although I knew with certainty neither woman would be able to take that advice. "Is there anything we can do for you? Bring you anything?"

Lord Hughes shook his head. "I'll be fine." He looked at Redvers, seeming to know that he had questions. "Go ahead and ask."

Redvers leaned one shoulder casually against the wall, crossing his arms. "The investments look bad, Your Lordship. Especially since it looks like Simon Marshall had uncovered them and was holding them over your head. He talked to people about it."

It wasn't a question, but Hughes sat down on the wooden bench and rubbed his hands over his face. "It looks bloody terrible. I know." He sighed and looked between Redvers and I. "When I invested the money I didn't realize that the company was making deals with German distributors. It's entirely my fault, and I should have been more circumspect in my investments, more diligent in researching the company. But James requested it of me." Hughes's face twisted into a bitter smile. "My brother was somewhat more functional at the time, and he said he needed me to make this investment for him. He promised not to ask for any more favors."

Redvers studied him for a moment, piecing together the rest of the story. "But what he was really trying to do was ruin you."

Lord Hughes looked at the ground. "Indeed. My own brother. He hoped that when word got out, I would be ruined and he would somehow take over my business investments. I'm not exactly sure how he thought it would work."

"What kind of company was it?" Perhaps Lord Hughes was overreacting about the impact it had during the war.

Hughes gave me a hollow look. "Munitions."

It really was that bad. "How did you avoid word getting out?" I asked.

"I withdrew my money once I realized what the company was doing and where its business interests truly were. It ran the distribution through several shell companies, but it was still horrifying to learn that I had invested in munitions that were going to fight against our own men." Hughes ran a hand through his hair. I had never seen the man so agitated. "James was the only one who knew, and I paid him off to keep his mouth shut about the investment. I also threatened to expose his role in it, although that didn't carry any weight. He has very little to lose."

We were all quiet for a moment, and then Lord Hughes continued. "Unfortunately, the investment had already made a fortune by the time I realized what was happening." Hughes gave a bitter laugh. "I'm sure James didn't intend for me to make even more money. He was furious when he found out. Tried to demand that I owed him some of it."

I thought about how awful it was to have your own brother so determined to see you ruined. It painted a very poor picture of Poppy and Alistair's father—it was a wonder the two had turned out even half as well as they did.

"How did your brother find such an investment?"

Hughes's face darkened. "He has more than a few . . . unsavory contacts." Redvers nodded at this.

Something else occurred to me as well. "Is that why you staff your estate with veterans?"

Hughes gave a sad nod. "It's the least I can do."

"How did Simon find out?" Redvers asked the question that had been on the tip of my tongue.

Hughes shook his head at this. "I don't know for certain. I suspect he rifled my office. There were scratches on the desk drawer that I keep locked. It's where I keep all my financial information. He had to be very clever to piece it all together, but I wouldn't put it past the boy."

"Was he blackmailing you?"

"Simon was a good lad. He never brought up the investments actually. But he did say he wanted my help in learning how to make money himself." He grimaced. "And my permission to court Lillian."

I was surprised he would allow it, especially since Lillian seemed to think he wouldn't have. He read my face. "Lillian has a mind of her own. If she really wanted him, what choice did I have? Her happiness is all that matters."

"I suspect most fathers wouldn't feel the same." Mine perhaps, but only if it occurred to him to think about. He was a bit absentminded, especially when it came to matters regarding his daughter.

Hughes shrugged. "Lillian is a blessing." He gave me a significant look. "As is your aunt."

I certainly didn't want to argue with the man, but I had to restrain myself from asking him how well he really knew my aunt. I loved her, but I thought calling her a blessing was a bit of a stretch.

But it did make his feelings about Millie clear. I opened my mouth to ask about his intentions, but Redvers headed me off.

"Is there anything else we should know?"

Lord Hughes looked at him for a long moment. "Whatever my sins may be, I had nothing to do with this mess."

At that pronouncement, Redvers seemed ready to go, but I had a few last questions first. "Do the police have any reason to suspect you would want to hurt Marie?"

Hughes rubbed his cheek. "What possible reason could I have to hurt that girl? She's been with us for so long that she seems part of the family." He gave a wry smile. "Well, maybe blends with the wallpaper is more accurate. But I'm happy for Lillian to have a companion—it gets lonely for her out on the estate otherwise. It's often just she and I and the staff otherwise."

I regarded him for a long moment, wondering how much he knew and how much of Marie's secret to let out. I didn't want the girl to find herself evicted from the Hughes's house as she had been evicted from her family home. I would have to tread carefully.

"And you don't mind how much time she spends with your niece?" I watched his face for a reaction.

Hughes's face creased in confusion. "They're just silly girls having a good time. Isn't that what girls their age do?"

I smiled and gave him a vague nod. It seemed as though he genuinely didn't suspect that Marie was anything other than what she appeared—a friend of Lillian's with neglectful parents. It also meant he had no reason to attack her.

Chapter 40

We checked back in with Inspector Greyson, giving him the basics of what we had learned, but nothing he wouldn't be able to discover on his own. I wasn't sure if Redvers was being deliberately vague, but it didn't seem like he was being entirely forthcoming with the inspector anymore. I wondered if it was for Hughes's benefit or some other purpose. Knowing Redvers, that could go either way.

Back in the car, I turned to Redvers. "Did it seem to you that Hughes was telling the truth? Do you think he really doesn't suspect anything about Marie?"

He glanced from the road to me for a second as we pulled back onto the main street leading through the village. "I think he was."

"And everything else?"

"That's a bit trickier." Redvers gave a small sigh. "It's hard to say whether he actually had no idea what he was investing in, or whether he has convinced himself of that after the fact. It's clear he's carrying a great deal of guilt with him."

"Do you think he'll be released soon?"

"Hopefully."

I wasn't looking forward to going back and contending with my aunt Millie. She would likely be full of recriminations that I hadn't yet solved this or protected Lord Hughes from being arrested. Despite the fact that this was all out of my hands, and I had done my best to work out who was behind the attacks.

I sighed.

"What's the sigh for?" Redvers gave me a sidelong look.

"I'm not looking forward to facing Millie."

"I don't blame you." He was quiet for a second, then pulled the car into a small drive leading to a gate, a field of grazing sheep beyond. We rolled to a stop, and he turned off the engine. "Let's put it off for a few more minutes."

I nodded, suddenly nervous, keeping my eyes straight ahead on the sheep. One small ewe came trotting up to the fence expectantly. Despite my anxiety, I smiled at it, wondering what she thought was coming.

"Jane." Redvers had half turned in his seat, leaned against the door, and was studying me intently. My heart sped to a gallop. We hadn't finished any of the serious discussions we had begun, and I was terrified he was going to tell me something I desperately didn't want to hear.

"Lillian will be upset of course, but even though she'll be worried I think she'll take things in stride." The words just started pouring out of me. "It's Millie I'm more concerned about. You know the temper she has, and she's going to be angry since she asked me to look into things . . ." I started talking faster and faster until Redvers leaned over and put a long finger on my mouth to stop me. The touch on my lips was electric and I stopped speaking immediately, frozen in my seat, unable to so much as breathe.

"Jane. Let me explain." His voice was quiet, but I'm pretty sure my heart stopped beating. "The woman I was engaged to was a friend of the family. It was a sort of . . . understanding between our parents, and neither of us was very interested in actually going through with it."

My heart pumped once or twice. He removed his finger from my lips and I stayed quiet as he leaned back against his door. I felt the loss of his proximity immediately.

"She is now happily married and living in Newcastle with her baby and husband."

I started breathing again as I let that sink in. "So, you're not in love with her."

"I'm not in love with her." His voice was very quiet and I could feel his eyes boring holes in the side of my head as I continued staring at the friendly sheep that was now nosing around the browning grass. The only time I had felt such relief was when I learned I was cleared as a murder suspect. This felt equally as important somehow.

I snuck a peek at him as my shoulders drooped with the loss of tension. "I'm glad," I said quietly. I was still staring at the sheep, but from the corner of my eye I could see that a smile had crept onto his face.

I took a deep breath and continued. "I suppose I should also admit that you were right."

"I will mark this date on my calendar." His brow was raised and his eyes were full of humor.

I turned to face him fully, leaning back tentatively against my own door. I pursed my lips and gave him an arch look. "You should. It's quite an accomplishment for you."

His full lips pursed into a straight line and I could tell he was choking back a laugh.

I smiled for a moment before I became serious. "When you said that I run from things. You were right." I chewed my lip for a moment, and those dark eyes went to my mouth. My voice dropped. "I just . . . after all that happened with Grant . . . I crave safety." I sought the correct words to explain further, my eyes searching his for understanding. "Not that I don't feel safe with you . . ." I hurried to explain. "I do. I just . . . it's just that . . ."

He nodded, his voice gentle. "I understand." I had told him only a little of what my deceased husband had been like—a sadistic monster who took pleasure in causing me pain. Those years of cowering before him put steel in my spine now. I didn't want to be put in such a vulnerable position ever again, and it made me wary of men.

But it also made me weary. Keeping one's guard up like a battle shield at all times was exhausting. I turned back to the sheep, who now had several companions, and studied them, wondering what else I should say to Redvers. Should I admit that he tempted me to stop running? That I had more feelings for him than I ever anticipated I could have again?

Could I make myself that vulnerable?

The decision was taken away from me, when a distant rumbling became louder behind us. A tractor pulling a small wagon stopped, obviously needing to go where we had just pulled in. Redvers sighed as he moved back into position behind the steering wheel and turned the car back on. More sheep waited at the gate.

"They were waiting for hay," I said absently.

We reversed, and pulled out, the farmer giving a friendly wave as we vacated his land and pulled back onto the main road. Redvers gave a small sigh.

"I would prefer if this conversation wasn't over."

This time, I couldn't argue with him.

Chapter 41

The spell between us had broken and my thoughts went back to the case at hand. There had to be something we were missing, some link we weren't seeing. This couldn't be just a random series of terrible events.

We pulled up to the house and went inside, leaving the car in the drive. The family was in the drawing room, and I was pleased to see that Alistair had joined them. The young man was still a bit pale, but since he was up and about, he was obviously feeling better. A thin cloud of smoke hung in the room near where the young people sat—they had obviously been nervously chain-smoking for some time, judging by the full ashtray. We hadn't told anyone what was happening before we left for the police station, but it seemed they had worked it out anyway. No one was saying much, pensively waiting to hear what news we had.

Tears began streaming down Lillian's face as soon as she heard that her father was being held at the jail. We did our best to reassure her that he would be released soon, and that he had the very best solicitors—even if he didn't now, he certainly would hire an entire cadre of them. As Redvers spoke, I watched Millie's face become more and more stoic. I could tell she was struggling with her own emotions, but she would never admit to it.

Alistair held one of Lillian's hands in his own. His face was creased in concern as he gazed at her. "It's a hanging offense, since Simon was killed." We all looked at him in shocked silence. Even Millie was staring at him in horror, no biting response at hand. "But whatever happens to Uncle Edward, I'll take care of you, Lillian."

Lillian's tears came faster now, punctuated by a few sobs. "Tha-thank you, Alistair." Alistair pulled a handkerchief from his pocket and handed it to the girl.

I saw Millie looking at Lillian, and I could tell she was trying to make her mind up about something. I caught her eye and gave her a nod. Her face softened slightly, and she gave me one in return.

"Lillian, perhaps it would be good for us to get some fresh air."

Lillian gave a vague nod as she blew her nose in the linen handkerchief. "I'll come along." Alistair stood, reaching down for Lillian's hand once more.

For once, Millie handled things with something approaching diplomacy. "I think I should be alone with her just now, Alistair. But thank you for offering." Alistair's face darkened, and I thought a fit of temper would follow, but he gave a brisk "Very well," before excusing himself from the room.

Lillian and Millie left not long after, Millie's arm wrapped around the girl's shoulders despite the awkward height difference. Redvers raised an eyebrow at me and I whispered, "I think Millie is going to tell her that she's her birth mother."

Redvers kept his voice low. "She hasn't told her yet?" I shook my head. Lillian knew of course, but they hadn't discussed it. I felt certain Millie would care for Lillian if anything was to happen to Lord Hughes, and now was a good time for her to offer that reassurance. Lillian was of age to care for herself, but she would undoubtedly feel adrift without a parent—I was glad Millie was willing to officially assume that role.

Hammond was the only one left in the room, and he strolled

over to join us as we took a seat near the window. Hands in pockets, he was the picture of relaxation, but his brow was furrowed.

"Do you know, there is something I forgot to mention to you."

Redvers and I looked at him with interest.

"That first day that the police came after Simon was killed, I came to the drawing room, and Alistair was lurking outside. Listening." Hammond took a seat. "He looked guilty when he saw me, and scurried off."

I cast my mind back and tried to remember that morning. So much had happened since then that it was a bit of a blur.

"That's odd," I said. "I think he excused himself from the room, didn't he?" I looked to Redvers, who nodded. "Why would he listen at the door instead of staying behind?"

Both men gave a shrug. "It could be anything," Redvers said.

"I only thought of it because of his . . . little display just now."

"Wildly inappropriate," I said. "Did he think he was making her feel better?"

"He's a bit of an odd goose, that one," Hammond said.

We were all quiet for a moment when Martha stepped in the room. I noticed that her eyes brightened when they landed on Hammond.

"Chris, can I talk to you?"

Hammond blushed and hurried from the room.

I looked at Redvers. "Is something going on there? I've never heard her address anyone by their first name before. Except me, but that was only after she helped me into a bath."

Redvers didn't say anything, but his eyes were twinkling.

Hammond returned moments later, and I decided it was long past time to ask him about his strange behavior.

"Chris. Is something going on between you and Martha?"

Now Hammond's face turned the color of a ripe tomato.

He stammered a bit before I jumped back in to save him. "She's lovely, really, and I'm happy for you." When I thought about it, I realized they were probably only a few years apart in age. And Martha was quite an attractive woman when she wasn't so pinched with worry—and those lines had disappeared once her brother was released from jail.

He smiled shyly. "Thank you."

"Is that why you returned here so suddenly? And why you were wandering around in your stocking feet?"

He ducked his head. "We've been sneaking out to spend time together. It started really innocently—just taking her out for dinner on her off nights. But she takes care of everyone so well . . ." He trailed off for a moment. "I came back early to see her, but I didn't want anyone to know, so I was sneaking back to my room. I was supposed to take her to the pub for a late lunch once she had served the family."

Well, that explained his weird behavior and awkward disappearances. There was something else I wanted to know, however.

"Did you know about her brother on the grounds?" It would have saved us quite a bit of investigating if he had been up-front about it. But he shook his head.

"She was keeping that from me as well." Chris frowned. "The woman really can keep a secret. But I knew something was off. I kept trying to convince her to tell me, but she refused."

It was something of a relief to know that all the intrigue surrounding Hammond was cleared up. At least my instincts regarding one person on the grounds were correct.

But there were more questions and I started speaking my swirling thoughts aloud. "Who had reason to kill Simon, poison Alistair, attack Marie, and cut the line of the plane?"

"And assault you at the stream."

Hammond's eyebrows shot up. I figured it was now safe to

include him on all the details, so I gave him a quick rundown of my being pushed into the freezing water.

"So, the plane and the stream were probably linked to me, don't you think? Trying to stop me from asking questions?" I put my chin in my hand, elbow resting on the arm of the chair.

Both men nodded. "Most likely," Redvers said.

But none of us could come up with an explanation for the rest.

"I will say, it feels personal," Hammond said. "Attacking people close to either Lord Hughes or Lillian."

That felt true. And it was an explanation that would eliminate Lord Hughes's business enemies from the mix. But it didn't offer up many other alternatives.

Something was tickling at the back of my memory. I thought about everything we had done, and everyone we had talked to.

I shot to my feet. "I'll be right back."

Both men raised their eyebrows and started to stand from their seats but I waved them back down and headed out of the room.

I went down the hall toward the kitchen, glad the men hadn't followed me. I thought it would be less intimidating to talk to Sergei Fedec without them hovering over us. I poked my head into the kitchen and found Sergei nursing a cup of tea at the table, Mr. Shaw seated opposite him. I stepped all the way into the room, looking around for the ever-present Martha.

"Hello, Mr. Shaw. Sergei, where's your sister?"

Sergei started a bit and looked at me warily.

"She ran to cellar for vegetables."

"Do you mind if I join you?"

Sergei gave a casual shrug, but Mr. Shaw upended his cup,

slurping down the rest of his tea, and stood. "Take my seat. I've got to get back to it." He put his cup and saucer into the sink before disappearing back belowstairs.

Sergei watched me as I took the seat Mr. Shaw had just left.

"You seem to be getting on well with everyone."

Sergei gave another shrug, eyes still wary.

I decided to skip the small talk and come straight to it. "I remembered that you said you saw someone else on the property one night."

Sergei's face was even more closed off. "Yes."

"Do you remember when it was?"

Sergei didn't say anything for a while. I decided to confide in him in the hopes of gaining his trust. "I'm trying to find out who that might have been. Lord Hughes has been arrested, and I would dearly like to get him out of jail."

Sergei's face relaxed a bit. "Martha told me about trouble here. Lord Hughes is good man." He paused. "For aristocrat."

I conceded the point. "Can you help me?"

Sergei considered me for a moment before offering another shrug. "I do not see the person very well. But I know they are not staying in house."

"How do you know that?"

"Because I follow them from the barn when I see them. I stay back, but I do not want someone to break in and hurt my sister. I make certain the man does not go back to the house. I worry they are thief."

"And this was before Simon died?"

Sergei nodded. "Before, yes. A day or two? Is hard to say."

"And did you see where they went?"

"The person did not go into big house. They go down driveway and up road. I wait to make sure they do not come back, and after time I hear vehicle."

Whoever it was had been staying off the property but had the means for transportation.

"You didn't see the car?"

"Is far away. But the noise, it carry here."

I nodded. Sound did carry out here. But it couldn't have belonged to another household because the nearest was several miles away. The sound of a starting car wouldn't have carried that far. Whoever snuck in to cut the brakes on the Lambda had come from outside the grounds and left a vehicle down the lane as a means of escape.

"Did you tell all this to the police?"

Sergei nodded, then lifted a shoulder. "Most of."

I was a little surprised the police knew all this and arrested Lord Hughes anyway—signs were pointing to someone outside the house having sliced those brake cables. Although the poisoning and the attack in Marie's room were probably enough for an arrest by themselves.

"Thank you, Sergei. I appreciate you telling me."

Sergei took a drink of his tea. "I hope you help Lord Hughes."

I nodded and left.

I returned to the drawing room where Redvers sat waiting for me. Hammond had gone back out to the barn. With all the uncertainty, he wanted to check on the Moth.

Redvers' mouth twisted. "I think the man is going to start sleeping out there with that plane."

"I'm sure he only wants to fix it once." I was too restless to sit down, and I paced around the room by the windows.

"Where did you go?" Redvers watched me walk back and forth.

"To talk to Sergei. I remembered that he had seen someone else on the grounds. I wanted to ask him about it." Redvers nodded, and I related what Sergei had told me.

Redvers let me talk, and

when I had finished he spoke up. "Yes, I heard most of that from Greyson."

I rolled my eyes. "Two questions in that case. Why didn't you stop me? And why didn't you fill me in on it?"

Redvers shrugged. "The police were looking into the possibility but weren't getting anywhere with it." I pinned him with a look. "And I forgot to mention it."

It was awfully convenient. I had to wonder how many times Redvers "forgot" to tell me things.

"Let's head into town," Redvers said.

I stopped moving for a moment. "Why?"

"Because you're making me dizzy. And because we have someone else to talk to."

"Who is that?"

"Someone I think we've overlooked."

Chapter 42

We got redressed for the brisk fall air and returned to Redvers' car. As we settled in, I asked again who it was we had overlooked. I had been going over it in my mind but hadn't come up with anyone.

"Queenie Powell."

It took me a moment to place the name. "The maid?" Redvers nodded and I thought about the girl. I had only caught glimpses of her a handful of times and had never really spoken with her. She was quiet and efficient and came in twice a week from the village. "She doesn't live in the manor, so I forgot she was even connected with the house."

"As did I, frankly. I know the police questioned her at the very beginning, but I'm beginning to wonder if she might know something useful."

Maids did see quite a lot, so he was probably on to something there. I thought about the little I knew about the girl and recalled what Martha had said to me about Queenie calling up and giving her notice. "Martha told me that she quit over a boy."

Redvers gave me a sidelong glance before returning his eyes to the narrow road. "I hadn't heard that."

I pursed my lips and thought about Alistair's boyish good looks. "I could give a guess as to what boy it was." It would make sense why Queenie hadn't wanted to come back to the house and had quit her position over the phone—the boy had been in residence at Wedgefield Manor.

We motored into the small village and parked on a narrow side street, walking several blocks to the old stone pub that sat near the river. The outdoor seating area overlooking the water was charming, but it was already too cold in the season for it to be used comfortably.

My steps slowed. "Are we going for a drink?"

Redvers looked at me, eyes sparkling. "I wouldn't think you would be up for one yet."

I could tell he was teasing me, and in fact, the idea of having a drink turned my stomach. He gave a small chuckle—I must have turned slightly green.

We entered the pub, Redvers ducking under the low wooden lintel. We approached the bar, and I hung back a bit, taking in the cozy atmosphere. Thick wood beams lined the ceiling, but the whitewashed plaster walls kept the dark wood from overwhelming the space. A small fireplace sat at the opposite end of the room from the bar, although it wasn't in use at the moment. Two elderly patrons perched on stools at the far end of the wooden bar, their eyes flicking between Redvers and I.

"Is Queenie about?" Redvers asked the barkeep.

"What you want with 'er?" The man was bald with a large moustache beneath a bulbous nose. He stopped wiping the counter for a moment and regarded us.

"Just wanted to chat with her about her work. We were thinking of hiring her—we're going to be renting one of the cottages, and we need a maid." I realized what Redvers was playing at, and I stepped next to him, wrapping my arm around his side and smiling at the barkeep. Just a happy couple in need of cleaning help.

The man nodded once and then jerked his head toward the

back room. "She's back there. Could use a new job cleaning since she quit the last. Stupid girl."

I reluctantly removed my arm from Redvers' taut waist and followed him into the back. We found Queenie Powell cleaning a table, stacking dishes crusted with remnants of lunch. She was a pretty girl, with fair skin and a smattering of freckles across her pert nose. Thick blond hair was cut short and styled with pin curls around her face.

"Hello, Queenie," I said softly.

"Mrs. Wunderly! What are you doing here?" She looked from me to Redvers and her spine straightened.

"We have a few questions for you, Queenie. Can we sit down?"

Queenie avoided meeting my eyes and went back to stacking dishes. "I've told the police everything I know. And what I know ain't much. I was only at the house twice a week."

I decided to take a gamble on my hunch. "We're here about Alistair, Queenie."

The girl's shoulders slumped and she heaved a sigh, motioning for us to follow her to a clean table in the back corner. She pushed her hair back behind an ear. "How did you find me?"

Redvers answered. "I heard that your father owned this pub. I took a chance that you might be working here as well."

Queenie nodded. "It was stupid of me to quit working at the estate. My da's right angry about the lost wages." Her eyes misted over. "But I couldn't keep working there."

"Why not, Queenie? What's happened?" I kept my voice soothing.

"Alistair and me, well, we been sneaking out together whenever he comes to stay with his uncle."

My hunch had been correct. I nodded for her to continue.

"But this time he said he was going to marry his cousin

Lillian." Her tears started in earnest, and Redvers reached into his pocket and handed her a white handkerchief. "Then he said after they were wed, we could still be *friendly*. We could keep on just as before, but he would be married to someone else."

Queenie blew her nose. "I told him I'm not that kind of girl. And it was me or nothing." She sniffled. "He chose her. I couldn't keep working there, not when I never want to see him again. And then with what happened to poor Simon . . ." Queenie's voice trailed off.

"When did he tell you this, Queenie? Before Simon died?" Redvers' voice was equally soothing, but Queenie started a bit.

"No, I think it was after. Alistair had a rented room in the next town over. Said I couldn't tell no one, but it was so we could be alone together." I winced as I hoped the girl wasn't in trouble. Her father would have something worse than lost wages to be upset about. "We used to meet there a couple times a month. But when he showed up at the estate, and Miss Martha wanted me to make up a room for him . . . well, we had a big fight. That's when he told me about him and Miss Lillian. I only found out later that Simon had been in that accident." Her tears started again, and Redvers shifted in his seat. "She's a nice girl, Lillian is, but I thought he loved me."

I patted her arm and made sympathetic noises, but looked at Redvers. If Alistair had a room in the next town over, he could have easily come to the estate and cut the brake cables on Simon's car. Chances were good he also knew how much Simon used the car.

Unless he was trying to kill his uncle.

"Did you tell the police about this, Queenie?"

She blew her nose. "I told them that I hadn't seen anything suspicious around the house. And that was true." Her chin lifted a bit, and her watery eyes met mine. "But I didn't think it was any of their business about me and Alistair."

I could understand why she might not have wanted anyone to know she was spending time alone with Alistair, but we might have saved considerable time if she had been honest with the police in the first place.

We asked Queenie a few more questions, then excused ourselves. Before we left, Redvers insisted that the girl keep his handkerchief, and she tucked it into her apron with a wobbly thanks and stars in her eyes as she gazed at him. I suspected Queenie would get over Alistair before too long.

We were only steps from the pub when I turned to Redvers. "What was Alistair's alibi for the night Simon was killed?"

"Poppy claimed he was home with her."

"I wonder if that's true. And if he got her to lie for him."

Chapter 43

We returned to the car, and I was opening the driver's side door before I remembered that we were in England.

Redvers, arms crossed, leaned against the side of the car and cocked his head at me. "Did you want to drive?"

I shook my head and went around to the passenger side, thoughts whirling. The crazy notion I'd had when Alistair was poisoned was starting to look much less crazy. Could Alistair have done it to himself? If he had poisoned himself, everything else made sense. Especially if he had designs on getting Lillian to marry him.

"What if Alistair poisoned himself?"

Redvers pulled out onto the main road. "I'll admit the thought has crossed my mind. But why take such a risk?"

"Because the stakes are high. Perhaps he thought a little murder attempt would get him enough sympathy from Lillian that she would agree to marry him." I cast my mind back to our conversation while he lay in bed. "He kept insisting that Lord Hughes was innocent, and that he thought the servants were responsible."

"Given his feelings on the hired help, I suppose he would consider either scenario a win. Either one of the servants is arrested, or his uncle is blamed."

"It's the only way I can see that the rest of this makes

sense." I frowned. "He knocks off Simon and loses competition for Lillian's hand. Simon was obviously looking to court the girl as well—Lord Hughes said as much. But did Alistair plant the arsenic bottle in Lord Hughes's room? If he did, he was obviously trying to frame his uncle."

"I suspect Alistair might have taken after his father more than we may have realized." Redvers sounded grim. "With Hughes out of the way, Alistair would inherit everything."

"But not if Lillian . . . oh." If he was able to convince Lillian to marry him and then get rid of Lord Hughes, Alistair would have control of the estate. All that money his father had lost, now at Alistair's fingertips.

Of course, if she refused marriage, an "accident" could remove Lillian from the line of inheritance; Alistair had already made strides to remove Lord Hughes from the equation. If he succeeded, the Hughes estate and fortune would most likely go to Alistair's family without him having to marry her.

"I wonder if he cares about Lillian at all," I muttered, watching as the countryside passed in an increasing blur.

Redvers glanced at me, gently pushing harder on the gas, and I watched the speedometer spike a bit higher. "I hope so. Otherwise she may be in danger."

The tires had barely stopped before I was out of the car and rushing into the house, but there was nothing but silence to greet us. We checked all the downstairs rooms before advancing to the bedrooms upstairs, which were locked and appeared unoccupied since no one answered the repeated knocking. We paid special attention to Alistair's room, Redvers applying his lock-picking skills to let ourselves in, and found that while Alistair's suitcase was still there, he was not.

"They're probably outside." I could hear my hopeful tone, and Redvers glanced at me. It didn't need to be said aloud, but we were both concerned that Alistair might have already done something rash. I wondered where Mr. Shaw and Martha were, but was feeling too anxious to spend any time looking for them.

We headed out onto the grounds. The cold air scorched my lungs as I sucked in great lungfuls, trying to keep up with Redvers' long legs. He finally slowed, and when I looked up I could see the figures of Poppy, Millie, and Lillian in the distance. Rascal bounded toward us, tongue flapping in the breeze.

"Thank God," Redvers muttered.

"But where's Marie?"

He indicated with his head toward the woods that framed the lawns where I saw Marie pushing through some brush, a small white ball held aloft.

We continued toward the ladies at a more reasonable pace, and I was able to catch my breath.

"Where's Alistair?" Redvers asked as soon as we reached them, his tone not quite casual.

The girls gave him an odd look, but Millie's glance was far more speculative. I wondered whether she would be surprised by our suspicions.

Poppy spoke up. "He said he was going for a drive! Maybe going in to the village?"

"What's wrong?" A worried crease pulled between Lillian's brows. I glanced at Redvers; we hadn't discussed how much to tell the girls or whether we should warn Lillian that she might be in danger from her own cousin. This would require some diplomacy—especially with Alistair's sister here.

I narrowed my eyes at the girl, thinking. Poppy and Alistair were close, but how far did that extend? Would he have confided in his sister? Poppy saw my face and looked to the ground, flushed.

"Poppy," I said quietly. "Do *you* know what's wrong?"

She refused to look at me, her fingers tugging at her skirt. The others turned to look at her, and she became more nervous, glancing toward the woods as though she was looking for an escape.

"Alistair is in some trouble, isn't he?" I kept my voice soft.

Poppy refused to look at me and fumbled in her pockets for a moment before she nervously pulled a cigarette case from her coat pocket. I watched as she tried to light it with shaking hands before Marie came forward and helped her. Stepping back, Marie shot me a look, and I tried to convey with my eyes how important this issue was. I must have been successful because Marie touched Poppy's free hand, wrapping it in her own. I raised my eyebrows.

"Poppy, I think this is important," Marie said, squeezing Poppy's hand.

"But I don't want to get him in trouble." Poppy blew out a stream of smoke.

"I think he's already in trouble," Marie said quietly.

Poppy looked at her uncertainly, but finally gave a small nod.

The girl still wasn't going to speak, so I picked up the thread Marie had started. "What happened, Poppy?" She gave her head a little shake, so I continued. "I heard you arguing with him. Telling him to stop." I could feel Redvers looking at me in surprise. I hadn't given him the details, because I had assumed it was a childish squabble and then forgotten about the whole thing. But I kept my eyes on Poppy. Her eyes misted over and she finally looked at me.

"He didn't mean to hurt anyone!" Poppy's hand clenched into a fist, nearly crushing her cigarette. "But I think he might have."

"Who do you think he hurt, Poppy?"

"Maybe Simon." Her voice was quiet and she wouldn't meet anyone's eyes.

I didn't point out that Simon was well beyond hurt—the man was dead. And I didn't believe for a second that Alistair hadn't meant to hurt anyone, but Poppy naturally wanted to believe the best of her brother. There was no kind reason to disabuse her of the notion right now—she would have plenty of time to deal with the hard facts later.

"And where is he now?"

"I don't know!" Poppy wailed. "He wouldn't tell me! He just said he had to leave."

I could feel Redvers' tense frustration next to me.

"Poppy, I know this is difficult. But when you told the police that Alistair was home with you the night Simon died, was that true?"

Tears streamed down Poppy's face in earnest now. She shook her head.

"Did Alistair spend a lot of time away from home? Maybe you didn't know where he was?"

Poppy glanced up at me and swiped at her wet cheeks. She didn't need to answer for me to know the answer was yes. But she reluctantly nodded. Marie plucked the forgotten cigarette from Poppy's small hand and put it out.

We were all quiet for a moment, then Redvers spoke.

"Ladies, I think it would be best if we went inside and talked things over."

I looked around. He was right—the women were easy targets out on the lawn. I didn't think Alistair would try to take all of them on to get to Lillian, but it was better to be safe. It would be easier to guard everyone inside the manor.

Lillian started to argue, but Millie put her hand on Lillian's arm and shook her head. Millie and I exchanged a look, and Millie gave me a small nod. It told me she knew how serious things were with Alistair, although I doubted she knew just how much was at stake—she wouldn't be so calm if she did.

We got Millie and the girls back to the house and settled into the drawing room. I extracted a promise from my aunt to keep everyone where they were while Redvers placed a call to Inspector Greyson and I alerted the staff to the situation. Martha was easy to find in the kitchen, and she promised to round up her brother and Mr. Shaw. I trotted back outside to locate Sergeant Barlow. I found him sweeping out the stables, and I came upon Group Captain Hammond in the barn checking over the Moth. Both men agreed to come directly to the drawing room with the others.

Redvers and I returned at nearly the same time and we spoke quietly together outside the drawing room door. "Greyson will have his men out looking for Alistair. Although who knows how far he could have gotten by now."

"Do you think he'll try to come for Lillian?"

Redvers shrugged. "It's hard to say what he's thinking or even what he's capable of at this point. Although if he knows the police suspect him, he'll be desperate. He'll think nothing of killing or hurting someone else."

I nodded. "Do we need to search the house?"

"We'll do that directly after this meeting. I'll split up the men and search. Then we can send Millie and the girls to collect bedding and pillows for tonight."

I raised my eyebrows.

"They'll all need to sleep here tonight. We can't risk everyone sleeping in their own beds."

"I agree." Redvers sketched out the rest of his plan, and I could find no fault with it except the part where I would be sleeping with the other women. "I'll keep watch over the ladies tonight while they sleep."

Redvers looked for a moment like he would argue but decided against it.

I went back to where the girls were gathered nervously while we waited for everyone to arrive. I did my best to soothe them without giving much else away. Millie stood behind them with a shot of whiskey in her hand. She caught me looking at it.

"Just the one for my nerves," she muttered. "I know we need to stay sharp."

I nodded in relief.

Shaw ambled through the door, hands in pockets, moments before Martha arrived with Sergei in tow. Barlow was not far behind, and Hammond arrived last, a slight frown on his face. I looked at him and he shrugged. He was probably concerned that something might happen to the Moth in his absence, but we needed everyone's help. Redvers gestured for everyone to find a seat. When they had, he took a deep breath and plunged forward.

"We have reason to believe that Alistair might try to harm Lillian."

"NO!" Lillian cried out. "He would never—"

Redvers cut her off. "I know you care about him. But he's backed himself into a desperate situation." Redvers was trying to spin it as positively as he could. The ladies had settled in and were listening closely, while the staff in back shared concerned glances with one another. "We just need to keep everyone here safe until we can find him and ask him some questions."

Despite Redvers' best efforts, Lillian's jaw was still set at a mulish angle, and Millie and I watched her nervously. It would be hard to keep her safe if she didn't believe that Alistair was dangerous. But trying to convince her of that might push her closer toward him, if her expression was anything to judge by.

Poppy turned to Lillian. "No, Lillie. It's true." It was as serious as I had ever heard the girl.

The mulish expression faded from Lillian's face. "It's not a stupid prank of his?"

Poppy shook her head and reached for Lillian's hand, grasping it tightly. The girl had pulled herself together since our conversation earlier and a quiet strength radiated from her now.

Redvers and I glanced at each other. Sometimes help comes from the most unexpected places.

Lillian studied her cousin for a moment before she sighed and turned to us. "Very well. But only if you promise he won't be hurt once you do find him."

We agreed readily, knowing full well it was an empty promise. We had no control over how the police would treat Alistair once they found him, but it seemed to ease Lillian's mind.

The meeting wrapped up fairly quickly after that. Redvers didn't give any more information to the group than was absolutely necessary—just enough to convince everyone that their role was crucial and needed to be taken seriously. It was decided that Hammond would stay in the barn with the vehicles and the plane—including Alistair's motorcycle, which was still tucked behind the door. Since Alistair had a key to the house, Shaw, Barlow, and Sergei would cover the entrances on the ground floor, and Redvers would provide occasional relief to the men while patrolling the rest of the house. The women, including Martha, would gather in the drawing room overnight. There was a great deal of argument from Millie and the girls, but Redvers was quietly insistent that we should stay together.

The pieces fit together with Alistair as the culprit, but until we could find him and talk to him, we couldn't be absolutely certain. Until then, all we could do was protect Lillian and the rest of the household.

I looked around at the assembled faces in the drawing room and hoped we were right about Alistair. Otherwise we could be locking ourselves in with a killer.

Chapter 44

There were still several hours before nightfall, so we had time to put our plans into action. If the police caught Alistair, all the better, but in the event that they didn't find him, we needed to be prepared. And the first step was ensuring that Alistair hadn't secreted himself away somewhere in the house. The men split into pairs and searched the house top to bottom, but as expected, Alistair was nowhere to be found.

Once that task was completed, Millie and I marshalled the girls to the upstairs bedrooms to pull together bedding for our makeshift beds in the drawing room. I would be keeping watch and had no intentions of sleeping, but in an act of solidarity I went to my own room and started to gather whatever I would need for the night.

I was interrupted by a pounding at my door, and Millie's voice shouting my name. I made my way over and as soon as I unlocked it, the door flew open and Millie pushed inside, nearly knocking me over.

"Lillian's room is locked and she isn't answering the door." Millie was trembling and her voice was overloud in the room.

"When . . . when is the last time anyone saw her?"

"About twenty minutes ago, when we came up for bedding. Marie says she locked the connecting door as well and wouldn't answer her when she called."

I muttered a curse, and Millie was too distraught to even bother with a glare. "Where's Redvers?"

"He's in the hall trying to get in."

I flew down the hall, catching Redvers just as he was about to push open the door. He had made short work of the lock with his picks, and it struck me again about how flimsy these door locks were.

It was the first time I had been inside Lillian's bedroom, and I quickly glanced around the large space with its spare furnishings. Her father would give her anything she wanted, but her space was decorated sparsely with a large bed and enormous wooden wardrobe, but little else. A putter was leaned in one corner near the marble fireplace and a few scattered balls told me she practiced even when she was alone in her room. I wasn't sure I had ever met someone so single-minded.

But perhaps the most important feature of the room was that it was empty. I noticed a white sheet of paper on the end of the bed and hurried over to snatch it up, my eyes quickly skimming over the dashed off note Lillian had left us. Redvers was already standing near the open window.

"This says she didn't believe Alistair could have meant to hurt anyone. She was going to find him and try to talk him into turning himself in so this can be sorted out." I ignored the cries of alarm from both Millie and Marie and went to stand near Redvers at the window.

"Could she be involved?" Redvers asked quietly.

I shook my head, certain of her innocence. Despite how it looked, I knew in my gut that Lillian wasn't working with Alistair. She was too upset by the harm that was coming to those around her. That wasn't faked.

And while escaping out a window was incredibly foolish

on her part, it also made sense. Lillian thought this was simply a misunderstanding, and she didn't want Alistair to be hurt in the process of capturing him. I wondered if it would have helped had we been more explicit with her in explaining what he was suspected of doing. Of course, she still might not have listened. As standoffish as the girl could seem, I knew that she cared deeply about the people in her life. She would want to believe the best of her cousin.

Redvers' head was mostly outside the window and I bent over to peer out. We were on the second floor, but Lillian's room had a ledge with easy access to a drainpipe. For an athletic girl like Lillian, she would have had no trouble climbing down.

"It looks like this is how she got out. And she has a head start on us now." Redvers was already moving toward the door and I was close on his heels.

"Where should we look first?"

"I was thinking we'll head over to the barn and see if Group Captain Hammond happened to see her leaving. He headed out not long after we searched the house. Perhaps he saw her exiting her window."

We hurried into our coats and burst outside, the cold air stinging my cheeks. I hadn't bothered with gloves or a hat, and I felt the lack of them as we hurried toward the barn.

As we drew closer, I could see that the sliding door was pushed wide open. Redvers and I both frowned and picked up our already grueling pace. Hammond wouldn't have left it that way, especially not when he was trying to keep Alistair out.

We cautiously approached the door, Redvers motioning for me to stay behind him. I wanted to roll my eyes, but then I saw the shiny black revolver he pulled from his coat pocket.

Standing behind him was fine, after all.

"Group Captain Hammond?" Redvers called out, sweeping his pistol across the interior immediately before us. He moved inside cautiously, and I took one more look around the landscape outside before following him in. The car bays were empty, the Moth sitting in lonely silence. On the far side of the plane, I could see a crumpled form on the ground.

"Chris!" I whispered loudly, trying to push past Redvers, but he held me back. He finished his sweep of the large room and then let me go.

I ran to Hammond's side, quickly finding the gash on the back of his head. There was quite a bit of blood, but it didn't look fatal. I gently rolled him over and he moaned.

He was still alive.

"Chris, can you hear me?" His eyes fluttered open and he moaned again, one hand moving to his head and touching it gingerly.

Redvers had gone up the stairs and quickly cleared the second floor before returning to my side.

"Looks like he took the Daimler. He must have come back for Lillian after all."

"That was a risky move on his part." I considered for a moment. "Perhaps he never really left the grounds at all." It was possible that the boy had simply hidden in the woods; we had only searched the house for him. It would make sense since all the vehicles in the barn had been accounted for when we returned from town and now the Daimler was missing. Somehow, he must have let Lillian know where to meet him.

But we had more pressing concerns now that he had my cousin with him. "How long ago do you think they left?"

"Lillian has been gone for close to thirty minutes, so probably something close to that. I think we'll have a devil of a time catching them. They've quite a head start."

I looked around in panic, even as Redvers came over to help Hammond sit up.

"Do you know what happened?" Redvers asked.

Hammond's hand was still on his abused scalp. "Lillian came in and was talking to me. I asked her why she was out of the house. Then everything went black."

Redvers' black brows drew into a storm and he turned to me. "He used her as a distraction."

I nodded, distracted myself. I stood and went to the barn door, pushing it wide open.

"What are you doing?" Redvers asked.

I hurried back and positioned myself behind the Moth. "Help me with this."

Redvers didn't ask again, but got into position and helped me push the Moth outside the barn.

"Jane . . ." Redvers started what I assumed was going to be an argument, but I ignored him. I moved to the side, and attached the wing into place, running around and attaching the other. I gave them firm pushes to make sure the mechanism held.

"Jane . . ."

I just shook my head. I did a cursory inspection and then cast my eyes to the heavens, saying a quick prayer that Hammond's vigilance over the little plane had been enough.

"This is the only way," I said. "We'll never catch them otherwise."

"Who's going to fly it?" Redvers looked at Hammond, still insensible inside the barn. "He's in no shape."

I took a deep breath. "I am."

Chapter 45

"Are you sure you've had enough lessons?"

I wasn't sure, but I knew how to take off, turn, and land. I crossed my fingers that would be enough. As I stood on the wing and peered into the front cockpit, Hammond staggered out of the barn. One hand still held the back of his head, but he was carrying my helmet and goggles.

"You can do this." He handed me my gear and gave a nod that was entirely more assured than I felt, but I appreciated the vote of confidence.

I thanked him and clambered into the backseat where the instructor normally sat, thankful I had left my gear in the barn after our last flight. They were cold as I pulled them on, but the fog on the goggles cleared quickly.

"This isn't the cinema! We should just call Greyson!" Redvers called.

"Get in!" I yelled. I didn't have time to argue with the man and I would take off without him if I had to—I wasn't willing to risk Lillian's safety by delaying any longer. Redvers' lips were pulled tight, but after a moment's hesitation he did what I said. He hoisted himself into the front seat and pulled on the helmet and goggles Lord Hughes had obviously left there.

Hammond stood at the front, ready to spin the propeller. He noticed the apprehensive look on my face.

"You'll be fine!" he shouted, then winced. I gave him a thumbs-up and he spun the propeller as I clicked the starter over. The Moth burst into life.

My stomach was somewhere around my feet and felt as though I had swallowed something made of cast iron. But I pushed the little plane forward, and onto the track that we used to take off.

"Which way would they have gone?" I shouted. The silence went on so long I thought he wouldn't reply, but just as we lifted off the ground I heard him shout over his shoulder.

"To the left!"

I glanced down and saw the dirt road that led around the long side of the estate. Even as we climbed, I pulled the plane around in that direction. I could see Hammond watching from the ground below us, and I gulped. I was used to having his expertise in the plane—I needed to put it from my mind that I was suddenly on my own.

I followed the dirt track. It made sense that Alistair would have taken the long way off the estate—if he had come anywhere near the house, we would have heard the motor. The only saving grace was that Alistair would have been drastically slowed by taking this route—the dirt road was mainly for farm equipment. Not well-built cars, no matter how carefully maintained they were.

We followed the route, the hum of the plane's engine keeping time with the anxiety in my veins. I was anxious for Lillian but also for Redvers and I—every time I tried to look down, I nudged the stick in that direction. It took a great deal of concentration to keep the plane steady without moving the stick when I looked below us. I had only ever really concentrated on keeping the plane level with the horizon before—not keeping it level and tracking someone on the ground.

Minutes passed before we came to the place where the dirt track met the road. It left us two options for which way Alistair might have turned, and I made the snap decision to follow it to the left, assuming he would have turned away from the estate, instead of toward it. Redvers was silent for so long that I felt compelled to call out to him and ask if I had taken the correct route, but then he turned in his seat and gave me a quick nod of approval before he went back to surveying the ground.

The countryside stretched out below us, and our shadow crossed over rolling hills and grazing sheep, the landscape dotted with the occasional farmhouse, but no vehicles that I could see. I was beginning to worry that I had turned in the wrong direction and we would need to double back when I heard Redvers's shout.

"There!"

I glanced down, the Moth giving a little jerk in that direction, and saw the Daimler speeding down the narrow road before I straightened us back out. I surveyed the land and moved the plane slightly to the left, lining up with the car in front of us, then pushed the throttle as I tried to overtake it. It seemed that Alistair heard the plane because even from our height, I could see his car pick up speed. It was dangerous on these narrow roads to be traveling so fast. I hoped he could keep control of the car, or he and Lillian would be killed in an accident—just like poor Simon.

I needed a place to land and cut them off. Alistair came to an intersection, barely slowing before barreling off to the right. I gave a grunt of frustration as I lost some of the gains we had made, and turned the airplane in the direction he had gone. We pulled level with the car and then slightly ahead.

Redvers was silent the whole time, and I appreciated his trust. I didn't know many men who could have refrained from trying to direct the whole operation, but he was leaving this effort entirely in my hands. Although as far as the plane was concerned, he didn't have any choice.

"Do you see where we might land?" I shouted.

"I think up ahead." I barely heard the reply as it was whipped into the wind, but my gaze followed where his hand had pointed.

I tracked the route Alistair would be forced to take, and in the distance saw a pull-off much like Redvers and I had used earlier in the week, leading from a farmer's field onto the road. The field had already been harvested, but I could see the broken stalks and browned foliage of the aftermath left on the ground. I pulled the plane into a turn and then another, bringing our altitude lower while praying that we had enough of a lead on Alistair.

"Brace yourself!" I shouted to Redvers. I didn't dare take a look at him as I lined up for a landing. There was no dirt track like we had at the estate—we would have to rough it on the field.

And rough it we did. As the wheels came close to the ground, I could feel the thrush of stalks hitting the wheels of the plane. The first jolt of the ground came hard, lifting us slightly back into the air. I ground my teeth together and brought her down again, this time staying on the ground as we bounced along, the impact and the shock of the uneven ground sending me slightly airborne with each jolt. We slowed but I maintained our forward momentum, switching to the foot pedals at my feet as I navigated the plane toward the track that would take us to the road.

We hit a hard dip, and my teeth chattered together once before we came back up and I navigated the plane onto paved road. I cut the engine once I had the little plane in place—we were now blocking Alistair's path entirely. The Daimler's engine was loud in the sudden silence, and I realized my heart had jumped into my throat. They would come around the last curve at any moment, and I prayed they would be able to stop before crashing into the side of the Moth.

Chapter 46

Redvers was out of his seat almost before I brought the Moth to a halt. He clambered down and removed his pistol from his jacket, pointing it down the road toward the oncoming car. I unbuckled and climbed from my own seat. If the Daimler hit the Moth, I didn't want to be inside it when it happened.

The car came around the final curve and didn't appear to be stopping. For a long moment I watched, convinced Alistair was going to drive straight through Redvers and into the side of the plane. But at the last moment, Alistair hit the brakes, the car screeching and sliding sideways in its sudden effort to stop. The front wheels hit the right ditch and came to an abrupt stop, a long line of rubber on the road leading to that point. Alistair climbed from the car, a small streak of blood running from his forehead, and moved like he was about to run, when Redvers grabbed him, throwing him to the ground. Redvers pocketed his gun and roughly pulled Alistair's hands behind his back.

I ran to the car while Redvers dealt with Alistair, but I didn't see Lillian. She wasn't in the passenger seat where I had expected her to be, nor was she in the backseat.

"The boot," Redvers called to me. I grabbed the keys from the ignition and ran around to the back of the car, hands shaking so badly I could barely get the key into the lock. I finally opened the trunk and found Lillian curled in a ball. She was unconscious, but still breathing. I checked her pulse and smoothed her hair away from her face. I didn't see any wounds on her head or body, but there was a faint chemical smell coming from the trunk.

"She's here!" I called to Redvers. "She's unconscious." I peered around the car at Redvers. "How are we going to get them back to the house to call the police?"

"I don't know," Redvers' voice was tight as he was holding on to a still-struggling Alistair with a knee in the boy's back while tightly holding his wrists. I was surprised Alistair had any fight left in him, but his body had been pumped full of adrenaline. Much as mine had.

I turned back to Lillian and began hunting around for the source of the chemical smell, but I couldn't see anything. Instead, I monitored her breathing and murmured soothing words, although she likely couldn't hear them.

It was only minutes before we heard the sound of approaching cars from the other direction. I panicked, thinking that someone was going to hit us from the other side, and I sprinted past Redvers and the Moth to flag down the approaching car. But I needn't have worried—as the line of three cars slowed and pulled to a stop on the side of the road, I realized the police had arrived.

I breathed a long sigh of relief.

Inspector Greyson leapt from the lead car and raced forward. I pointed to where Redvers crouched over Alistair, and I returned to the back of the car to keep an eye on Lillian. She still wasn't responding, but she seemed to be breathing normally, and my cursory inspection didn't reveal any blood—although she was likely to be banged up from her ride in the trunk.

Once Alistair was secured, I insisted that a police car

should be dispatched to pick up Millie so she could be with Lillian. I knew she was frantic with worry, and it would be cruel to keep her guessing about Lillian's safety any longer. I also insisted that an ambulance was called. Even though there wasn't any blood, I thought it would be safer to have the girl taken to the nearest hospital instead of the local doctor—and the nearest hospital was many miles away. I was concerned that Lillian was still unconscious, but when a burly policeman lifted her gently out of the trunk, we saw a white handkerchief beneath her. I picked it up gingerly and held it away from my face, but I could tell it was where the chemical smell was coming from. Lillian had been knocked out with some sort of anesthetic, not a blow to the head, and something tight in my chest loosened. My cousin would most likely be okay.

As soon as Millie appeared I stepped out of the way—she moved in like a tank and destroyed everyone that stood between her and Lillian. I felt sorry for the ambulance crew; Millie was shouting at them from the moment they arrived, ensuring Lillian was getting the best treatment, and I could still hear my aunt once the doors were closed with her and Lillian inside. The noise must have broken through Lillian's consciousness, because as she was loaded into the vehicle she began coming around. This of course, didn't make Millie any quieter. I watched the ambulance drive away, and climbed into one of the police cars headed to the station, slumping against the seat as the adrenaline began to leach from my system.

By the time we got to the police station, I felt completely wrung out, but I pulled Inspector Greyson aside and asked if it would be possible to have Lord Hughes released so that he could be with his daughter.

"Under the circumstances, I think we can do that." Greyson made the arrangements to have Hughes let go and for one of his men to drive him to the hospital.

"You look done in. Can I get you some coffee?" The inspector was as solicitous as ever.

I was tempted but shook my head. "Let's see what Alistair has to say for himself." I put one hand up to my head and realized I was still wearing the flying helmet with the goggles pushed up, and I pulled them off, swinging them nervously from one hand.

I expected an argument about sitting in on the interview with Alistair, but apparently the inspector thought better of it, because he simply turned and walked toward the interview room. Perhaps he was coming around to my usefulness, despite my gender. I followed quickly into the room where Redvers was already waiting with the young man.

Alistair was insolent, sitting behind the table with his arms crossed, a fresh scrape across one cheek from when Redvers had taken him down to the ground, and dried blood from the gash on his forehead. There were tears in his trousers, and I imagine his coat hadn't fared too well, either.

I leaned against the wall in the back of the room, afraid that if I sat down I might fall asleep now that I was drained of adrenaline. Redvers and the inspector sat across from Alistair and regarded him for a moment. I had no doubts this would be a difficult interview, judging from the stubborn set of Alistair's jaw.

Greyson started right in. "We have you bang to rights on kidnapping."

Alistair gave a careless shrug. "Maybe she wanted to go with me."

I rolled my eyes. "Knocked out and in the trunk of your car?" I couldn't help but interject.

Alistair glared at me. "She would have agreed to marry me. I just had to make sure I could get her there."

"Get her where?" the inspector asked.

Alistair pinned his lips shut, blue eyes glittering angrily. Gone was the carefree playboy whose only concern was the welfare of his cousin—Alistair's normally slicked hair was ruffled and all signs of geniality were gone from his face, leaving only hatred and anger in its wake. It was as if we were seeing behind the mask for the first time, and what we saw wasn't pretty.

Greyson continued. "I can imagine why you wanted to force her to marry you. Once you were married, you would inherit Lord Hughes's estate. And by setting Lord Hughes up for a murder and your own poisoning, you could expedite that process."

Alistair shrugged but refused to say anything.

I knew I should let the inspector do the interrogating, but it was hard to keep myself quiet. "Look, Alistair. Everyone here knows it's true. Once you kidnapped Lillian, you pretty much admitted your guilt for the rest of it."

He turned his angry glare to me, intending to intimidate me, I was sure, but I met that challenge and then some. I was angry, too—he had murdered an innocent veteran, implicated a kind man, and kidnapped my cousin. I pushed off the wall and stalked forward, arms crossed over my chest.

"I can't believe you were stupid enough to poison yourself with arsenic." I guessed that attacking his intelligence might make him angry enough to come back with an answer.

"That was the easy part," he replied arrogantly. "I tested the amounts on a number of rats and noted whether they died or just sickened. Then I did the math to account for my own body weight." My face twisted in horror, and Alistair smirked. "Oh, don't worry, Mrs. Wunderly. It was still a risk, but it was a rather small amount that I used. I was never in any real danger."

He'd misinterpreted my look. I was horrified for those poor rats, not worried that Alistair might have died.

"I suppose you pushed me into the stream."

"You were getting in the way of my plans. Asking too many questions. I thought a little scare would do you good."

I had been right. The point had not been to kill me—just to scare me.

"Why attack Marie?" Redvers interjected. I glanced at Inspector Greyson to see if he minded that we seemed to have taken over his interview, but he seemed content as long as he was getting answers. He was busy taking notes on a pad of paper.

Rage boiled up through Alistair's veins. His face turned red and when he spoke, spittle appeared. "That unnatural little whore! Messing around with my *sister*! I'm only sorry she wasn't in the bed when I tore it apart. It's exactly what I want to do to her. There's nothing wrong with my sister. She would be normal if it weren't for *her*."

I doubted that was the case, and I was sorry that Alistair felt that way about either of the girls. What was between them was their business only. And it made both of them happy—Marie was the most cheerful I had ever seen her with Poppy around. It was hard to say what Poppy was like ordinarily since I had only just met the girl, but it was a shame that Alistair couldn't accept his sister and be pleased for her happiness.

"Must have been quite the disappointment to find it was only pillows in that bed." I hated to admit it, but I was enjoying pushing Alistair's buttons.

His face darkened even further. "If I could have found her alone after that. Just once . . ."

I shuddered, thinking that Marie had been lucky indeed that she had spent the nights in Lillian's room after the attack.

"I thought you got along with your uncle. Why frame him for all this?"

Some of the redness bled away from Alistair's face as he seemed to regain control of himself. "I hate my uncle. For what he did to my father." His voice had a thrum of dark and lasting anger.

Redvers stepped in. "And what exactly is your uncle responsible for doing? It seems to me your father brought his fortunes upon himself."

"But he could have helped Father. At any time! Instead we lost the house and all our money. And Uncle Edward has *everything*. He could have spared some to help his only brother."

I shook my head and went back to my post against the wall, grateful for the little bit of distance from the toxic young man. Alistair had adopted a rosy view of his father and failed to see the truth. Lord Hughes *had* tried to help his brother, but ended up investing in scandal as a result. I could only imagine how many times before that Hughes had tried to step in and help, only to have his efforts rebuffed or resources drained away. And Alistair had accepted the poison from his father's lips without questioning whether it was true or whether his father was culpable in any way. It was hard to fault him—no one wants to believe the worst of their parents. But he had let that poison rot him from the inside, and then taken extreme measures to right some imaginary wrongs.

I nearly felt sorry for him. Nearly.

"And Simon?" Redvers asked.

Alistair's lip curled. "He was a nobody. That my uncle was helping instead of me and my family. And Simon thought he could *court* Lillian. My cousin may be adopted, and not truly blue blood, but he still needed to learn his place. She was above him."

Interesting. Alistair didn't seem to realize that Lillian was Lord Hughes's blood daughter. He only knew that she was adopted.

I shook my head. I had heard enough. The men could finish with Alistair and fill me in on the rest. I was tired of listening to the hatred that welled up out of this boy.

Chapter 47

I left the interview room and asked where my aunt and Lillian had been sent to. With all the excitement, a number of constables still milled around, and it wasn't difficult to convince one of them to drive me to the hospital. On the ride there I fell asleep against the door, my goggles pressed against the window, and the officer gently shook me when we arrived. I groggily thanked him for the ride and went inside to find my cousin.

I knocked on the door to Lillian's private room—I would guess Millie had insisted on it—and gently pushed open the door. Lord Hughes and Millie stood at Lillian's bedside, their hands clasped and fingers entwined. When I came into the room, Millie saw me notice but ignored me. Lord Hughes gave me a brief nod but turned his worried face immediately back to the doctor.

It looked like Lillian's exam was just finishing up. The doctor clicked off the light he had been shining in her eyes and turned to Lillian's parents. "She'll be perfectly all right in a few hours; I think it's fine for you to take her home. Just keep an eye on her." Millie and Hughes both nodded solemnly, eyes on Lillian's drawn face.

As the doctor passed me on his way out, I came fully into the room.

"Lillian," I said gently. My aunt glared at me, but I ignored her. "Why did you go out to find Alistair?"

She looked at me from her hospital bed, her eyes still slightly glazed. "I didn't think he could have done those things on purpose. I wanted to talk to him before the police found him. See if we could figure out how to fix things."

I nodded, arms crossed over my chest. Millie released Hughes's hand and stepped forward, smoothing some of Lillian's hair back. "You don't need to answer any questions right now, dear." Lillian and I ignored her.

"You just wanted to believe the best of him."

Lillian nodded slowly. "And I didn't want the police to hurt him. We had a hiding place as children where we would leave notes for one another in a hollow tree. After I left my room, I went there and found a note telling me where to find him."

I nodded. Alistair had stayed on the grounds after all. "And what happened in the barn?"

A frown creased Lillian's face. "Alistair said he needed the car. He had me go in and talk to Group Captain Hammond. I thought he would just take the car while I distracted him. Instead he hit him on the back of the head. I didn't see with what. I screamed and started shouting at him that that wasn't what we agreed. I started to leave the barn and that's when he came up behind me with a white cloth. I don't remember anything else."

Lord Hughes looked at me. "The doctor seemed to think it was chloroform on the handkerchief."

That made sense. I had another question for Hughes. "Will you call Alistair's father?"

Hughes shook his head and gave a small, sad smile. "There's little use in doing that. He won't be interested in helping. But I'll hire a good solicitor for Alistair."

"He's going to need one." I thought about whether I

would be able to extend such kindness toward someone who had kidnapped my daughter and tried to frame me for murder. I was glad my initial impression proved correct after all. Lord Hughes might have carried some secrets, but he truly was a good man.

After all, we each carried some secrets.

Lord Hughes had officially been released, so he and Millie took Lillian home. I rode back with them in the car that Shaw had brought to the hospital. It was dark by the time we left, and Lillian and I both nodded off even though Millie was squeezed into the backseat between us.

Even though I was exhausted, I paced the front hall and waited for Redvers to finish up with Alistair and Inspector Greyson and return to the estate. I didn't have long to wait—soon after I left the room, Alistair had demanded representation. There wasn't much more to be learned from him that night, and Redvers had left the inspector to his paperwork.

As soon as Redvers came through the door, I rushed forward. "The Moth! We need to get it back to the estate. And make sure I didn't damage it."

Redvers looked bemused. "Didn't anyone tell you? Hammond was sent for. He was supposed to get the plane checked out and back where it belongs."

I worried at my lip. "Even with his head bashed in?"

"Group Captain Hammond is a war veteran. I think he's tougher than you're giving him credit for. In fact, he probably has the Moth back in the barn already."

If I hadn't been so tired, it would have occurred to me to simply go out to the barn and check, but I hadn't. Then I gave a small sigh of relief. All I wanted was to relax and have a stiff drink, not chase around the countryside cleaning up loose ends. A selfish impulse, but there it was.

It seemed everyone had much the same idea. Despite the late hour, Lord Hughes and Millie were seated in front of the fire in the drawing room, each nursing a drink. I could see that Millie had gone for straight whiskey instead of her usual highball, and Hughes had something similar.

"Where are the girls?" I stopped to talk to my aunt on my way to the bar cart, surprised that she had been able to tear herself from Lillian's side.

"They're upstairs looking after Lillian."

"Without you?"

Millie shot me a dark look and I put my hands up in surrender. "I was just wondering, Aunt Millie." Lord Hughes gave me a conspiratorial smile. I left them and continued on my way to the bar cart where Redvers and Hammond were speaking in undertones.

Hammond gave me a wry smile. "Can I fix you something?"

"A gin rickey if you will. How are you feeling?"

"I've the devil of a headache, but I'll be fine. The Moth is safely back in the barn." He gave me a sidelong look as he fixed my drink. "Only a few scratches."

My face reddened slightly. "I'm sorry. I hope there wasn't a lot of damage."

He chuckled. "It would have been worth destroying her to catch them. I'm not worried about it in the slightest." He looked slightly proud. "Besides, I hear you did a damn fine job flying and then landing in that field. I'm impressed with how far you've come."

I blushed and thanked him. I cast a quick glance at Redvers and he shot me a wink. He must have been reporting to Hammond on how I had done on my first solo flight. I wondered if he had mentioned all the times I'd made the Moth dip when I tried to look at the ground. I would come clean about that myself—keeping that stick steady was something I wanted to work on next time Hammond and I went up.

To my everlasting surprise, I heard my aunt's voice from the chairs behind us. "I suppose I have to admit it's a good thing that you were able to learn to use that contraption, Jane."

We all turned to face Millie and I smiled.

"You should mark this day on your calendar," Redvers whispered in my ear.

"What was that, Mr. Redvers?" Millie gave him a sharp look.

"I told her that she had done well."

Millie looked slightly mollified. Then she cleared her throat. "And I suppose I am sorry about the damage it incurred."

I frowned. "When I landed it? I think we were lucky the crops had already been harvested. The damage could have been much worse."

Millie looked into her drink, swirling the last few swigs in the bottom of the glass. "Not exactly," she muttered.

I looked at Redvers as realization dawned upon us. "Aunt Millie! *You* sabotaged the fuel line."

She huffed. "Not me personally. I simply talked with Mr. Shaw and asked him to ensure that you couldn't take the infernal thing up anymore. You were taking such unnecessary risks." She took a long drink. "I admit I wouldn't have gone the route he did, a little dangerous tampering with the fuel line, but it all worked out in the end. Mostly." She shot Hammond a dark look, no doubt since he had already fixed the damage.

That was one last mystery solved, then. I heard the sound of Hammond trying to muffle his laughs behind me. It seems he was amused at my aunt's brazen interference, even though he'd been the one to have to clean up her mess. I didn't know whether to be amused or angry myself. Perhaps I was a little bit of both—it seemed to be the way with my aunt.

We all settled into chairs around the fire.

"What will become of Poppy?" I hoped Lord Hughes would step in.

"She'll stay here with us." Lord Hughes met my eyes, and his voice was firm. I nodded and smiled. I was glad he was going to take care of the silly girl, and not hold her brother's actions against her.

We were all quiet for a moment, thinking about what would become of Alistair. None of us wanted to say, but he would probably spend most of the rest of his life behind bars—and that was if he was lucky.

Lord Hughes was still gazing into the fire when he broke the silence. "I'm sorry you were all caught up in my nephew's foolishness. And I'm sorry Simon lost his life to it." His voice was quiet, and his face twisted with pain.

"This isn't your fault, Edward." Millie reached across the small space and took Lord Hughes's hand in her own. He turned and gave her a warm smile. I had a feeling Millie might be staying here longer than she had initially planned.

I turned to Hammond. "And what will you do, Chris? Return to the Aero Club right away?"

He gave a small smile. "I think I'll stay a bit longer." He glanced at Lord Hughes, who gave him a smile and a nod. "We haven't finished your lessons, Lord Hughes." Chris looked to me. "And we can continue yours if you like, Jane."

I wasn't sure I would go all the way and complete the training needed to get my license—I certainly wouldn't have time before I had to leave—but I definitely wanted to get back up in the sky, even after the day's events. I grinned at him. "We probably should practice emergency landings. So that it goes a bit smoother next time."

I heard Redvers groan a little as Hammond laughed.

The evening was winding down, and we were all quietly lost in our thoughts when Redvers stood.

"If you'll excuse us for a moment." Redvers took my hand and pulled me from my chair. Carrying his whiskey in one hand, he led me down the hall and into the library.

I raised my eyebrows in question.

"I just wanted to speak to you alone for a minute." Redvers closed the door behind us as butterflies started a dance in my stomach. "I'm afraid I only have a few more days here before I have to go back to work. I don't have more time for a holiday."

"Holiday?" I could hear the incredulous tone of my voice. "I thought you were here on some kind of case." I realized I had never followed up on *why* Aunt Millie had called him here. I had only worked out that she'd summoned him.

He smiled, that dimple winking at me from his cheek, and my heart skipped a beat. "You never finished interrogating your aunt about what I was doing here."

I gave him a slow smile in return. "In all the excitement I did forget. You mean to tell me you were on vacation?"

"Indeed, I was."

"Why come here?"

"To see you."

For a long moment, I was struck breathless. I had never once imagined that Redvers had taken vacation and come to the estate for the sole purpose of seeing me.

"Well . . . I . . . I'm sorry we spent your entire vacation chasing down a murderer."

"I'm learning that things aren't relaxing when you're around."

There were several ways to take that, but I decided to let it go.

"I'll be heading back to America soon. I was hoping to be back in time for Christmas."

Redvers nodded and took a step closer.

My mouth twisted in a wry smile as I tipped my head back to look at him. "Although, the way it looks with Millie and Lord Hughes, I think I'll be traveling home by myself."

Redvers turned and set his whiskey on a side table. "Oh, I wouldn't say that."

I caught my breath and stared at him. "Why not?"

He gave me a mysterious smile in return.

And then I forgot what we were discussing in the first place.